Father John's

Father John's Gift

R. Allan Worrell

Copyright © 2017 by Rodney Allan Worrell

All rights reserved. This book or any portion thereof may not be reproduced or used in any manner whatsoever without the express written permission of the publisher except for the use of brief quotations in a book review or scholarly journal.

Cover art created by Karl Brandt.

First Printing: 2017

ISBN-13: 978-1542664462

Dedication

This book is dedicated to everyone who has ever looked at the billions of stars in the night sky and wondered if there was an alien species, on some distant planet, looking back at them.

Famous Quotes

"We make our world significant by the courage of our questions and the depth of our answers" [1]
— Carl Sagan, Cosmos

"Reality is merely an illusion, albeit a very persistent one." [2]
— Albert Einstein

"Facts are stubborn things; and whatever may be our wishes, our inclinations, or the dictates of our passion, they cannot alter the state of facts and evidence."[3]
—John Adams, 'Argument in Defense of the Soldiers in the Boston Massacre Trials,' December 1770

Contents

Disclaimer...viii
Chapter 1: The Prison...1
Chapter 2: The Phone Call..7
Chapter 3: The Trip..11
Chapter 4: The Wilkin's House....................................17
Chapter 5: Recovery...22
Chapter 6: The Playoff Game......................................26
Chapter 7: Confession...29
Chapter 8: Katie McLeary..34
Chapter 9: The ER...39
Chapter 10: Chief Perlman..50
Chapter 11: The Reporter..53
Chapter 12: The Newsroom..59
Chapter 13: A Trail of Healing.....................................65
Chapter 14: Hospital Executives..................................69
Chapter 15: The Athlete..73
Chapter 16: The Bears Coach.....................................77
Chapter 17: The Hook...79
Chapter 18: The Club..83
Chapter 19: Trouble in the Rectory.............................86
Chapter 20: The Meeting...93
Chapter 21: The Chain of Command...........................98
Chapter 22: The Gifts...101
Chapter 23: The Super Bowl......................................107

Chapter 24: The Interview 112
Chapter 25: "Cardinal Gino" 116
Chapter 26: The Call from Rome 119
Chapter 27: The News Media 122
Chapter 28: Father Mark 129
Chapter 29: The Check 146
Chapter 30: The Project 151
Chapter 31: Tina 155
Chapter 32: Maria Lopez 168
Chapter 33: Carlos Martinez 174
Chapter 34: Sergio's Call 182
Chapter 35: The Warning 184
Chapter 36: Lamar's Mother 199
Chapter 37: The Hacienda 201
Chapter 38: The Conclusion 213
Author's Note: The Quest for ET 220
References 226

Disclaimer

This book is a work of fiction. The names, characters, ideas, organizations, situations and philosophies portrayed in this book are either fictional and are the product of the author's vivid imagination and conjecture, or if real, they have been used as a part of the story without implication that the characters or organizations actually behave in the way described in this book. Any resemblance of the characters in this book to real persons living or dead is purely coincidental.

Chapter 1: **The Prison**

"Asshole priest!"

The insult came from convict, Jeremiah Rhodes, an inmate who was waiting his turn on death row. Father John turned and looked back toward the cell from which the comment had come. As he stood at the bars of his cell, a young man in his twenties flipped Father John the finger, and gave him a look that could kill. John was unnerved by the look and the remark. He turned back to his guard escort for an explanation.

"Just ignore him." the guard said.

"What's his story?" John inquired.

He's been here, on death row, for three years waiting for the results of his latest appeal. The State of Illinois can't decide whether or not to kill him."

"What did he do?" John couldn't help it. His curiosity got the better of him, and he knew the guard knew everything there was to know about the inmates under his watch.

"After years of physical abuse, he finally snapped and killed his stepfather one night after his stepfather got drunk and beat his mother to within an inch of her life. He was only sixteen at the time, but the system treated him as an adult, which is why he is here. That was five years ago."

"But what has he got against priests?"

"Well, believe it or not Father, Jeremiah is Catholic. His lawyer asked the judge for leniency at his sentencing. He claimed Jeremiah was sexually abused by a priest and had been beaten by his step father

Father John's Gift

for years, but the judge would hear none of it. It almost makes me feel sorry for the guy. He's not normally so nasty ... No offense, Father."

"None taken. I understand." John was serious. He had heard a few rumblings in the church of pedophile priests, and although he was initially shocked by the stories, he thought those priests should exit the priesthood and get the psychological help they needed before returning to work. That is, if they could be reformed. John had to admit he really didn't know if they could be reformed or not. His seminary training dealt with a lot of sexual issues inside and outside of marriage, but the training did not include reforming pedophiles, particularly pedophile priests.

John felt sad for Jeremiah. He could only imagine the anger he must have felt after suffering abuse from his stepfather and from an authority figure he trusted. It was no wonder Jeremiah had snapped.

This was only the second time John had been to the maximum prison, and it was the first time he had ever visited anyone on death row. John volunteered for the assignment when it was offered to all the priests at St. Andrews by his Monsignor who got a call from the Warden. The Warden requested a priest when another death row inmate, Lamar Johnson, specifically asked for a Catholic priest instead of the default nondenominational prison pastor.

They walked down the long gruesome cell block and received no additional remarks from the other fifteen inmates, most of whom were sleeping in their bunks, or quietly reading to pass the time. As they walked towards the end of the block, John contemplated the mental state of the men who would soon meet their maker. How different were they then he? How did they get here? He could only guess what their lives were like. When they reached the last cell, Lamar Johnson got up from his bed and walked toward the front of the cell.

The guard barked, "Hands!"

Lamar said nothing but placed his hands through a waist high slot in the bars and the guard placed handcuffs around Lamar's wrists.

"Back off."

Lamar took three steps back from the door as previously instructed. The guard took the keys from his belt and opened the door. John and the guard stepped inside the cell. John looked back at the guard, expecting him to leave.

"I have to stay in the cell with you for your protection. It's the law." The guard glanced at his watch. "It's now 9:35. You have fifteen minutes with the prisoner." With his right hand on his baton, the guard retreated to the left front corner of the cell and stared at the floor.

John nodded towards the guard and looked at Lamar who now stood directly in front of him. "May I call you Lamar?"

"Yeah."

"Lamar, please sit down." John turned and grabbed a wooden chair from the corner of the cell opposite the guard. He pulled it close to Lamar who now sat on the edge of his bed.

John sat down and leaned towards Lamar. He spoke to Lamar in a muted tone to give the semblance of privacy. "My name is Father John Danek. I am a Catholic priest from St Andrews Parish. How can I help you?"

With his elbows on his knees, Lamar leaned towards John and looked directly at him. He whispered, "Thanks for coming Father. You know, I don't have much time... They will kill me tomorrow."

He spoke about it in a matter-of-fact tone, as if he were reading a fact from a newspaper article about someone else. He tried to show he was resigned to his execution, but it was only for appearances. Lamar tried to be strong, but knew if he allowed himself to come to grips with his impending death, it would tear him apart inside.

John replied, "Yes, I know. I read over your file before I came here this morning. Would you like to make a confession?"

"Yes Father."

Father John reached down and pulled his stole from his black leather bag, kissed it, and placed it around his neck. "Let's begin."

Lamar followed John's lead in prayer and made the sign of the cross with him. Lamar was Catholic after all. "In the name of the Father, and of the Son, and of the Holy Spirit, Amen"

Knowing they had little time, John was straight to the point. "Lamar, I want you to listen to me. This is important. You can lie to

Father John's Gift

me, and you can lie to yourself, but you can't lie to God. He will know what is in your heart, Lamar. Do you understand?"

"Yes Father."

"What would you like to confess?"

"Well, I had a bad life, and I did a lot of bad things.... I, I, I don't know where to begin."

"Did you kill the drug store owner that they said you did?" Lamar's file discussed the drug store robbery and the killing that took place nearly two years ago.

"Yeah, I killed him."

"Are you sorry for what you did?"

"Yes Father. I had over a year in here to think about it. There is not a day that goes by that I don't wish I hadn't killed that man. It was just crazy. The voices made me do it. I didn't want to, but they made me. They said he had to die, because he was bad and would change the world for the worse."

John was disturbed by Lamar's mention of, "the voices". Lamar's file said nothing about mental illness. Knowing he had little time, and believing Lamar's mental illness would make no difference to God, John decided to continue with the Confession. "Did you tell anyone you were sorry? Did you write to the victim's family?"

"Yeah. The prison shrink suggested I write them and I did. I never heard back from them though. I don't know if they even got my letter."

"That's OK Lamar. I'm glad you wrote them, and I'm sure your letter will help them, as I am sure it helped you. God will forgive you, that is, if you are truly sorry for what you did."

Lamar looked sadly up at Father John. It was all becoming too real for him now. "Oh God, Father. I'm sorry, and I don't want to die." He dropped his head, stared at the floor, and began to cry.

John placed his left hand on Lamar's shoulder. "It's OK Lamar. Let it out. I forgive you, and God will forgive you too. Lamar, you have already been saved your repentance today, and by Christ's death on the cross. Do you have anything else you would like to confess?"

"No Father."

"Let me bless you Lamar."

As Lamar looked up at Father John, John blessed him with his right hand, and said, "Lamar, I absolve you of your sins, in the name of the Father, and of the Son, and of the Holy Spirit. Amen."

"Thank you, Father." Lamar wiped a tear away from his right eye.

"Is there anything I can do for you now? Is there any message you want me to give to someone on the outside?"

"Yes Father. But can I ask you a question first?"

"What is it?"

Lamar sat up straight and said, "Do you believe in free will?"

John raised his eyebrows. He was surprised. He never expected such a philosophical question to come from a convict out of the blue. "Yes, I believe we have free will. We can choose right from wrong. Why do you ask?"

"Father, I'm confused. I have thought a lot about why I did what I did, and I am sorry, but the religion just doesn't make sense to me."

"What do you mean?"

"If God is all knowing, and He already knows what we will do, then why should He make us, only to send us to hell when we fail Him? And if he knows what we will do before we are born, then aren't we predestined to fail?

John thought about how best to answer his question and then said, "Lamar, that's a deep subject philosophers and religious men have struggled with for centuries. But I will give you two answers.

First, we can't know what God knows. It is beyond our understanding. We only know what the Bible tells us, that God loves us and wants us to choose Him over evil." John paused to let it sink in.

"And second, we know it is God's plan that we each should have a choice in what we do; to either choose Him, or not to choose Him. Even if you fail, your soul will still be saved by being truly sorry for what you did, and for having reversed your course, and choosing to be with God."

Lamar looked at John with a blank face and was unconvinced. "I don't know Father. I want to believe you are right, I mean... what choice do I have now," he said sarcastically.

Father John's Gift

Lamar's sarcasm made John wonder if he had just been deceived. Did Lamar really believe in God, or was his confession just a cry for help? "Lamar, you do have a choice. It's up to you."

Lamar changed the subject. "Can you tell my mother that you saw me, that I love her, and that I'm sorry for everything? She hasn't spoken to me since the trial."

"Yes, I can do that. How can I reach her?"

"I wrote her a note. Can you see that she gets it? It's important."

Lamar got up and retrieved a letter from the table next to the bed and handed it to Father John. "It has her address for you to reach her. I put it in an envelope, but I don't want to mail it. I'm afraid she might just throw it away. I think she will read it if it comes from you. She always was a religious person. She still goes to Mass every Sunday. ... My younger brother, Jamal, said she won't come to see me die tomorrow. I don't blame her. I don't want her to see me die anyway."

John looked at the note and said, "I will see she gets it Lamar, and I will tell her what you said."

"Thank you Father. "

"Is there anything else?"

"No... I guess not."

"OK Lamar. I want you to be strong and know I will pray for you."

"Thank you Father."

They both stood and Lamar shook Father John's hand. John couldn't help but think it was such a waste of a life for the state to kill Lamar, but he said nothing. It was out of his control.

John took off his stole and placed it and Lamar's letter in his bag. He turned towards the guard. "I'm ready."

The guard nodded and instructed Lamar to stand back.

* * * * * * * *

Chapter 2: **The Phone Call**

After returning to the St Andrews Rectory, John entered his private room, set his bag on the end of his bed, opened it and retrieved Lamar's letter. He then placed the letter on his desk to remind himself to contact Lamar's mother, and he picked up a copy of *The Investigator*, a newspaper tabloid Margaret, the rectory housekeeper, had left for him. He shook his head in disbelief as he gazed at the full page photograph of the "little green men" on its cover. The cover story was entitled, "My Mother was Abducted by Aliens!"

Father John chuckled as he looked over the article. Margret was always reading such garbage and leaving it for him! He never understood why she loved to tease him with such outrageous articles. This was not the first time. She must get some sadistic pleasure by leaving them, and he did think that, in itself, was oddly funny. Was it something he had said? If so, he couldn't remember it. He was glad he could laugh at himself along with Margaret. Though he never said as much, he was glad she did not make her thoughts public.

Being a religious man, John could not imagine how otherwise intelligent people could believe in aliens. The thought of little creatures with large heads and big black bug eyes arriving in space ships from other planets was so absurd, John dismissed it outright. Aliens? From other planets? Does anybody take these ideas seriously? Why would people like Margaret ever buy these cheap tabloids? It had to be pure entertainment. The paper was entertaining;

Father John's Gift

he had to give it that. John concluded it was harmless enough, and he tossed the paper in the trashcan next to his desk.

He wiped the cheap newspaper ink off his hands and sat down. He picked up a white three ring notebook which held the beginnings of a sermon he had started on the life of St Paul. He had started it months ago, but it wasn't quite finished. John had several other sermons he could use for tomorrow's service, but he had recently given the St Paul sermon some more thought, and believed he could finish it with just an hour or two of work. It would be nice to have some fresh material for his ten o'clock Sunday morning service. He grabbed a pen and flipped through the pages to recall what he had written.

John loved to write more than he loved to pray. Writing sermons, in the quiet of his room, helped him to clarify his thoughts. It helped him to think about life and spiritual ideas in a structured way, free from other distractions. He hoped... no, he believed he could reach those in the congregation who might never otherwise apply abstract religious concepts to their lives. John knew if could get his thoughts down on paper; if he could see them in black and white, the truth of his ideas would be revealed. Father John believed fervently that God spoke to him through his writing.

John loved his life as a St Andrews priest, but it wasn't always this easy. He had seen and heard much in his early years. Dealing with extreme poverty in Costa Rica, during his missionary work at age twenty-three had been hard. But now, in 1960, at the age of forty-one, he enjoyed his life and his job in downtown Chicago at St Andrews Parish. The problems of a parish priest were varied enough to make ministering to middle class Catholics interesting and occasionally challenging, but however difficult, there was a rhythm to his work, a routine to his life, and Father John felt he had everything under control.

"Father John."

It was the shrill voice of Mary Margaret Winkle, the 56-year-old rectory secretary and housekeeper. Although she normally didn't sleep there, "Margaret" as she liked to be called, was always there to do whatever needed to be done to keep the lives of five priests and the Monsignor on track. John first met Margaret when he came to St Andrews over ten years ago, and he relied on her more than anyone else throughout his career as a priest. For him, she was an institution all by herself, and he couldn't imagine doing his job without her.

"Yes Margaret", Father John replied.

"There is a phone call for you. It is Mrs. Wilkins. She said it's urgent."

"Thank you Margaret. I'll be there in a minute." He finished his last sentence, put down his pen, exited his small bedroom, and walked down the long hallway leading to the phone in the foyer.

Despite its large size, the rectory had only two phones for the five resident priests who lived there. There was one for receiving public calls in the foyer, and one for making private calls located in the study. The priests complained constantly to Monsignor Eckhart that they needed more phones. After all, they reasoned, the phones were their connection to the parish, and each of the five priests received several calls a day. But the Monsignor felt that two phones were sufficient for the frugal lives of the priests. He stated that sharing the phones served to bring the priests closer together, and two phones were enough for them. Of course, the priests all knew the Monsignor had his own private line in his residence at the back of the rectory.

"This is Father John."

"Father, this is Barbara Wilkins." Her voice trembled with emotion as she said the words she dreaded to hear herself say. "Father, my Jeremy is very sick. I've had the doctor here and he says Jeremy may not make it through the night. I know the weather is awful, but can you come out to our house tonight?"

Father John knew the Wilkins family well. They were a devout farm family, attended Mass every Sunday, and despite a long drive into the city, Jeremy was a sixth grader at St Andrews Elementary.

"Yes Barbara, I understand. I will leave right away and will be there as soon as I can. What is your address?" John glanced at his watch. It was already half past eight.

"Thank you Father. Our address is 155 Mulberry Street. We live on the West side of Chicago off of Route 17, about five miles beyond the entrance to the new Cloverdale subdivision. Do you know where that is? "

Father John's Gift

"Yes, I think I can find it. I will leave right away. I expect to see you in about half an hour."

"Thank you Father."

Jeremy had been sick with childhood leukemia for nearly two years, and Father John had talked often with Barbara from the beginning about Jeremy's illness and her reaction to it. She had taken the news of Jeremy's leukemia hard. She could not understand how God could take her only son away from her. Still, even though both knew this day would come, it was impossible for Barbara to accept that Jeremy was finally dying. Administering Last Rites to a child was never pleasant, but Father John knew it was some comfort to the family to know their child would go to heaven.

"Mary Margaret! Please let Monsignor Eckhart know that I had a call and I may be back late tonight."

"Already done, Father." John smiled when he heard Margaret's reply from down the hall. He sometimes wondered why he ever bothered to speak to her. It was as if she could read his mind and anticipate his every move. It was uncanny how Margaret was always one step ahead of him.

* * * * * * * *

Chapter 3: **The Trip**

St. Andrews parish had expanded into nearby suburbs as the city of Chicago grew and pushed farther into the countryside. No new parishes had yet been established on the West side of Chicago, and Catholic farm families who lived on the outskirts of Chicago had no choice but to join St Andrews. Father John had to drive thirty five miles to get to the Wilkins household.

The weather was typical for Chicago in February. The city was hit with three inches of snow which fell on top of five inches received the previous day. The army of city plows could not keep up with the constant snowfall, and though all the city streets had been plowed once, there were too many streets to keep them all passable. To make matters worse, the constant traffic packed the new snow into the pavement and made the outlying roads icy and dangerous.

Although the parish had done well financially in the last few years as the congregation grew, Father John was still driving a ten year old, 1950 Buick. The car was left to him a year earlier by a younger priest who had suddenly left the priesthood in disgrace, just when John's old Ford had died of engine trouble. Monsignor Eckhart was happy to give the Buick to John in lieu of buying him a new car. But with 120 thousand miles on the odometer, and with its body rust and cracked vinyl seats, the car showed its age. Nevertheless, it still ran well and John never complained; he always accepted whatever his superiors saw fit to give him. But when he saw a much younger priest, Father Jim,

Father John's Gift

get a new car, he felt a sudden pang of jealously. He had to remind himself that he was a priest and taken a vow of poverty. And after all, it was only a car.

Father John could see his breath after he climbed into the cold car. John had not used the car in a few days, and the temperature was now in the teens. He adjusted the throttle and he turned the key. The engine oil was thick, and the engine did not turn over on the first try but came to life on the second. The engine backfired once and then roared to life loudly with a hole in the muffler. The Monsignor had told him months ago to get the muffler replaced, but there was never time for such mundane things. John subconsciously procrastinated when it came to maintaining the old car.

"OK Willie, hang in there with me. We have to make a late run tonight. We have an important job to do." Though he knew it was silly, John liked to name his cars. Only his second car, he had named it "Willie" in honor of an old dog he had and loved as a child. Like his dog, the car was faithful and had never failed him.

He turned on the car's lights and as he revved the engine, blue smoke poured out of the tailpipe and he heard a brief squeal from the fan belt. He ran the car a minute to warm the engine and then grabbed an ice scrapper from behind the passenger seat. He exited the car to clear the windows of ice and snow. With the windows cleared, John jumped back in the car and slammed the door. He gently stepped on the accelerator to avoid spinning the tires, and as the car pulled away from the curb, he heard the snow crack under the wheels. "Thank you, Willie," he said. He kissed his fingers and patted the dash. He then glanced upward and whispered, "And thank you Lord". He looked his plastic Jesus on the dashboard and made a quick sign of the cross.

The sun had set hours ago, and most people were at home trying to stay warm after battling the slow traffic on their way home from work. With the inner city streets now mostly clear of traffic and plowed, Father John had little trouble navigating the city. However, when he got to the edge of town, the covered roads looked unfamiliar, became more treacherous, and he slowed to five miles an hour in two or three inches of new snow.

R. Allan Worrell

Being a city priest, most of his work was close to home and Father John rarely ventured into the countryside. He thought he knew where the Wilkins family lived, but the sun had set over an hour ago, and in the dark snowy roads, he was now unsure about where he was and how to get to the Wilkins house. He turned on the car's interior dome light and fumbled with a map as he creeped down the road. The distraction of the map and snow proved too much for John. When glancing at his map, he failed to notice the road had narrowed, and the car's front right wheels suddenly slid off the road and onto the shoulder. He stepped on the brakes and jerked the wheel to the left as he tried to keep the car on the road, but he was too late. The wheels locked up on the underlying ice, and the car slid off the road at less than five miles per hour into a shallow ditch filled with snow.

"Damn!" Father John rarely swore, but he was anxious to get to the Wilkins house on time and he now regretted telling Barbara he would be there in half an hour. He glanced at his watch and noticed it was already nine o'clock. He had less than five minutes left to reach his destination. To make matters worse, he knew he was lost and he didn't know how much farther he would have to go. Still in the car, Father John looked to the road ahead and then turned and looked out the rear window and saw there were no other cars on the road to help him. He was all alone. "What am I going to do now?" he said out loud to himself.

Determined to get to the Wilkins's house, he turned off the ignition, grabbed his black priest bag from the passenger seat and exited the car. He was now glad he had put on his heavy boots and had dressed warmly. It had stopped snowing, and he thought he could walk several miles if he had to. He saw a distant light from a farmhouse about a half mile up the road. If the farmer let him use his telephone, he could call for help with his car and then call Barbara to tell her he would be late. He recalled passing a gas station at an intersection a few miles back. Was it a Sunoco or a Sinclair? He hadn't looked at the sign carefully enough and he couldn't remember which it was, but he thought it was green and he was sure it was not an orange Exon. The farmer would know. He banged the Buick's heavy door closed and began his trek to the farmhouse.

Father John's Gift

With the snow stopped, the night sky was unusually clear, and now that he was more than five miles from the edge of Chicago, he could see stars not visible in the glare of city lights. He looked up at the night sky in utter amazement. Living in downtown Chicago, John had not seen so many stars since he was in Costa Rico so long ago.

"Father in heaven, help me get to the Wilkin's house tonight."

No sooner had his prayer left his lips, a bright light zipped across the night sky and in no time at all, a space saucer descended silently in front of him and hovered ten feet off the ground about fifty feet up the road from where he stood. It arrived so fast it seemed to have come from nowhere. Scared and stunned in disbelief by what he saw, Father John stared straight ahead and didn't move a muscle.

"Holy Mother of God."

He stood transfixed.... bewildered by what was before him and he wondered what would happen next.

No sooner than it had arrived, the ship turned a bright light directly on him. It was so bright against the dark night sky John turned his head and shielded his eyes with his hand so as to not look directly at it. As agile as it was, the ship was enormous. It stretched ninety to a hundred feet across and was not quite circular. It rotated slowly and reflected the moonlight off one side of the ship as it turned. The ship had creases at its edges and appeared to be made of some blue-green metal. John guessed the ship was a hexagon or maybe an octagon, and it looked to be thirty feet thick at its center and tapered to five or six feet at each side.

The ship suddenly stopped its rotation, and with the light still on him, John felt himself levitate a few feet off the ground and his black bag slipped from his right hand and dropped beneath him. With his arms at his side, he was at once paralyzed and suspended in mid-air about five feet off the ground. He felt as if he was locked in a strange embrace with the ship from which there was no escape. He knew it was doing something to him, but he didn't know what it was.

The ship emitted a high pitch tone which oscillated with another tone of a lower frequency every other second. With each change in tone, blue and white lights turned off and on, alternating at the edges of the ship. The sound was so loud it hurt his ears, and he wanted it to stop. He wanted to cover his ears with his hands, but John could not raise or move his arms. He felt the tips of his fingers tingle, but painfully so, as if his hands were being pricked with pins or needles. With tears in his eyes, he blinked and squinted in the bright light. He was able to move his eyes, but the rest of his body was frozen… frozen not from the cold, but from an unseen force ~~which came~~ from the ship. The ship hovered ten feet off the ground in front of him with no apparent means of support, and did not move.

John felt a warm sensation and tightness in his chest which grew and grew until he thought his chest would explode. He felt like his heart was racing out of control, and he wondered if he was having a heart attack. Sweat now dripped off his forehead, and it burned as it dripped into his eyes. He thought his life was over and that the alien ship was killing him. He had thought often about how he would die, and ~~it never occurred to him~~ he could never imagine that his life would end this way. He screamed for help as loud as he could into the night, but there was no one for miles around to hear him. If he died tonight, who would find him? He closed his eyes and said the 'Hail Mary' prayer out loud to himself.

"... Holy Mary, Mother of God, pray for us sinners, now, and at the hour of our death. Amen."[2]

Before John blacked out, his last thought was that he was now prepared to die, and he thought he would finally see God.

When it was over, John opened his eyes and found himself lying on his back in the middle of the road staring straight up into the night sky. He had not seen the ship leave, but it was now gone. He didn't know when the ship left, or how long he had laid there. He felt nothing but the stinging cold winter air blowing on his face. He saw only the ~~beautiful~~ stars twinkle above him, and the sight of his ~~own~~ breath in the cold, reflected by the headlights of his car.

Father John got up and looked back at his car, now about twenty feet behind him. Somehow, strangely, the car was back on the road, the lights were on and it was running! He turned around and looked at the road ahead and saw no one. He was still truly alone. He pulled off his right glove and scratched his head in the cold night air as he tried to remember what had happened and to make sense of it all.

Father John's Gift

His mind was full of questions. Didn't his car slide off the road and get stuck in the ditch? How did it get back on the road? How long had he lain on the road? Did he imagine the whole thing? How did he end up on his back in the middle of the road? Didn't he just see what he thought was a space ship ahead of him? He turned and looked at the road ahead. Whatever it was, it was gone, and he was OK. It was as if he just had a terrible nightmare, or perhaps his mind was playing tricks on him. Did he imagine the whole thing? The entire experience was so unreal, that for a moment, John questioned his sanity, and wondered whether or not the ship was ever there. He looked down at the street beneath his feet and stared at impression he had made in the snow to confirm his UFO experience was real. It was. Confused, he shook his head in amazement, made the sign of the cross, picked up his black bag and returned to his car.

Father John did not know or understand what had just happened, but after all, he was a religious man, and whatever it was, he believed it must be part of God's design. Like so many things John did not understand, he accepted it as a matter of faith, and he trusted it fit into God's divine plan and John was His obedient servant. He accepted things he could not change, and knowing it was futile, he never questioned the will of God.

* * * * * * *

Chapter 4: **The Wilkin's House**

The Wilkins house was exactly two miles up the road from where Father John encountered the UFO. His mind was so numb from the UFO experience Father John didn't remember driving to the Wilkins house. His thoughts were now of the task at hand; saving the soul of a twelve year old boy named Jeremy Wilkins. He located the house number on the mailbox at the end of the drive and was pleased to see fresh tire tracks in the long driveway. It had not been shoveled, and without the fresh tracks, the driveway would have been obscured by the blowing snow which was now starting to make drifts on the road. He remembered Barbara telling him of the doctor's visit, and he surmised the tracks must have been made by the doctor's car when he left a short time ago. *He exited the car* ✓

John turned right into the driveway and immediately saw there were lights lit on both floors of the old farm house. The driveway meandered back and forth for a few hundred feet between several large trees in the side yard before it reached the side of the old farm house. He parked next to a tractor covered with snow in front of an old wooden garage at the end of the driveway and walked a short snow covered path to the front porch. He stepped up on the wooden porch of the old house and looked through a large picture window where he saw a dimly lit room with a nice fire burning in the fireplace at the closed end of the room. Despite the fire, no one was there. He smelled the smoke blowing down from the chimney and he felt a sharp stinging wind on his face. John was cold and anxious to get inside. He set his case down on the porch

Father John's Gift

and looked through a diamond shape window in the front door and saw the light of a single lamp on an end table next to a large green sofa in the living room. The fireplace at the other end of the room looked warm and inviting. He tried the doorbell, but when he pressed it, he heard nothing and he concluded it must be broken. He opened the metal storm door, pulled off his right glove, and knocked hard on the heavy wood door to make himself heard. After a few seconds, he saw a couple come down the back stairs and walk to the front of the house to let him in. *and recognized her immediately*

Mrs. Barbara Wilkins, a woman in her mid-thirties, opened the door to greet him. He bent forward to pick up his case, and when she opened the door he looked up at her. He saw how tired and distraught she was by the impending death of Jeremy. She had dark circles under her eyes and looked as if she had been crying. Her clothes were wrinkled and hung on her as if she had slept in them and had worn them for several days. When she saw John look at her in the doorway, she became self-conscious, and she ran her fingers through her unkempt hair. But Barbara was a religious woman, and she felt immediate relief by the presence of Father John. At this moment in time, she needed to believe in a benevolent God and life after death for her son, Jeremy.

"Thank you for coming Father."

"Don't think anything of it Barbara", Father John replied. "I am here to help you."

James Wilkins, Jeremy's father, was a hard-working and proud man in his early forties. He greeted Father John as the priest entered the front room of the modest farmhouse. "Hello Father. The doctor left about an hour ago. We don't know how much time we have. Please hurry. Can I take your coat? Let me show you to Jeremy's room."

Father John smiled at the humble farmer. "Of course."

He handed his coat to James who placed it carefully over the back of the sofa in the living room. James turned back to face Father John and said, "Please, follow me." John followed James through the hallway and up the narrow set of stairs at the back of the house to Jeremy's bedroom. *and Barbara*

The bare wooden floor of Jeremy's room creaked as they entered it. The room was decorated with the expected fixtures of an active twelve year old boy. There were posters of sports figures, shelves with model racecars and airplanes, and baseball trophies, evidence that Jeremy had played Little League Baseball in each of the last three years.

Wasting no time, Father John went immediately to Jeremy's bedside. He set his black case on the floor, opened it and began removing the articles necessary to the sacrament of Extreme Unction. He had holy water, holy oil, a crucifix, a Bible, and his holy stole.

Jeremy had a high fever, and he mumbled something softly…incoherently. His face was red, and there were small beads of sweat on his forehead. It was obvious the boy was gravely ill.

Father John kissed his stole and placed it around his neck. He kissed the crucifix and placed it on the blanket covering Jeremy's chest, and he then placed his Bible on the nightstand next to Jeremy's bed. John looked at Jeremy's distraught parents, now at the end of the bed and John said, "Let us begin." He then looked back at Jeremy and began to pray.

"In the name of the Father, and of the Son, and of the Holy Spirit." Father John made the sign of the cross. As he started his prayer, James and Barbara Wilkins blessed themselves along with Father John. John bowed his head and said,

"Heavenly Father, we ask you to forgive your son, Jeremy Wilkins all of his trespasses, and upon the hour of his death, allow him to enter the kingdom of heaven. In Jesus name we pray the Lord's prayer." Father John again looked back at Jeremy's parents and nodded his head for them to join him in the prayer. Each bowed their heads, cupped their hands, and said the Lord's Prayer with Father John.

When the Lord's Prayer was done, Father John reached for the small vessel of blessed olive oil he had brought with him. He removed the cork, applied some of the oil to his right thumb, and began to apply it to Jeremy's forehead. As he touched Jeremy's head, John felt a sudden surge of energy which started in his chest and passed through his arm and hand and into Jeremy. Jeremy unexpectedly arched his back and with eyes closed and a grimace on his face he groaned, "Oh!" as if in pain. John was startled by Jeremy's exclamation and sudden movement. Barbara grasped out loud, and out of the corner of his eye John saw her grab the bed post for support, but he continued the

Father John's Gift

sacrament and made a small cross on Jeremy's forehead with the blessed oil and prayed:

"Through this holy anointing, may the Lord in his love and mercy help you with the grace of the Holy Spirit."[4]

He then anointed Jeremy's hands, and said,

"May the Lord who frees you from sin save you, and raise you up.[2] Amen."

"Amen." echoed Barbara.

Father John made the sign of the cross to end the brief sacrament, and then turned to face Barbara and James. "It's done. Jeremy is in God's hands now."

John collected his articles and place them gently back into his black bag. As he got up to leave, he noticed Jeremy resting easily. He motioned to Barbara and James to join him in the hallway outside Jeremy's room.

"Thank you Father." said Barbara.

"Yes…Father, thank you." repeated James.

"Is there anything more you would like me to do? Would you like me to stay the night?"

"No Father. I feel better now, just knowing that Jeremy will be with God in heaven." Barbara's statement was genuine. They both looked at James who could only nod in agreement. Seeing his son dying before his eyes, and having just given him up to God was more than James could bear. James said nothing but started to softly cry. Barbara turned and embraced her grief stricken husband.

"Well then, please call me tomorrow. Let me know how Jeremy is doing. OK?" His words masked his real belief that Jeremy would die and he would have to begin preparations for Jeremy's funeral service. It was horrific to think of burying such a young boy.

"Yes Father, we will."

John's ride home was uneventful. Father John could not get the sight of Jeremy and his distraught parents out of his mind. He had nearly forgotten the encounter with the UFO, but as he walked back into his room at St Andrews, he glanced at the trash can next to his desk and saw *The Investigator* newspaper he had discarded earlier in the evening. A shiver ran down his spine as he recalled his UFO experience from just a few hours earlier. His hands trembled as he leaned over and picked the tabloid out of the trashcan. He stopped and stared at what he had thought was a ridiculous headline, but now he looked at it with new eyes and a new-found respect. He folded the paper and carefully placed it in the large bottom right-hand drawer of his desk. Maybe the article wasn't so silly after all, and maybe Margaret wasn't so dumb for reading *The Investigator*. He would have to reread the article tomorrow.

* * * * * * * *

Chapter 5: **Recovery**

The next day was as busy as most others. Father John was up at five AM. He dressed and downed a quick cup of coffee before making his way to the church. He held Mass at five forty, and attended a prayer breakfast immediately afterwards in the St Andrews school cafeteria. His schedule was full of the duties of an inner city priest: visit with the children in the elementary school classrooms; hear confessions for an hour in the church; attend an hour of prayer and reflection which was immediately followed by lunch with any of the other St Andrews priests whose schedules allowed them to join him. The afternoon would be spent with a trip to a homeless shelter where he met with the residents and helped manage their food bank, and, if there was time, he would stop by Chicago General. It was Chicago's largest hospital, and John visited it every Tuesday to attend to the spiritual needs of sick and dying patients. However, no sooner had his prayer breakfast ended at eight twenty when John looked up from his table and saw Mary Margaret burst through the cafeteria door and come running toward him.

"Father John! Father John! You must come! Something wonderful has happened! I have Mrs. Wilkins on the phone in the rectory! She said her Jeremy is better this morning and she insisted on speaking to you."

Surprised by Margaret's exclamations, Father John stood up and excused himself from his breakfast parishioners. He took one last gulp from his coffee. The liquid was still hot, but he was thankful he felt no molar pain as he had the night before. He noted it, thought it was odd, but then rushed with Margaret back out of the school and across the street to the rectory.

"This is Father John."

"Father John? This is Barbara Wilkins. I have the most amazing news! Jeremy woke up this morning with no fever! He started talking to us like his old self. We called the doctor who told us to bring Jeremy immediately to his office. The doctor ran Jeremy's blood work early this morning, and he wants to redo the test, but it looks like Jeremy's illness is gone! The doctor said he believes Jeremy is now in remission! It's a miracle, Father John! We still can't believe it. I put my trust in the Lord, and I know that you made all the difference by coming last night. The doctor told us last night Jeremy would die, but I didn't give up hope! I stayed up all night and prayed for Jeremy to get well and he did! It's a miracle Father John! It's a miracle!"

Father John was speechless. He had personally witnessed several children die from cancer in the hospital, and he had all but given up hope that Jeremy would survive the night. Doctors were rarely wrong when they warned the parents that their child would die.

Collecting his thoughts, John said nothing.

"Father John? Are you there? Did you hear what I just said?"

"Yes. Yes. Barbara. I'm here, and I heard every word. That's wonderful news, Barbara. That's wonderful. Thank you for calling and letting me know."

Father John paused briefly and stared down the hall as he hung up the receiver.

"How's the Wilkins boy?" The question came from Monsignor Eckhart who had just entered the long hallway from his private quarters at the other end of the rectory.

"He's fine Monsignor." Father John said with a hint of disbelief in his voice. "That was his mother calling to tell me it appears that Jeremy is now in remission. They are running more tests to confirm the findings, but Barbara said the doctor thinks he may fully recover. It's remarkable."

Father John's Gift

"That's great to hear! Thank you Father." The Monsignor, with briefcase in hand, disappeared into his office across the hall.

Father John placed the receiver back on the hook and headed down the hall towards his room. He couldn't help but think it had something to do with his UFO encounter. He had told no one of his encounter and believed it was so fantastic a story that he dared not tell anyone about it. He had heard of UFO encounters and read of alien abductions in Margaret's "Investigator" newspaper. It was the stuff of science fiction movies which he never took seriously, and he thought it was convenient that the encounters always took place at night, under the cover of darkness. No, he thought, only crackpots and uneducated people really believed in such things. He believed the scientific community's verdict on extraterrestrial life was still out. Though he didn't know much about Science, John knew enough about astronomy to know the universe was immense... that there might be life on other planets, in other solar systems, in other galaxies. But are they visiting us here and now? It was a question he couldn't answer, and one he didn't want to think about.

Though he now knew it was real, he would not tell anyone about the UFO. He thought if he spoke a word of it to anyone, he might never be taken seriously again. If he did, it would mean the end of his career as a priest. Besides, it had all happened so fast, that on some subconscious level he doubted it really happened at all. The encounter seemed like a strange dream, an odd memory of something which was not real. John was in denial. He didn't want to believe it. He decided to just put such thoughts out of his mind. Tomorrow was another day. He wanted his life and his routine to continue the way it always had.

Life at St Andrews continued normally the next several days for Father John. But word of Jeremy Wilkins remarkable recovery from leukemia spread like wild fire through the parish. The parish had a tight network of active women, and several of them were at the parish breakfast with Father John when Margaret had interrupted them. Margaret's emotional outburst provided them with new material which they were more than happy to know about and tell their friends. They had little else to do but to spread parish news and church gossip.

Though such news rarely if ever got back to any of the St Andrews priests, the network was now a buzz about Father John. It didn't hurt that John was a tall attractive man, and was secretly cherished by many if not most of the Club's female members, all of whom perceived him to be a rising star at St Andrews.

* * * * * * * *

Chapter 6: **The Playoff Game**

As he walked to the huddle for what would be the last play of the game, the Bears quarterback, Ted Reiner was so nervous, he pissed in his pants. It had happened a few times before, but never in a playoff game. His pants were dark black so Ted tried to pretend it didn't happen, and he hoped no one would notice. But now in the huddle, Ted caught a knowing grin and a little chuckle from Gary Bowman, his star receiver. Ted shook his head slightly and sneered at Gary through his helmet, hoping Gary would get the message, and just shut up about it.

The Green Bay Packers and the Chicago Bears had been neck and neck with each other all season long, and today's game was no exception. It was the NFC Championship game and the winner would go on to play the Pittsburgh Steelers in the Super Bowl. The score was 21 to 17 in favor of the Packers, but the Bears had possession and were on the Packers 30 yard line. It was the third down and eight yards to go. With only fifteen seconds left in the game, everyone knew it was now or never for the Bears, and Ted knew that Gary was his best bet to score. The entire team knew it.

At age twenty four, Gary Bowman was the fastest tight end in the league, and the Bears had paid dearly for him and for good reason. His hands were magic. At a height of six foot five, Gary could catch anything thrown in his vicinity.

Ted looked around the huddle at his team. He could see it in their faces; they were all ready and anxious to see what play he would call.

"Let's got to go for it. ... Let's do the 'Sugar Loaf Right'... on twenty five."

Ted had discussed the play with the coach and had practiced the pass with Gary more times than he could count. The play was simple enough. Gary would run straight up field, head fake to the inside, then cut back to the sideline and look for the ball over his right shoulder. It worked again and again in practice. It had to work now, or the season would be over for the Bears.

Now down on his haunches, Ted looked up at Gary. "You ready?"

"Yeah, I'm pumped!" Gary could hardly contain himself.

Ted made a final glance around the huddle. "Any questions?" There was nothing but silence. Everyone was on board for the play.

"OK guys. Let's do this! ... Remember, go on twenty five."

Ted stood up and placed his fist in the middle of the huddle and each member piled their hands on top of his. Pumping his fist up and down the team joined in as Ted yelled the chant as he had a thousand times before:

"One!"

"Two!"

"Three!"

"Go Bears!"

They broke their huddle and all walked slowly to the line of scrimmage.

As the Bears lined up for the play, the roar of the crowd was deafening. Ted took two steps back from his center, looked left and right into the stands and motioned with both hands for the crowd to quiet down. The crowd understood. The Bears fans went quiet, but the Packer fans kept up the noise. Ted stepped up to his center and began his call as loud as he could,

"Fifteen! .... Thirty two! .....Seventy four! ...... Twenty five!"

The snap was good and the play was in motion. Ted fell back deep and ran around his left side. He had to throw the ball diagonally across the remaining length of the field. It was a long pass, but not beyond his capability. By running left Ted drew attention away from Gary, who was now breaking right towards the sideline. The play only lasted ten seconds, but to Ted, it was an eternity. Ted could see Gary was at least

Father John's Gift

three steps ahead of the Packers defensive receiver. Now in position, Ted let the ball fly with all his might and then he dodged a Packer lineman who dove at him just before he released the ball. Ted had done his part. It was up to Gary now.

The crowd fell silent and held their breath while the ball was in flight. With his adrenalin flowing, Ted had thrown it long.

As the ball approached, Gary jumped as high as he could with his arms outstretched. He caught the ball ten feet in the air, but as he pulled it toward his chest he felt the crushing blow of a Packer's defender who came from behind and slammed his helmet and shoulder pads into Gary's legs. Gary's string bean body tumbled over the tackle's back and did a backward summersault in mid-air. He had jumped for the ball at the fourth yard line and he would have landed on the second, but the hit from behind propelled him forward causing him to land on his back and right leg, just over the goal line.

The crowd went wild about the spectacular catch and touchdown, but fell silent when Gary did not get up. He had done his job. He had scored the winning touchdown for the Bears, but his right leg was now broken, and he lay twisted on the field. His leg was bent backwards at an angle which no healthy leg could possibly make. As he laid on his back in the Packer's end zone, Gary stared at the stadium lights and yelled out when he felt a searing pain from his right leg. The pain was so intense Gary was immediately nauseous. He released the ball, pulled off his helmet and puked on the field in front of 50,000 stadium fans and countless more on television. He knew his season was over.

Thanks to Gary, his team would go on to play Pittsburgh in the Super Bowl, but he would not be a part of it. His dream of a lifetime was over.

* * * * * * * *

Chapter 7: **Confession**

Christine O'Roark, age fifteen, was a petite, shy redhead and was physically developed for her age. She was the only child of Helen Fitzpatrick, an insurance company secretary, but she had never known her father. Her father abandoned her mother and moved out of state as soon as he learned her mother was pregnant with Christine. Left to raise Christine by herself, her mother was so disillusioned with men she consigned herself to a single life; she never married, and she never dated again. Life was hard for Christine and her mother, but Christine didn't know any better. Her mother saw to it her physical needs were met, and despite the lack of a father, Christine was a relatively happy teenage girl most of the time.

It was a Friday afternoon and Christine went to church right after school. Christine rarely ever went to church on a Friday, but the next Wednesday was "Ash Wednesday" which marked the beginning of the Catholic Season of Lent. She wanted to go to confession in preparation for Easter. Sister Agatha, who taught Christine's religion class at St Andrews, had talked at length about the importance of Easter to the Christian faith, and had stressed the need for always making a good confession before one entered the Lenten Season. Christine was a good Catholic, and she took Sister Agatha's instructions seriously. But on this occasion, Christine had a dual purpose in coming to Confession. Christine wanted to confess her sins, but she also felt a strong need to unburden her soul with thoughts which had been troubling her.

Father John's Gift

Christine entered the St Andrews confessional and closed the heavy wooden door as quietly as she could. Despite her best effort, the confessional door closed with a loud click which echoed throughout the almost empty church. She sat down on the hard wooden bench, and then knelt before the semi-opaque yellow window which separated her from Father John. As she did, a dim light came on revealing the shadow of the priest on the other side of the window. Though the image was indistinct, she knew it was him. Christine knew Father John said Confessions every Friday afternoon, but this was the first time she confessed to him since she made her first confession, nearly nine years ago. She didn't try to avoid him, but somehow she always managed to get Father Jim or Father Pete whenever she went to confession on a Wednesday after school, or after a late Saturday afternoon Mass, just before going home for dinner.

Father John slid the small door open revealing him to Christine as a dim shadow through the milky yellow glass. He began the sacrament with the sign of the cross.

Christine started the Sacrament of Penance as she learned it at age seven. The church required their second graders to go to Confession in order to cleanse their souls from sin before they made their First Communion. Christine had gone to Confession many times since then, and making a confession was ordinarily easy for her, but today, knowing her priest was Father John, Christine was nervous. "Bless me Father, for I have sinned. It has been one month and two days since my last confession. These are my sins. I talked back to my mother twice, and lied about doing my homework to my History teacher."

"And what else my child." Father John knew her confession was too short to have covered a full month since her last confession, and her quick recital of her sins sounded rote, as if she had memorized them in preparation for the sacrament. Her delivery was not unlike many he had heard from several other nervous teens from St Andrews. John knew there had to be more.

Christine hedged in her reply, "Nothing else..."

Father John pressed her to continue, "Are you sure? Is there something else you wish to confess?"

R. Allan Worrell

"Well..." Christine was hesitant to continue. She had rehearsed this confession a dozen times in her head, but now that she was actually in the confessional, she was afraid to say what she knew she must. She hesitated, and she struggled to think of something else to say to avoid telling Father John her real problem, but her mind went blank. Father John said nothing and waited for her to reply.

Ten seconds... fifteen seconds... twenty seconds of silence passed between them before Christine could no longer stand the silence. She could think of nothing else to say, so in a whispered voice she blurted out what had been troubling her. "Father, I have dreams about Jesus."

Her remark was unexpected, but Father John felt the psychological door was now open, and he believed her. He echoed her statement to get her to elaborate. "You have dreams about Jesus?"

Christine paused briefly as she thought of what to say next. She could not now retract her statement. She had said it, and she had to move forward and tell Father John what was bothering her. "Yes Father, Jesus comes to me in my dreams."

"And that troubles you?"

"Well, He makes love to me."

Father John was shocked. Although he knew her from school, Father John didn't recognize Christine's voice, but he guessed his confessor was a young girl at St Andrews High School. Christine's confession of sexual dreams about Jesus was not unheard of. He had been warned of such confessions when he attended the Seminary, but this was a first for Father John. He knew sex was a sensitive subject to such a young woman, and her telling him this secret took a great deal of courage. Father John kept his composure and took a deep breath, but tried hard not to let Christine hear him. Once again, he echoed her last thought in his most calm and non-judgmental voice. He wanted her to talk, but he didn't want to upset her.

"Jesus makes love to you in your dreams?"

"Yes Father."

John had to know how much his confessor understood about sex. He knew there were many school yard myths which might be accepted as fact by a young, naive teenager. Could she simply be dreaming of kisses? He had to find out.

Father John's Gift

"Tell me my child; do you know what a virgin is?"

"Yes Father."

"Are you a virgin?"

"Yes Father."

Father John felt a sigh of relief at her answer. There had been an out of wedlock pregnancy by a young teen in the parish last year, and it had caused much pain to the family who needed counseling and had to get help to deal with the pregnancy. The young girl's parents agreed to allow her to deliver the baby and put it up for adoption, but she had to be transferred out of St Andrews parish, to a home and school for pregnant girls on the outskirts of Chicago. Her family had suffered much humiliation and pain by the episode, and Father John did not want to see it repeated if it could be helped. He pressed on.

"It is normal for all of us to love Christ."

"Yes Father."

"But our love for Christ and his love for us is not sexual. You must think of Him as a Father who loves you, yes, but only wants you to be happy… free from sin in the eyes of God. Christ wants you to enter the kingdom of heaven, to be with God when you die."

"Yes Father."

"Do you understand what I am saying?"

"Yes Father."

"Good. I want you to pray about this, and ask for the Lord's guidance. Can you do that?

"Yes Father. I can do that." Christine was relieved the sacrament was about to end and she didn't have to say any more.

"For your penance, I want you to say five, "Our Fathers" and five, "Hail Marys".

"Yes Father."

Ten prayers for penance was the standard fare for Christine's confessions. She always received this penance from all the other priests, regardless of the sins she confessed. She once thought they must have established some priestly pact; a penance rule book established for confessed minor infractions. As a young teen, Christine often wondered what the penance would be for a person who committed some terrible evil sin against God and man.

R. Allan Worrell

"Your sins are forgiven. Go in peace."

"Thank you Father."

Christine made the sign of the cross with Father John as he ended the sacrament as it had begun. Father John slid the window shut between them, and as Christine got up to leave she felt frustrated that her confession had ended this way. It did not go as she had planned. She had bared her soul to her priest, but he did not understand what she was trying to tell him. Father John did not know Christine had just lied to him about having a love affair with Jesus. Her secret love was not Jesus, it was Father John.

Christine didn't know what to do. At the tender age of fifteen, without a father at home, Christine didn't know how to gain the love and affection she desperately needed from an adult male. Although all her girlfriends at school had fathers, they rarely talked about them with Christine. Christine didn't know their fathers, and she had never even seen her friends interact with them. Taught since the first grade in a Catholic school, all of Christine's teachers had been Nuns. Father John was the only adult man she really knew, and now, at the age of fifteen, she found herself strangely attracted to him. The fact that he was a priest and had taken a vow of chastity had never occurred to Christine. She didn't know what to do, but Christine left the confessional frustrated and more determined than ever to get Father John's love and attention. She would have to find a way.

* * * * * * * * *

Chapter 8: **Katie McLeary**

It was now early March, and true to form, the Chicago weather started to behave erratically. It was that transitional month between winter and spring, when nature flirts with warmer weather and winter loosens its grip. It had been a hard winter, and Chicagoans were anxious for the arrival of spring and the warmer weather they knew would follow. And so, all felt relief when the thermometer finally rose above forty degrees for a few days in a row and heavy coats and boots were left behind.

Katie McLeary, age fourteen, and her brother Bill, age eight, were on their way home from school on a Monday afternoon. Though it was still cold outside, the sun was bright, the snow was melting, and there was a hint of spring in the air.

"Katie...let's take the shortcut home!" Bill was in a hurry to see if the package he had ordered from Sears had arrived. He had shoveled sidewalks and driveways all winter for neighbors and had saved his money so he could afford the latest addition to his WW II model airplane collection. The Sears catalog stated that delivery could be expected in six to eight weeks, and more than seven weeks had passed since he had placed his order.

Katie was older and wiser, and knew the dangers of taking the shortcut on such a warm day. The route included a brief crossing of the Des Plaines River, a tributary of the Chicago. The Des Plaines always froze during the winter and could be easily crossed, but it was always dangerous in the spring when the ice began to melt.

"OK Bill." Katie knew it had been a harsh winter and that parts of Lake Michigan had frozen. It was still early in the season and there had not been much time for the river to melt. And so, when her little brother made the suggestion they take the shortcut, she relented. What Katie did not know, and could not know, was that Harken Steel, a large steel manufacturer three miles up the Des Plaines River, had received a major order from Chrysler Corporation. Chrysler had expanded their Valiant line of compact cars and had doubled its normal order from Harken. In order to meet Chrysler's demand for steel, Harkin had been running their mills at 100% capacity for more than two weeks. Cooling the newly forged steel resulted in the discharge into the river of millions of gallons of warm waste water. Although the Des Plaines River would ordinarily have been safe to cross at this time of year, the ice was made thin by the warm under-currents running downstream from the steel foundry.

When Katie and Billy reached the river, it looked harmless enough. The river was still snow-covered from last week's five inch snowfall. The sky was a beautiful blue, and the bright sun light glistened off the still pristine snow which covered the river ice.

"Race you across!" Bill yelled to his sister as he took off across the ice.

Katie loved the view of the snow on the river, but she now had second thoughts about crossing it. "Bill!" Katie screamed at her kid brother, but it was too late. Bill was already ten to fifteen feet on the ice, running with all his might to beat her to the other side.

The river was only fifty feet wide at the crossing point, and at first it looked as if there would be no problem. Bill could not see that the ice beneath the snow had melted to less than an inch near the middle of the river where the warm waters from the steel plant had been running.

When he reached the middle of the river, Bill fell through the ice and snow in the blink of an eye. It was as if he had disappeared by magic. Katie watched with horror as her brother vanished before her eyes. She had not even left the river's edge.

Father John's Gift

"Bill! Bill! Oh God no! Oh God! Oh God!"

Her heart raced in disbelief at what she had just witnessed. She knew the dangers of following her brother out onto the ice. She dropped her red book bag to mark the spot where Bill had crossed and started running along the bank of the river to the nearest bridge, located about one hundred yards up the river. "Why didn't we take that bridge!" she cried.

"Bill! Oh God, Bill!" Katie was mature for her age and her mother reminded her often to watch out for her younger brother. How could she have let this happen?

When she reached the base of the bridge, Katie started up the hill to the road fifteen feet above her. Her shoes slipped on the melting snow and she muddied her hands and the knees of her pants on the side of the hill during her climb to the street. When she reached the road, she looked both ways and saw no one. She turned to run down the middle of the street towards town for help. Just then a black and white police car came around the bend in the road doing about twenty five miles an hour. The car almost hit Katie, but the driver saw her at the last moment and slammed on the breaks, swerved to the right, and stopped just past her. She ran up to the car waving her muddied hands and arms wildly and as tears streamed down her face.

"Damn!" The driver exhaled deeply and swallowed hard from his near miss.

The driver, a fifty two year-old police chief named Jim Perlman, had just ended his shift and was on his way home when he nearly hit Katie. He was still dressed in his police uniform. Katie ran up to the car door crying as the Chief rolled down his window.

"Help! Help! Help me please!"

The Chief had encountered many emergency situations in his career and he recognized the real thing when he saw it. Now at the side of the road, he turned on the police car's cherry red flasher and quickly exited the car. At six feet five inches tall he towered over Katie. He placed his two large hands on Katie's shoulders and spoke in a slow, deep voice in a deliberate manner. "OK. OK! Calm down now.... We will fix this. What's your name, and what's the problem?"

"My name is Katie McLeary... and my little brother Billy just fell through the ice on the river!"

"Where?"

"Down the river near that large tree!" Katie pointed to her red book-bag on the river bank. "I dropped my red book bag over there to mark the spot! Do you see it?"

"Yes, I see it."

Chief Perlman then looked further down river and saw that the river took a sharp bend just beyond the point where Katie had said her little brother had gone under. He made a mental note of a two story white colonial which backed to the river. The house had a large blue spruce in the side yard which he believed would be easy to spot from the street side of the property. The Chief noticed none of the adjacent houses had one like it.

"OK", he commanded as he opened the back car door. "Get in."

They jumped into the car and the Chief turned on his siren and yelled, "Hold on!" He stomped on the gas pedal. With the steering wheel in his left hand, he grabbed the police radio microphone with his right. "Linda, Chief Perlman here! Send an ambulance to the two hundred block of Oak Street. Have them look for my car. I will leave the cherry on."

"You got it Chief!" the radio replied.

The black and white sped down to the next corner on the other side of the bridge and made a sharp right turn into a quaint old neighborhood with big houses on Oak Street. The chief stepped on the gas once again, and the car sped down the street a quarter of a block. He spotted the large white colonial with the tall blue spruce and he came to an abrupt stop in front if the house. He cut the siren and yelled again at Katie, "OK, let's go!" He left the car running and the car's red cherry flashing for the ambulance driver to see.

Katie followed Chief Perlman as he ran between the houses to the back yard adjacent to the river. The yards were large, and each ended with a few trees and a small dock at the edge of the river. The couple ran to the river, and the Chief looked back towards the bridge where they were, just moments ago.

Father John's Gift

The Chief pointed to the large oak tree on the opposite side, a hundred feet up the river from where they stood. "Is that it? Is that the tree?"

Katie looked hard and spotted her red bag in the snow beneath the large tree.

"Yes! That's it! That's it!"

"OK!"

The Chief grabbed a snow shovel that had been left on the dock. Local boys had used it to scrape the river ice to play hockey a few weeks before. Jim began shoveling the snow along the side of the dock which faced the sharp bend in the river. The Chief was in luck. His calculated guess of the water flow was correct. Looking down through the ice he could see the body of Billy McLeary. Bill was caught on a pylon holding up the dock.

The dock surface was only a foot above the ice. The Chief turned the flat shovel end for end, and he began to smash the ice with the handle. When the hole was large enough, the Chief lay down on the doc, reached through the hole in the ice, and grabbed the frigid bluish body of Bill McLeary. He pulled Bill up onto the wooden dock, laid the small boy on his back, and began mouth to mouth resuscitation as Katie looked on in horror at her nearly frozen little brother.

As the chief worked hard to revive Billy, they heard the distant siren of an approaching ambulance. Linda had done her job, and help was on the way.

* * * * * * * *

Chapter 9: **The ER**

The police called Billy's mother at home at 3:00 in the afternoon.

"Mrs. McLeary, this is the Chicago Police Department. My name is Officer Fletcher. Do you have a daughter named, Katie and a son named, Billy?"

"Yes? What is it? Is something wrong?" Sally McLeary had never received a call from the police department and the officer had her full attention. Sally didn't know what to think.

"Mrs. McLeary, I'm afraid I have some bad news for you. There has been an accident, and your son Billy fell into the Des Planes River this afternoon. He has been rushed to Chicago General ER in an ambulance."

"Is he OK?"

"I'm sorry Mrs. McLeary, I don't have that information. You will have to speak to someone at the hospital about that."

"What about Katie? Is she OK?"

"Yes. I understand Katie is OK. Our police chief took her to the ER after Billy was put on the ambulance. Katie is waiting there to meet you. Can you or your husband go to the hospital now?"

"My husband is out of town, but I will leave right away."

"Good luck, Mrs. McLeary. I hope your son is OK."

"Thank you... I'm sorry, I forgot your name."

"It's Officer Fletcher. I work at the 32nd Precinct."

"Thank you Officer." Tears started to flow as Sally processed what she had just learned. With her husband out of town she thought of Father John. He had helped her when she had a miscarriage two

Father John's Gift

months ago, and had spiritually guided her through her ordeal. If anyone could help her, she thought, he could. She dialed St Andrews.

"St Andrews Rectory, Margaret speaking."

"Hi Margaret. Is Father John there?"

"Who is this please?"

"I'm sorry Margaret. This is Sally McLeary."

"No, Mrs. McLeary. Father John is at Chicago General Hospital right now. He volunteers there every Wednesday afternoon."

"I just got a call from the Chicago Police. They told me my son Billy fell into the Des Plaines River this afternoon and was taken to Chicago General. Can you reach Father John and ask him to meet me there?"

"Yes, of course! I'm so sorry to hear about your son. Is he OK?"

"I don't know. I'm still at home now, but I'm leaving for the hospital now."

Margaret paused, and thought about what she could do. "I will call the hospital and have Father John paged. They can let him know to meet you in the ER. Will that work?"

"Yes. Thanks Margaret."

Sally hung up the phone and realized she had not said goodbye.

Father John was nearing the end of his rounds when he heard his name over the hospital PA system. He located a hospital house phone and was told to proceed to the ER to meet Sally McLeary when she arrived. John didn't know Billy McLeary had arrived ten minutes earlier, breathing but still comatose, and the doctors were working hard to revive him.

Father John arrived in the ER just as Sally McLeary entered through the outside door.

"Father John! Thank God you are here!"

"What is it Sally? What's wrong?"

"It's Billy. He fell through the ice in the Des Plaines River on his way home from school with Katie. He and Katie should already be here. Father, I'm so afraid!" She wiped the tears from her eyes.

"OK Sally. Let's not jump to any conclusions. Let's find out what's going on. Have you called Dan?"

40

"No Father. Dan is out of town on an important business trip. I don't want to call him until I know what to tell him."

"OK Sally, that sounds right. Let's see what the nurse knows about Billy."

He and Sally turned and approached a large desk, the ER check-in point. A nurse was seated behind the counter doing paper work. As they came close to the desk, the nurse put down her pencil and looked up at them. Sally was the first to speak.

"Nurse, do you have a patient named Billy McLeary? I'm his mother."

The nurse's phone rang and she glanced at a light on the phone and saw the call was from an outside line. Knowing the call would roll over to the hospital operator, she ignored it. She stood up from behind her desk and looked back at Sally and said, "Yes Mrs. McLeary, Billy is here. He arrived about ten minutes ago, and the ER doctors are working on him now. Your daughter Katie is here too. A policeman brought her here just after Billy arrived. I will take you to Katie, but I need you to fill out your health insurance information for Billy." She grabbed a clipboard with the necessary forms.

"Can't I see him? How is he?"

"Mrs. McLeary, the doctors are doing all they can for Billy. We must let them do their work without any interference. Let me take you to Katie, and I will keep you informed about Billy's condition. Please come with me."

Unable to do anything else, Sally looked at Father John for support.

"She's right Sally. I will see what I can find out about Billy after you meet with Katie."

The nurse walked around from behind her desk and handed Sally the medical insurance forms on a clip board. "Please fill these out and give them back to me when you are done. Now follow me, and I will take you to Katie." She then led Sally and Father John across the waiting room which was half full of patients to a closed door marked, **"Private: Hospital Staff Only"**. Before entering, the nurse stopped and turned to whisper to both Father John and Sally, "You should know that Katie is quite shaken up. She faults herself for Bill's accident."

Father John's Gift

Sally looked with fear at Father John who gave her a solemn nod. With that, the nurse opened the door and allowed Sally and Father John to enter the room where Katie was waiting for her mother. The nurse then closed the door behind Father John to return to her desk in the ER.

When Katie looked up and saw her mother enter the room, she jumped out of her chair and rushed into her mother's open arms. "Oh Mom! I couldn't help it. Bill just ran out onto the ice and then he was gone! It happened so fast, there was nothing I could do! Oh Mom, it was awful! The policeman helped me, but Billy was so blue!" Katie started to cry.

"Don't worry honey. I know it wasn't your fault. Shhh, stop crying now. I know you did your best, Katie." Both mother and daughter were crying and hugging each other.

Father John started back to the door they had just entered, "Sally, I'm going to go check on Bill." Sally started to get up to accompany him, but he raised his hand to stop her. "No Sally, you stay here with Katie. I can go places in the hospital where you can't go. I'll find out what's happening to Billy, and then I'll come back to let you know."

Sally gave Katie another squeeze and replied, "OK, thank you Father. We will stay here."

Because he had been there for years, Father John was a fixture at Chicago General, and almost all of the one thousand, two hundred and thirty hospital staff members knew his face, if not his name. John had little trouble moving about in normally restricted areas of the hospital. He walked back into the waiting room and passed through a pair of swinging doors marked, "Hospital Staff Only." He saw a long row of curtains on both sides of the room. Behind each curtain was a patient in a bed or a chair waiting their turn to see a hospital resident. It was business as usual at Chicago General. All the curtains were currently occupied, and more patients were waiting their turn in the waiting room.

Father John walked down the hall of curtains and turned the corner looking for Billy. Doctors and nurses were clustered around a patient. He walked quickly over to peer through the hospital staff to see if Billy was there. As he approached the group he heard a doctor say, "He's stable. That's all we can do for now."

R. Allan Worrell

The nurses and doctors suddenly backed away from the bed revealing a small boy in a light blue hospital gown. It was Billy McLeary; alive, but comatose. An oxygen mask covered his mouth and nose and a clear hose ran to a green oxygen bottle with a gauge mounted on the leg of the gurney.

The primary ER doctor turned to Father John and gave him a look of recognition. "May I help you Father?"

"Is that Billy McLeary?"

"Yes. That's Billy. Is the family here?"

"Yes Doctor. His mother and sister are outside in the ER waiting room. What can I tell them?"

The doctor was unusually blunt. "Billy is comatose, but stable for now. He may or may not ever come out of his coma. There is no way for us to know for sure. We will keep him overnight in the ICU and monitor him closely. If there are no complications for the next twenty four hours, we will feel better about his long term prognosis, and he will be moved to a standard hospital room tomorrow."

"I understand. May the family see him now, doctor?"

"Yes. We have done all we can. You can ask the family to come back here. Billy will be admitted, and we will have him moved to the ICU."

"OK. Thank you Doctor, I'll go get his family."

Father John returned to the waiting area. As he entered the small room, both Sally and Katie jumped up to learn Billy's status.

"Father John! How's Billy? Can we see him now?"

John looked at Sally with a serious look on his face. "Yes, you can see him. I will take you to Billy now. But Sally, you should know Billy is still in a coma, and the doctors say he is still in great danger. They want to keep him in the Intensive Care Unit tonight so they can monitor him closely." Sally nodded with sadness and fear in her face. Katie starred at the floor, squeezed her mother's hand and said nothing.

Father John led the couple back through the waiting room to the hall of curtains where he last saw Billy. As they approached Billy's bed, Sally ran up to her son calling his name over and over again, "Billy! Billy! Billy!" Father John and Katie watched as Sally stroked her young son's Irish red hair, squeezed his hand and kissed his forehead.

Father John's Gift

"Billy, it's Mommy! I'm right here Billy. I'm not going to leave you Billy."

Katie stood silently next to her mother with tears in her eyes. She was shocked to see her active little brother lay out on the examination table in a hospital gown and was moved by her mother's tears. She was struck by the sight of Billy lying unconscious in a hospital gown and lay motionless before her, and she feared Billy might die. Less than an hour ago Billy was so full of life, such a thought was unthinkable. Would she ever see Billy run and play again? As she silently wiped away her tears, Katie was overcome with emotion and realized for the first time just how much she loved her little brother. She said nothing. She stood silently as she replayed the events of the day over and over again in her mind. Katie felt helpless as she looked up at her mother and saw her crying again. Father John placed his hand on Katie's shoulder to comfort and reassure her. She looked up at him and he said nothing but nodded to let her know he understood.

An ER nurse walked up, pulled back Billy's curtain exposing the group and said, "We will transfer Billy to a room on the ICU floor now. You may come along if you wish."

Father John replied, "Thank you Nurse."

A hospital transportation aide suddenly appeared and helped the nurse place Billy onto a gurney for his ride from the ER to the Intensive Care Unit. Sally, Katie, and Father John accompanied them as they moved Billy to his room down the hall and up in an elevator to the ICU on the fifth floor.

When they reached the room, Sally turned to Katie and asked her to wait in the room with Billy. When Katie was out of earshot, Sally turned to Father John. Still in the hall outside of Billy's room, Father John spoke up, "What is it Sally?"

"Father, I'm scared. I'm scared that Billy might not make it tonight."

"I know Sally. That's understandable, but you must not give up hope. The doctors say Billy could wake up at any time. Only God knows if or when he will wake up."

"Father..."

The look in her eyes spoke volumes. John knew where the conversation was going and understood how hard it was for Sally to say what they both were now thinking. "What if he dies without ever waking up?"

"Sally, do you want me to perform the Last Rites?"

It was all Sally could do to hold back her tears. "Yes Father. Can you do that please?

"OK Sally. I will have to get my things. I don't normally carry them around in the hospital. I keep them in my car for emergencies. I'll be back as soon as I can."

"Thank you Father." Sally pulled a chair up beside Billy's bed.

Father John left the group to retrieve his priest bag. When he returned, he stopped by the ICU nurse's station. There were several nurses there, and he quickly identified the nurse in charge.

"Nurse, my name is Father John. I am with the McLeary family in Room 517. Little Billy McLeary is comatose, and the mother has asked me to perform the Last Rites. I would like to do that now."

The head nurse turned around and scanned the charts which hung on the wall behind her and quickly found Billy's chart. She turned back to Father John and as she looked over the chart and said, "I don't see any reason why you can't do that. We are in a monitor mode for Billy. Thank you for letting us know, Father. How long will it take?"

"Not long. It's a short sacrament which lasts about five minutes."

"OK. Thank you Father. I'll let the other nurses know so you are not disturbed."

Father John entered Billy's room. While Father John was gone, Sally had told Katie what she had asked Father John to do, and she explained the sacrament of Extreme Unction to Katie who was fascinated to hear it. When Father John returned, they were waiting for him …anxious to see the Last Rites performed before them for the first time in their lives.

Father John went directly to Billy's bedside and began the routine which he had performed more times than he cared to remember. It had been less than two weeks since he had administered the Last Rites to Jeremy, and he was now saddened that he would have to do it again on yet another young boy.

Father John's Gift

As before, John began the sacrament with the Sign of the Cross and The Lord's Prayer. And as did with Jeremy, he applied the holy oil to his thumb and began to apply it to Billy's forehead.

"Through this holy anointing, may the Lord in his love and mercy help you with the grace of the Holy Spirit."

Father John had barely finished his sentence when Billy's eyes opened wide, he sat up in bed and yelled out his sister's name!

"Katie!"

Katie's name was the last thought Billy had when he went into the water, and it was the first thought to enter his mind when he suddenly and unexpectedly woke up.

Sally and Katie were both stunned by Billy's outburst, but no more so than Father John who jumped back away from the bed so violently he struck a table behind him, and he sent the ceramic table lamp crashing to the floor.

Sally immediately went to hug Billy. "Billy!" Both she and Katie were crying again, but this time they cried tears of joy to see Billy awake. Ignoring Father John, Sally turned to Katie and yelled, "Katie, go get the nurse!"

Katie ran out of the room and down the hall towards the nurse's station. "Nurse! Come quick! Billy's awake! Billy's awake!"

The three nurses at the station all heard Katie's cries for help. The charge nurse instructed Billy's assigned nurse to run to the room while she paged the doctor on call, Dr. Lund. He was attending to another patient in the ICU down the hall when he heard his page over the PA system. He excused himself, left the patient's room, and reached for the first white house-phone a few doors down the hall. He immediately dialed the nurse's station.

"This is Dr. Lund."

"Doctor, it appears our coma patient, Billy McLeary, is now awake in Room 517."

"Thank you Nurse. I will be right there."

Doctor Lund, a tall thin man in his fifties with bushy eyebrows, was present when Billy came in through the ER just twenty minutes earlier. Dr. Lund didn't work in the ER, but he was entering the hospital through the ER when Billy's ambulance pulled up. It was the beginning of a hospital shift change, and one of the ER docs was late. Since the ER was short staffed, Dr. Lund helped out by caring for Bill. He had seen many coma cases in his career, and knew they were all unique. Coma outcomes were always difficult to predict. Still, he was surprised when he was told that Billy was now awake. He had over twelve years of experience in the ER, and had he never seen a coma patient recover so quickly. He knew that usually they recovered in days or weeks, if at all.

Though groggy, Billy was sitting up in bed with his mother on one side and the nurse on the other as Dr. Lund entered the room. The nurse had already taken Billy's vitals: his temperature, his blood pressure, and she had made notes for the Doctor in Billy's chart.

Dr. Lund, grinned from ear to ear at Billy and said, "Billy? I'm Doctor Lund. You had us all worried young man! How do you feel?"

Billy looked up at the Doctor. "I don't know. Tired, I guess."

"Well, let's have a look at you." The Doctor sat down on the edge of Billy's bed and removed a penlight from his coat pocket to examine Billy's pupils. With the pen-light in one hand, the doctor tilted Billy's head back with the other and with his thumb held each of Bill's eyelids open one at a time to check his pupils. "Just look straight at me, Billy." He waived the penlight from side to side in front of Billy's eyes.

After checking Billy's eyes Dr. Lund relaxed and sat back and addressed Billy again. "Do you know where you are Billy?"

"In the hospital?"

"Yes, that's right. Do you know what happened to you? What's the last thing that you remember?"

"I was crossing the river, and I fell through the ice. I tried to swim, but I couldn't breathe! And the water was so cold!"

"That's right. Very good Billy."

He turned to the ICU nurse who had just finished writing notes on Billy's chart, recording what had just happened. Dr. Lund extended his hand and took the chart from the nurse.

"Everything look OK, nurse?"

The nurse handed the chart to the doctor. "Yes Doctor."

Doctor Lund scanned Billy's vitals, and looked for anything out of the ordinary. "Uh-huh, good, good, good... and good!" He stood up shook his head slowly, and raised his bushy eyebrows in disbelief at what he saw on the chart.

Doctor Lund then turned to Sally. "Mrs. McLeary, I have to say that Billy's sudden recovery is remarkable. Everything in his chart looks good. I want to keep Billy here overnight for observation. Coma is a strange thing. To be honest, we don't fully understand it, and I want to make sure there are no side effects from the coma. He seems to be fine now, and looks no worse for wear." With that remark Dr. Lund winked at Billy, who smiled back at him. "I will check in on Billy early tomorrow morning, when I do my rounds. If there is no change, then I think he can go home."

Sally replied, "Thank you Doctor! Is it OK if I stay with him tonight?"

"Sure. I'm afraid those chairs aren't too comfortable for sleeping. If you want to stay, you're more than welcome."

"Can I stay too?" Katie wanted desperately to know that her little brother was all right, and she didn't like the idea of going home to a baby sitter that she knew her mother would call.

Sally looked at the Doctor for an answer.

"Yes. I think that will be OK." He turned to the nurse. "Nurse, do you think you can find a cot for Katie to sleep on?" He then winked at Katie.

"Yes Doctor."

With that the Doctor turned and started to leave. "I'll see you tomorrow Billy. Get a good night's rest, OK?" Billy just looked at him and smiled.

"Thank you again Doctor." Sally replied.

Father John had been quiet during the entire exchange. He had restored the table he knocked over, and he began to collect his things upon Billy's awakening. After the doctor left the room, Father John turned to Billy. "Billy, we are all so glad that you are back with us." He then turned to Sally. "Sally, I'll be going now. Please call me tomorrow to let me know everything is OK."

Sally was so taken with all that had just happened that she forgot that Father John was even in the room. She dashed across the room to shake his hand and say goodbye. "Oh Father! Thank you for being here! I will call you tomorrow, I promise!" There were tears of happiness in her eyes.

Father John said his goodbyes once again and left the room just as the nurse was bringing in a cot for Katie and a maintenance man came in with a new table lamp.

With his hospital visit over, John drove back to St Andrews. On his return trip his head was swimming with questions. He had no explanation for Billy's sudden awakening or how Jeremy Wilkins could have recovered from the leukemia so unexpectedly. Why did these unexpected events happen? Were they somehow related? Could they be miracles? Was God working through him? How did he get this ability? Could the events be related to his encounter with the UFO? Was the UFO encounter real? Did God send the UFO? What really happened to him that night?

Father John felt something important had happened to him. He knew the implications of his UFO suspicions were enormous; to him, to the church, and to the entire world. His questions demanded answers. He would speak of them to no one, but now he would let nothing stand in his way to answer them.

* * * * * * *

Chapter 10: **Chief Perlman**

Chief Perlman had pulled a comatose Billy McLeary out of the Des Plaines River. He had administered CPR to him while waiting for the ambulance to arrive at the scene. He had both witnessed and participated in many such emergencies in his life, and he was always deeply moved when such events involved the life of a child. Billy McLeary was no exception.

After dropping Katie at the hospital, the Chief started for home. He planned to get a hot shower, eat a nice dinner, and have a quiet evening with his wife, Janet, who was always eager to hear the latest news of the day from her important husband. On his way home from the hospital, he anticipated his conversation with her and thought out loud to himself and said, "Oh yeah, she's gonna love this one."

Later that evening the Chief was sitting quietly in his living room front of a lit fireplace with his wife. He reached for the phone and called the hospital to check up on Billy. He expected that Billy would still be comatose.

"Hello, this is Police Chief Perlman. Do you have a patient named Billy McLeary checked in there?"

"Yes sir, he is in our Intensive Care Unit in Room 517. I can transfer you to the Nurse's station. Would you like me to transfer you?"

"Yes...thank you."

"Please hold."

"Intensive Care... Nurse Sarah."

"Hello Nurse. My name is Jim Perlman. Do you have a patient in Room 517 named, Billy McLeary?

"Yes we do."

"How Billy is doing?"

R. Allan Worrell

"Are you related to Billy?" Unlike the receptionist, the nurse was concerned about divulging private medical information to strangers.

"No. I am the police officer who pulled Billy out of the river this afternoon. He was comatose when I last saw him in the ambulance, and I would like to know if he is going to be OK." The nurse was satisfied he was telling the truth. She had enquired about Billy's story just as she had for all the patients under her care, and she knew few people would know about Billy's condition, or his fall into the river.

"One moment please." The nurse pulled Billy's chart off the wall and looked it over.

"Officer, I can tell you that Billy seems to be doing fine. We are keeping him here overnight for observation. The doctor wants to make sure there are no latent problems resulting from his coma."

The Chief was surprised. "Nurse, that's remarkable! Is Billy awake now?"

"Yes. He is wide awake and his mother and sister are with him."

"Oh, that's wonderful news. Thank you so much. Can I visit Billy tomorrow?"

"Yes. If his condition does not change he may be released sometime after noon tomorrow. If you want to see him, you should get here before then. Our visiting hours start at 10 AM tomorrow morning."

"Thank you again Nurse. I'll be there at ten. Goodbye."

The Chief rested his head back in his chair and smiled as he hung up the phone. It was the best possible conclusion: Billy was going to be OK. Days like this made his job and his life worth-while.

Linda, the dispatch operator who had called for the ambulance, knew of the Chief's heroic efforts. She called the hospital later that afternoon regarding Billy's progress and found out he was doing well. She told everyone at the PD's main desk about the Chief, and word spread quickly throughout the building. Linda then called the Chicago Tribune. After all, Billy's recovery was a great story, and since the Chief always said the Chicago Police Department could use all the good publicity they could get, he couldn't argue with her decision to call the paper. The editor at the Tribune assigned a young reporter,

Father John's Gift

Samuel Elms, and his best photographer to the story, and scheduled them to arrive at the police station early the next day.

Sam Elms arrived with the photographer at the police station the next morning just minutes before the Chief. As the Chief entered the station, the photographer's camera flashed and there was applause and cheers all around from the officers who waited for his arrival. A maintenance man who was on a ladder and was replacing overhead light bulbs in the back of the room let out a loud whistle, and everyone laughed.

The Chief was surprised by the unexpected attention he just received. He grinned and said, "OK, OK. Thank you everyone! I just did what anyone of you would have done under the circumstances."

Those were the words that the reporter, Samuel Elms loved to hear. He pulled out his notepad and started making notes about the Chief. It would make great print in tomorrow's paper. His was the first question.

"Chief! Chief! Sam Elms from the Chicago Tribune… Have you seen Bill? How is he doing?"

"No, I have not seen him. I'm planning to go to the hospital later this morning. Last I heard Billy was doing fine."

Sam furiously scribbled some notes to record the Chief's answer. "Chief? Are you saying Billy is awake?" Sam had just been assigned the story and had not heard the news of Bill's recovery.

"Yes, that's what I was told by the hospital last night."

"Do you know when Billy woke up?"

"No, I really don't know any of the details. You probably know more about it than I do. As I said, I am planning to go to the hospital later this morning. You are welcome to join me if you like. Now if you would excuse me, I have some work to do."

Samuel Elms grabbed a pay phone in the corner of the police office and phoned his bosses secretary. He asked her to let his boss know he would be busy working on Billy McLeary's rescue story for the rest of the day.

* * * * * * *

Chapter 11: **The Reporter**

At age twenty two Samuel Elms was fresh out of college. He had landed his first job with the Chicago Tribune as an investigative reporter, and he was eager to do well. True to his word, Sam hung out at the Police station until Chief Perlman emerged from his office promptly at nine o'clock. Sam had been to the station many times, and the Chicago Police Staff had taken to his innocence and naiveté. Sam was a welcome break from the older, more aggressive newspaper men and women who, more often than not, got in the way of their police work. Like so many of the other officers, the Chief knew Sam and liked him from the start.

"Sam, I'm going to the hospital now to check on Billy McLeary. You want to come along?"

The Chief wanted to foster his relationship with the young reporter. Aside from building a friendship with Sam, the Chief believed the professional relationship might help him in times of real trouble. The Chief knew any story could be slanted one way or the other, and he wanted Sam's trust and confidence which he knew might be invaluable under the right circumstances.

"Yes! Thanks Chief!" Sam was anxious to capture a story… any story, and though he was new at the job, he had great instincts as a newspaperman. He jumped at the opportunity to work with the Chief

Father John's Gift

directly. Despite his youth and inexperience, Sam could already smell a good human interest story.

Sam had questioned Linda Davis, the dispatcher who the Chief had radioed the day before. As one of the main Chicago PD dispatchers, there was very little that went on in the precinct that Linda didn't know. Linda knew the Chief well, and she had told Sam the entire story from start to finish as she knew it. At the time, Linda didn't know anything about Father John's involvement or Billy's miraculous recovery.

Chicago General was only a few miles away from the Police Station, and Sam and his photographer followed the Chief to the hospital in Sam's car. When they arrived at the hospital, they entered through the ER door. The waiting room was nearly full and the ER was bristling with the usual activity of an inner city hospital. Doctors and nurses were busy processing and servicing the constant flow of sick and injured patients who came through their doors.

The two quickly exited the ER and walked swiftly through the hospital's first floor halls and arrived in the main lobby. They logged themselves in as visitors at the main desk and found their way to Room 517 in the ICU where Billy McLeary had spent the previous night. As they approached Billy's room, Father John entered Bill's room just ahead of them.

Sitting up in his bed, Billy was bewildered by all the attention that he was suddenly receiving.

Sally McLeary greeted Father John as Chief Perlman and Sam Elms entered the room.

The single patient room was now crowded with people curious to know all about Billy's ordeal. The head ICU nurse would never have permitted so many visitors at once but she was preoccupied with new medications for a cardiac patient at the other end of the hall, and she didn't see them enter Billy's room.

"Can I help you officer?" Sally was alarmed to see the police chief in uniform.

"Mom! That's the policeman who pulled Billy out of the river!" Katie exclaimed.

"Oh, I'm sorry Officer, I didn't know! I'm Sally McLeary, Billy's mother." She nodded to Father John. "And this is Father John, our parish priest from St Andrews." And with a hand on Katie's shoulders she smiled and said, "And this is my daughter, Katie."

"I'm happy to meet you Mrs. McLeary and Father John, and I already know Katie! She and I are old friends now." The Chief smiled at Katie. "I'm Chief Perlman, and this is Samuel Elms from the Chicago Tribune. Sam wants to write a story about Billy".

The Chief turned to Billy. "You are going to be famous Billy! How are you feeling today?"

Billy was sitting up in bed in his pajama and looked at Sam. "Good... Wow! You really want to write a story about me?" He was excited about getting his name in the paper.

"You bet Billy! Everyone will want to know what happened to you. We are all so glad that you are OK." Sam retrieved his pen and notebook from his briefcase. "Do you feel like talking about it now?"

"Sure! ... I guess, I mean... if it's OK with Mom."

Sally smiled softly at Sam. "I don't think there would be any harm in that."

Standing quietly in the corner, Father John suddenly came to life. "Sally, I'll be going now." He then looked at Billy. "And I'll be expecting to see you back in school at St Andrews just as soon as your mother says you're ready."

"OK Father." Billy frowned at the thought of going back to school.

"It was nice to meet you gentlemen."

"It was nice to meet you too Father." The Chief started toward the door with Father John. "And now that I've seen that Billy is OK, I had better get back to work myself."

"Chief Perlman." Sally almost sprinted across the small room to catch the officer before he left. "I know Billy would not be here today if it wasn't for you." Her eyes welled up with tears with the thought that she almost lost her son. "Thank you." And with that she stood on her toes and kissed the tall Chief softly on the cheek.

The Chief took her hands, and looked down at Sally straight into her eyes. "You're so welcome. I'm just happy that everything turned out as well as it did, and Billy pulled through. And, oh by the way", the Chief smiled, "The real heroine of this story is Katie." The Chief

Father John's Gift

looked at Katie from across the room causing Katie to blush and look away shyly. "You have a remarkable daughter Mrs. McLeary."

"I know." Sally smiled at her daughter.

The Chief squeezed her hands one last time. "Good bye". He and Father John exited the room together.

Sam grabbed his pencil and paper and dragged a chair to the side of Billy's bed. "OK Billy. I want you to tell me everything you remember about the accident. Think you can do that?"

"Yeah, I guess so. I remember racing Katie across the river on our way home and I fell in! The water was so cold, and I couldn't breathe."

"OK. That's good Billy. Can I back you up a bit?" Sam had everyone's attention now. Sam looked straight at Billy.

"Were you coming home from school?"

"Yeah."

"What time was that?"

"I dunno."

Katie looked pensive and replied, "We get out of school at about 2:30 in the afternoon."

"Good." Sam started scribbling some notes. "Did you come straight home from school? Did you stop anywhere on your way home?"

Billy answered, "No, we went straight home. Mom gets mad if we go anywhere else."

"Do you always cross the Des Plaines River on your way home?"

"Sometimes we do during the winter, when the water is frozen. I'll never cross it again!" Billy said seriously.

"Was anyone else with you?"

"No. It was just Katie and me."

"Did Katie go out onto the river?"

"No…. I don't know." Everyone looked at Katie.

"No.", Katie said. "Billy ran onto the river before I could stop him. He went under so fast that there was nothing I could do. I immediately ran for help."

"What happened next?" Sam had heard the story from the police perspective. He wanted to hear it from the children's point of view.

Katie took over the conversation. "I ran toward the bridge and climbed up to the street for help. I was lucky when the police chief drove by."

"You sure were Katie. What happened then?"

"Well, I got in the car with Chief Perlman and we drove to Oak Street and ran in back of the houses to the river bank. Chief Perlman found Billy trapped under the ice near the dock. He used a shovel to break the ice and then pulled Billy out of the water."

Sally McLeary breathed deeply. She began to tremble as the picture of what happened to her children was suddenly made clear.

"The Chief breathed into Billy's mouth to get Billy breathing again, and then the ambulance came and took Billy to the hospital."

"Katie, did you ride in the ambulance with Billy?"

"No." Katie replied, "The Police Chief gave me a ride to the hospital."

"Was Billy awake before he went to the hospital?"

Sally jumped into the conversation. "I think I can answer from here. Billy was still unconscious until after he arrived in this hospital room." Her mind was replaying the events of the night before. "That was..." Sally looked away as she recalled the time... "About 25 or 30 minutes after Billy arrived at the hospital."

Sam's curiosity was peaked. "What happened to Billy? When did he wake up?"

Sally had anticipated Sam's question. "It was Father John! He met Katie and me in the Emergency Room and was with us when we brought Billy up to this room. We all thought Billy might die, so I asked Father John to give Billy the Last Rites sacrament which he did! That was when Billy suddenly sat up in bed and yelled Katie's name!"

Sam looked at Katie who was nodding in agreement with all that her mother had said.

Sally added, "Sam, I don't know how it happened. The doctor told us Billy's recovery was remarkable. I believe it's a miracle. Father John performed a miracle!"

Sam loved to hear such stories. It was sensational news, and he knew it. He lamented the fact that he let Father John go without

Father John's Gift

hearing his side of the story. Sam would have to catch up with the good priest later.

* * * * * * * *

Chapter 12: **The Newsroom**

After collecting his notes and saying good bye, Sam returned to the Chicago Tribune's newsroom or "The Trib" as it was called. The room was a sea of messy desks topped with stacks of notes, newspapers, dictionaries and typewriters. The newsmen were typing madly to make the day's deadline. Phones rang loudly in the background and cigarette smoke clung to the air. The writers were a rare breed. They loved their jobs and all thrived on the stress and adrenaline of putting out a daily paper. In short, they loved being "in the know" before everyone else, and they loved to see their name in print. For them, the newspaper article "by line" was everything.

Sam arrived at the office shortly before noon and went immediately to see his boss, Glenn Reddy. He passed the secretary station and waited just outside the glass door of his boss's office. Constantly busy, Glenn was always on the phone, and every reporter knew they would have to wait if they needed to speak with him in person. Glenn had been the Editor-in-Chief at the Tribune for the past twenty years and had a reputation for being a fair but tough boss. Recognizing Sam's passion and talent for writing, Glenn had hired Sam right out of school and Sam both respected and admired him. Glenn did not have a life away from work. Always at his job, Glenn knew he was a workaholic, but he didn't care. The Tribune was his life, and he was proud of the fact that no one worked harder for the Tribune than he did.

Glenn looked up from his desk at Sam through the glass wall, hung up his phone, and motioned for Sam to enter the office. As far as Sam was concerned, Glen's office was the military command post for the

Father John's Gift

Tribune, and Glenn was its Five Star General in charge of it all. Glenn had junior editors; lieutenants to help him screen and correct the work of over a hundred writers. But everyone knew Glenn had the final word. Nothing ever went to print without his blessing.

Glenn had three piles of papers stacked on his desk. Each was in a wire basket with a label indicating the status of a work in progress:

1) The "In" Box;
2) Needs Work!
3) Print it!

There was a sign on the back wall of Glen's office, posted there by his secretary which stated, "Get It Ready for Reddy!" It was put there affectionately, as a joke, and as a constant reminder of the ever present deadline which the reporters could never forget. Glen liked it, and he allowed the sign to hang behind his desk for the past six years.

Sam knew the Father John story was a good one, and he wanted to be the one to tell it. He didn't normally do stories for the religion page, but it didn't matter to him. Sam had already done the leg work and he felt the story was his. He wanted to run with it. Except for the miracle component, the story was like several others that he had previously done at the Tribune, and Sam was confident that he could do it well.

Glenn looked up at Sam. "Do you have a story for tomorrow's back page Sam?" Glen's question was sincere.

"Yes Glen, I can do it, but there's a strange twist to the story. You might want to give me another day or two on this one."

"What's the twist?" Glenn put his cigarette out in a paper coffee cup on his desk.

"I'm not sure boss, but this story might belong on the Religion Page. There's a Catholic priest involved with Bill's recovery. The family talks about it as if it was a miracle, and I want to interview a few more people about it."

Glen's answer was immediate. "Sam, that's Tom Judd's beat. You don't write for the religion page."

"I know. Glen, I like this story and I think you will too. It has such a strong human interest angle, and it may be even better if we write the boy's recovery as a possible miracle. Glen, let me have this one. I know I can do it. You won't be sorry."

Glenn looked straight at Sam and repeatedly tapped his pencil, eraser down on his desk as he thought about the situation. Glen's "pencil tapping habit" had annoyed Sam at first, but Sam learned it was Glen's way of thinking through an issue. Sam stared back at Glenn as if he could see the gears turning in Glen's mind. He waited for Glen's response as he counted the pencil taps. All the reporters debated how many taps it took for Glenn to give a positive response, and how many taps meant a negative one would be coming. Sam didn't believe there was any rhyme or reason to the number of pencil taps, but he couldn't help himself. He counted them all the same. Glenn spoke up after just eight taps.

"OK Sam, you can have it. I'd like to see copy by the Saturday deadline for Sunday's Religion page. If the miracle angle doesn't work, we will put it in the Sunday Life section. Have you talked to the priest yet?"

"No. That's next on my to-do list."

"Don't bother Sam. The priest will just deny it. He can't risk the church finding out about any alleged miracles; otherwise he would be in deep shit and I'm sure he knows it. I want you to talk to anyone who might know this priest. Get his history, his background, his life story if you can. Be as discreet as you can. But Find out everything about him without drawing a lot of attention to yourself. Who knows, if he's for real, then maybe this was not his first miracle."

"OK Boss. You got it!" Sam was now excited about the assignment. He loved his boss. He was happy to be given such freedom to do his job. It was investigative journalism projects like this one that consumed him until they were done. Sam knew he would work nonstop on it for the next few days. It would be a great story, and he would write it.

Sam went back to his desk and thought he needed to talk to some St Andrews parishioners. He needed to find out how much they knew about Father John. He looked up the church number in the phone book and dialed the church rectory.

Father John's Gift

"St. Andrews Rectory, Margaret speaking. How can I help you?"

"Hi Margaret, my name is Sam Elms. Can you tell me when your next service is?"

It was still a Wednesday morning, and Sam wanted to start interviewing the St Andrews church goers as soon as possible. He usually identified himself as a reporter, but he thought better of it when he called the rectory. After all, he didn't want to tip his hand, and he didn't want to get Father John in trouble. He wanted only to find out as much as he could about Father John.

"Well, during the week we only have an early morning service, so our next service will be tomorrow morning at eight o'clock."

"Can you tell me who will be saying the Mass?" Sam was curious to know if Father John would be there. He didn't want to encounter him and raise any suspicions if he could avoid it.

Margaret flipped through her schedule book. "Hmm, let me see. I'm showing Father Jim will be saying the Mass tomorrow. Sometimes the priests will switch with each other at the last minute and not tell me, so don't hold me to it."

Sam laughed at the way she said her last sentence, as if it was so important he would kill her for being wrong. "That's OK Margaret. That's all I needed to know. Thank you so much."

Sam got to the church at 8:30 AM and waited patiently outside the front of St Andrews church for the Thursday morning service to end. Not being Catholic, Sam Elms didn't know how long the service should last. He didn't want to ask Margaret because he knew she would wonder why he had to ask and she might suspect he was not Catholic. Sam glanced down at his watch every five minutes. When he looked up at 8:45, the front doors flew open and a small number of parishioners exited the church. He dodged a few of the older couples, and approached a well-dressed woman who Sam thought might be in her forties.

"Excuse me ma'am. My name is Sam Elms. I am a reporter for the Chicago Tribune." Sam pulled his credentials from his coat and flashed them high enough for her to see. "Do you have a few minutes to talk with me? Can I ask you a few questions?"

The woman was surprised but was flattered Sam had singled her out. She was happy to receive the attention of the young reporter and was naturally curious to see what he would ask her. "No, I don't mind", she said. What is this about? Are your questions about St Andrews?"

"Yes, in a manner of speaking, my questions are about St Andrews. First, can I ask your name please? And how long have you been coming to St Andrews?"

The woman smiled and said, "Sure. My name is Jenny Jenkins, and I have been coming to St Andrews for about fifteen years now."

Sam scribbled her answers on his notepad. "Do you know a St Andrews priest named, Father John?"

"Of course! Everyone knows Father John. He is well liked at St Andrews, and I'm not surprised you are asking about Father John."

"Why is that?" Sam didn't want to lead his informant by telling her what he already knew. He wanted to hear what she had to say without being prompted.

"I heard Father John paid little Billy McLeary a visit at the hospital a few days ago and he brought Billy out of a coma. Everyone in the parish is talking about it."

"Do you know the McLeary family?"

"No, I don't know them personally. I only know they have a few children who go to school here."

"How did you hear about Billy's accident and recovery?" Sam was curious to know how such information got passed around the church so quickly. It might help him with his investigation.

Jenny was very forthcoming. It was obvious she loved to be helpful. "Oh, I'm a member of the Club," she said proudly.

Sam scribbled some more notes. "What's the Club? Is that a church organization?"

"No, not really. It's not an official church group. It's just an informal group of St Andrews women who like to help out with church activities. You know, whenever there is a need."

"Have you heard anything else from the Club about Father John?"

Jenny looked down at the sidewalk and thought about the question. "Yes. As a matter of fact, the Club has it that Father John performed a

Father John's Gift

miracle on another little boy named, Jeremy Wilkins just a few weeks ago."

Sam was intrigued. It was the first he had heard of Jeremy Wilkins. He had wondered if there were more miracles and decided to pump her for information. "Really? What can you tell me about that?"

"Well, everyone knows that Jeremy had been sick with childhood leukemia for a long time, maybe two or three years, I don't know exactly. Jeremy was expected to die about two weeks ago. I guess everyone in the Club believes Father John cured him. I do."

Sam made more notes.

"Have there been any other miracles that you are aware of?"

"No. At least none that I know of. We are all watching Father John to see what he will do next!" Jenny grinned from ear to ear as if she had special knowledge and was happy to be so helpful to such a bright young man and she loved the thought she might get her name in the paper in an article about Father John.

"Thank you so much Mrs. Jenkins. Can I get your phone number in case I have any more questions?"

"Yes, I'd be happy to help you. We are all very proud of our Father John. He is a remarkable priest."

"It sure does sound like it!"

Sam took Jenny's name and number and thought he had made a good start. He decided to contact the Wilkins family to get to the source about the alleged miracle and to head back to the hospital to see what more he could learn about Father John from the hospital staff.

* * * * * * *

Chapter 13: **A Trail of Healing**

Father John and Chief Perlman left Billy's hospital room Wednesday morning and walked down to the hospital's main lobby. John was pleased that Billy was doing well, and from all appearances, Billy would completely recover. But Father John was disturbed by the presence of the newspaper man who, as far as he was concerned, could cause him trouble even before he understood what was happening himself. The Chief turned to Father John and extended his hand.

"Father John, it was very nice to meet you. I will say goodbye to you now because I need to use the lobby pay phone to check in with my precinct. I need to let them know I will make a few stops in town before heading back to work. I'm sure we will meet again."

John shook the Chief's hand. "Thank you Chief. I'm sure we will as well. It was nice to meet you too."

Father John watched the Chief walk over to the bank of pay phones on the far hospital wall, opposite the hospital cafeteria and gift shop. John then turned and paused in the main hallway to collect his thoughts and decide what he should do next. It was only 10:30 in the morning and John knew he did not have to be back at the church until three in the afternoon for a meeting with the women's out-reach program. John made his way back to the ER on the West end of the building. He had to discover if he was the instrument of God's hand. He had to know if he was the cause of Jeremy Wilkins's recovery from leukemia, and now Billy McLeary's sudden awakening from coma.

Father John's Gift

As usual, the ER was a busy place. Like any other inner-city hospital, Chicago General saw more than its share of accident and crime victims. The admissions staff was well trained in the art of triage. It was their job to recognize those who needed immediate help, and separate them from those who came to the ER with the common cold, flu, or mild fevers. Once identified, critical patients were quickly whisked away to the back room in a wheel chair or on a gurney while the waiting room served as a holding tank for less urgent cases.

Father John had come to the hospital from the church immediately after saying the eight o'clock Mass, and was still wearing his full length black robe with the small white priest collar. When he entered the ER, he drew the attention of the patients and their family members in the waiting room. After all, it was unusual for the patients to see a priest, dressed in black among the doctors and nurses who always wore white. Father John glanced across the room to size up the patients quickly proceeded through the door marked, "Hospital Staff Only", where he had found Billy behind a curtain the day before. He was greeted by a staff nurse just inside the door.

The nurse recognized Father John's face but she didn't know his name. She had seen him many times before around the hospital. "Can I help you Father?"

"Yes Nurse. Can I see the list of patients admitted to this area?"

The nurse had a million things to do and she didn't bother to question John's motives. She grabbed a clipboard hanging on the wall in front of her and handed it to him. "Here's the list of patients we have so far this morning. I'm sorry but I have to go. If you want some help ask the ER reception nurse at the desk just outside this door."

"Thank you Nurse."

She grabbed her stethoscope which she had tossed on the counter, placed it around her neck and walked back down the hall to join a doctor behind curtain number seven.

John looked over the list and glanced down the ER corridor. As expected, all ten curtains were pulled, and each curtain contained an urgent case. However, there were only three active ER doctors on call, and all were working on a critical patient behind curtain seven which the list showed was Kathy Looper, a young professional woman in her twenties who, when trying to cross Michigan Avenue in downtown Chicago, was struck by a car which ran a red light. The notes said the impact threw Kathy ten feet onto the street. She was unconscious and in bad shape. She suffered a concussion, internal hemorrhaging, broken ribs, an injured left shoulder and a broken left collarbone. The doctors were trying to save her life while surgery room number three was being prepared following an emergency appendectomy on a forty two year old man.

Though he wanted to help, John knew he could not intervene with the doctors. He would let them do their best, and he knew they would call him if she was Catholic, and if she was about to die. No, he would stay clear of the doctors and concentrate his efforts on the nine other ER patients.

John looked down the list and selected Lupe Rodriguez, a seven year old girl who had slipped on ice on her concrete driveway and by all accounts had broken both of her wrists when she tried to break her fall. John drew back curtain number two. There he found a Latino family of three standing over Lupe who was sitting up in bed crying softly and had both her arms in a single white sling, hung about her neck. All looked up at John as he opened the curtain, stepped inside, and like a doctor, he closed the curtain behind him. Looking at Lupe and her family, Father John was ready to do the work of God.

It was to be a long morning in the Chicago General ER, and it was one the ER doctors and nurses would never forget. John lightened their work load in a way they had not experienced before, and could not understand. If John made an impression on the hospital staff, the patients he cured were both stunned and amazed by his healing ability.

Most patients came to the ER expecting to see a doctor for specific problems: to have X-rays taken, to be given pain medicine, antibiotics, a splint or a cast, and to be sent home with a long recovery ahead of them. Instead, all of John's patients walked out of the hospital, cured of their illness or injury the same morning, without medicine, and without even having seen a doctor. All credited Father John with having performed a medical miracle of one kind or another, and all the

Father John's Gift

patients learned his name and the name of St Andrews Church before they left the hospital.

The hospital nursing staff was amazed and confused, not only by John's miracles, but also because he presented them with a new problem. The staff didn't know how to bill the patients or the insurance companies for the work he did.

John and the ER doctors were so preoccupied with helping patients they went about their business and were unaware of the accounting problem John had created. After all, John was a hospital volunteer. His services were free to anyone at the hospital. When they came to the ER, all the patients were concerned about what their ER visit would cost them, but all the patients John cured were delighted to leave the hospital without paying anything, and without owing the hospital a dime.

****

Chapter 14: **Hospital Executives**

Dr. Jim Jones had been Chief of Staff at Chicago General for over seventeen years. His name, reminiscent of the suicidal religious leader Jim Jones in Jonestown, British Guyana, made him defensive regarding both his name and his lack of religious convictions. He had nothing to do with the religious cult leader who led over 912 people to commit suicide by drinking Kool-Aide laced with cyanide. Dr. Jones had every right to his name, as the other, infamous Jim Jones did.

Dr. Jones was a competent physician, surgeon, and administrator. He had the respect of every doctor at Chicago General, and was often called by doctors all over the country to consultant on particularly difficult cases regarding his medical specialty, Neurology.

Jim was upset. "Darnn it Bob! We've got to do something! The medical staff is starting to complain! Father John is out of control! He's curing sick people all over the hospital!"

Robert Lieberman, CEO of Chicago General, stood quietly looking out the third story window of his plush office. His office window overlooked a busy downtown section with a view of the Chicago River just a few blocks away. He immediately saw the irony in what his Chief of Staff had just said. "What's your point Jim?"

"The point is that he's making a mockery of medicine! Look. Tell me why I studied medicine for eight years if this priest can come along and cure the sick and injured with a touch of his hand and a little bit of his religious mumbo-jumbo? I'm sure word of his magic has already reached the streets! If the media gets a hold of this, we will be the

Father John's Gift

laughing stock of all Chicago! Bob, I'm afraid if we don't put a stop to it, Father John could put us out of business! "

The president turned and looked at his Chief of Staff with some consternation. "Oh, come on now Jim, don't you think you are over reacting just a bit? After all, curing the sick is what we do! I don't think a priest who helps out a little bit here and there will really hurt us, do you? Actually, I think the publicity might do us some good. Something like this will get people talking about us." Bob grabbed the ledger on his desk and flipped a page. "I got the new stats just this morning. Our census was down twenty three percent last quarter. We could use some good, free publicity just now. All hospitals have doctors and surgeons, but let me ask you…. how many hospitals have a priest who performs miracles?" He looked right at Jim and grinned, and then continued. "True or not, I don't think it can hurt us…can it? Is there anything illegal or unethical about it?"

Jim just stared at his boss and said nothing. He didn't like what his boss was saying, but he didn't have a retort to offer.

Robert Lieberman got up from behind his desk and began to walk back and forth pacing the room as he thought out loud, working the issue over in his head. He was always at his best when he paced the room and stared at the carpet. It was a thinking habit and style which was well known to his Chief of Staff who sat back in his chair and just listened to his boss think out loud.

The CEO continued. "Of course we don't have to say that it's true. Officially, if we are asked, we can say that we do have a Catholic priest who ministers to the sick. What's wrong with that? Everyone knows hospitals have priests and ministers who help out terminally ill patients and others who may want their help. We can let people believe what they want! We will show everyone we are friendly to the church. Folks may come here just on the chance that there is some truth to the miracle rumors." He paused at the window and closed the blinds to block the rays of the sun which was just beginning to set.

"You know what Jim? I think our Father John may bring us more business than we can handle." Though he didn't say it, he smiled at the thought of reports about miracles at Chicago General on the six o'clock news, and how they might take business away from his Chicago competition. He continued. "Besides, are the miracle rumors true? I mean, do you actually believe them?"

Jim looked at his boss with doubt in his eyes. "Honestly Bob. You know I'm not a religious man. I've always been a man of Science. I believe in the germ theory of disease, and the power of Science and modern medicine. I don't believe in witchcraft, voodoo, or faith healing." He paused to collect his thoughts and let the idea sink in. "Oh, I know that sometimes the power of the mind can strongly influence the body. Let's not forget the "Placebo Effect" which cures people who were never really sick. And we need only look at hypochondriacs who make themselves sick by believing they are sick. Maybe Father John is curing the hypochondriacs by convincing them they are cured of their fake diseases. Hell, I don't know."

Jim scratched his head and continued his thought. "Well, it could have been staged. But why would Father John do that? Has he lost his mind? Is he trying to make some sort of religious point? We both know there are lots of religious fanatics in this country. Maybe Father John has gone over the edge!"

The president was not convinced. "Jim, let's not jump to any conclusions. Have you even met the man?"

"No."

"Tell you what. I'll have Alice give Father John a call, and I'll have her set up a meeting for me with him. I'll talk to Father John about what's been going on when he comes back next week. Let me think about it some more. Maybe we can take advantage of the Father John situation."

Bob opened the office door to let Jim know that the meeting was over. He smiled, gave Jim a pat on the back as Jim exited the room. "And don't you worry about it, OK? I know you've got lots of more important problems to worry about. In the meantime, if any of the other docs ask you about our Father John problem, just tell them you talked to me, and that I said I'd take care of it."

Jim was not happy. He left the office unconvinced any change would be made. Still, he had done his part and had informed the

Father John's Gift

president of the problem. It was all he could do, and he had done it. It was out of his hands now.

****

Chapter 15: **The Athlete**

With his leg in a cast propped up on a second chair, Gary Bowman sat at his kitchen table and stared in disbelief at the Tribune article before him. Could this be true? Could this Catholic priest really perform miracles? He had to find out. All his life he wanted to play in the Super Bowl, and now that his team had made it to the bowl, he was out of commission.

Gary reached for the phone and dialed the operator.

"Operator."

"Hi. Do you have the number for Chicago General Hospital?"

"One moment please... The number is 217-555-9878."

"Thank you."

Gary dialed the hospital.

"Chicago General Information Desk. This is Gina. How may I help you?"

"Hi Gina. My name is Gary Bowman. Do you have a priest named Father John, who works there?"

"Yes, we do have a priest named, Father John, but he is not a hospital employee. He is a volunteer here at the hospital."

"Can you send him to come and see me?" Dealing with bureaucracy was not Gary's strong point and he knew it. He didn't know how he could make it happen, but he was determined to get Father John to come to see him.

"Well, Father John is a Catholic priest who works for the St Andrews Parish, and he is not here right now. You might try calling him at the St Andrews Rectory."

Father John's Gift

"OK. I'll do that. Thanks." Gary hung up the phone with a look of disappointment. "Damn, nothing is ever easy!"

Gary dialed the operator once again. "Can I have the number for St Andrews Rectory?"

"Thank you. The number is 217-555-7436."

Gary then dialed St Andrews. Someone with a high pitched voice answered the phone so quickly Gary did not hear the phone ring.

Gary looked at his receiver with a strange look on his face. "Hello? Is this the St Andrews Rectory?"

Mary Margaret was on the line. "Yes. This is the Rectory. My name is Margaret. Can I help you?"

"Do you have a priest named Father John who volunteers at Chicago General Hospital?"

"Yes. We do have a Father John here, and yes, he does volunteer work at Chicago General. Why do you ask? Is Father John OK?" Margaret had not seen Father John all morning, and she knew he was scheduled to visit the hospital. She wondered why she would get such as strange call.

"Well, my name is Gary Bowman. You might have heard of me. I play for the Chicago Bears. I broke my leg in a game against the Green Bay Packers last week. Do you think I can get Father John to cure my leg?" Gary was obviously NOT a religious person. He had no knowledge of the Catholic Church, and he had no idea how to make such a request.

"You want Father John to do what?" Margaret was genuinely surprised. Margaret had received gifts and notes from patients but she had not seen Sam's article in the morning paper and she really didn't know what to believe. This was the first request for a medical miracle she had received.

"Yeah, well... I saw in today's newspaper that Father John cured that comatose kid who fell in the river. I thought he might be able to fix my leg so I can play in the Super Bowl next month."

Margaret recalled Monsignor Eckhart telling her not to acknowledge or confirm any miracles by Father John if any inquiries were ever made.

"Look Mr. Bowman, despite what you may have read in the paper, our Father John does not do miracles on demand or otherwise. Are you a member of St Andrews parish?" Margaret did not know Gary Bowman, but the church had grown so fast in the last few years she knew she might not know all the new parishioners.

"No, I'm not a Catholic, but hey look; I could make it worth his while!" Gary's ignorance of church matters was blatant.

"You're not even Catholic?" Margaret was shocked that a non-Catholic person would call asking for the personal services of Father John. And she was offended that he would even think to offer money for the request. "I'm sorry, but what you are asking for is out of the question. Good bye Mr. Bowman." She hung up the phone with a look of disgust and disbelief. "Now I've heard everything. What's next?"

"God damn it!" Gary slammed the receiver down on his phone. He was flustered but still determined. He was not going to take "No" for an answer, not if there was even a chance he could still play in the Super Bowl. He thumbed through his little black book of phone numbers and then called his agent, Stu Pierson.

"Stu? This is Gary Bowman."

Stu was immediately apologetic. "Hi Gary! I'm sorry I haven't called you! I've just been so busy lately! How's the leg doin?"

"OK. Well, it still hurts now and then, and it itches awfully bad, but I think it will mend ... eventually. But hey Stu, I want you to do something for me."

"Whatever it is, you got it Gary. What do you need?"

"Did you read today's Tribune? There is a story about a Catholic priest named "Father John", who performed a miracle over at Chicago General."

"No, I didn't see it."

"Well, I called his parish, Saint Andrews to see if I can get Father John to bless my leg, and they just blew me off! If he can cure that kid, then who knows? Maybe he can cure me, and I can play in the Super Bowl yet!"

"Wow, it sounds like a fantastic story to me Gary, but I'll see what I can do." Stu was not going to say no to his star player, even if he did

Father John's Gift

have a broken leg. Stu had made a handsome commission when he negotiated Gary's last contract, and he was sure Gary would eventually heal. He thought about it some more. "Gary, what would it be worth to you? We may need to offer the church some money for the priest to make a house call. You know what I mean? Sometimes money talks!"

"Yeah, I already thought of that. What do you think it would take? I'd be happy to pay him. But, I mean, do you really think the priest will charge me a fee to come bless my leg?"

"No, my guess is that the priest probably won't take your money, but I'll bet his Bishop will." Stu knew something about the church hierarchy, and he thought he might even make a few bucks off the deal for his trouble. "Can I tell them you will donate $10,000 to the church for your Father John to pay you a personal visit?

"Shit Stu. I would pay $50,000 for him to get me to play in the Super Bowl!" Gary was now a millionaire. Pro football had been good to him, and even though $50,000 was a good chunk of money, Gary was determined. Thanks largely to Stu, Gary had invested his money wisely, and the stock market had done extremely well in the past few years. Gary didn't want to make a low bid and not get what he wanted. He also wanted to show Stu he meant business.

"OK. Well, Gary let's not go overboard. Let me handle this. I'll work on getting your Father John to see you. But remember, there is no guarantee that this will even work."

"I know. But Stu, I just gotta to do something! If I don't do nothing, I won't play in the bowl for sure!"

"OK Gary. Let me handle this. I'll give the Bishop a call, and "I'll let you know how it goes. OK?"

"Thanks man. I knew I could count on you." Gary hung up the phone with a renewed sense of hope and optimism. He just might play in the Super Bowl after all.

* * * * * * *

Chapter 16: **The Bears Coach**

Mark Winder had coached the Bears for the past five years. He was seasoned, and he knew how to motivate his players. He didn't get his team to the Super Bowl by accident; it took a lot of hard work. Mark dealt regularly with both the players and their agents. So it was no surprise when he received a call from Stu Pierson.

"Hi Stu. What can I do for you?" Mark knew Stu well. Stu had negotiated one of the largest football contracts the Bears had ever signed when they acquired Gary Bowman.

"Mark, how badly do you need Gary Bowman for the Super Bowl?"

"Stu, I don't understand why you are even asking me that. I know Gary will be out of commission for at least six months, and then he will need some serious physical therapy and training to get him back in shape for next season."

"Mark, I know you are right, of course. We both know Gary's leg is badly broken. But set that aside just for the sake of the discussion. How badly do you need him? I mean do you really think Jeff McCarthy can replace Gary?" Stu made it his business to know all the players and the needs of each team. He already knew Gary was a better receiver than Jeff, and that Jeff was Mark's only other star receiver. Stu was preparing Mark for what was about to come.

"Sure Stu, I'd love to have Gary in the game. But what is this about? It seems to me the question is academic."

"OK, I suppose it is … but just suppose for a moment, that I could wave a magic wand and get Gary back on the field in time for the Super Bowl. What would that be worth to you?"

Father John's Gift

Mark was amused. He didn't know where Stu was going with this line of questioning, but he thought he would play along to see what Stu was up to. "Well, I don't know how you expect to pull that one off! It would take a miracle, I'm sure. But just for the sake of argument, let's say you could do it. I'd be willing to put up an extra thirty grand to get Gary back in the game. Is that want you wanted to hear? Now tell me, what's this all about!"

"It's the longest of long shots Mark. I really can't go into it right now, but let me just say that your money could make a difference. Can I hold you to the extra thirty grand?"

"Stu... if you can pull this one off, I would gladly give you thirty grand to put Gary in the Super Bowl. But I think I am safe to say that I won't have to pay off on this bet. Still, I'd love to have Gary in the Bowl. You saw what he did for us against the Packers!"

"Thanks Mark. If I can make it happen, I will have Gary call you to say he is ready!"

Stu hung up the phone. He got what he wanted. He then dialed Bishop Carney.

* * * * * * *

Chapter 17: **The Hook**

"Chicago Archdiocese, Bishop Carney's office." It was Janet Henry, the Bishop's secretary.

"Hello, my name is Stu Pierson, who is this please?"

"My name is Janet. I'm Bishop Carney's personal secretary. Can I help you?"

"Hi Janet. Is the Bishop in today?"

"May I ask what this is regarding?"

"Yes, can you tell the Bishop that I am interested in making a large donation to the Chicago Diocese, but that I need to speak with him about it first."

"Let me see if the Bishop is available. One moment please."

Janet placed Mr. Pierson on hold and dialed the Bishop.

"Bishop Carney?"

"Yes Janet."

"I have a Mr. Pierson on the line who says he would like to make a large donation to the church, but he wants to talk to you about it first. Shall I put him through?"

The Bishop's morning had been uneventful. He had been looking over the church finances and was getting blurry-eyed staring at all the numbers. He thought the phone call would be a welcome diversion, and it might even help him out with his bottom line. He placed a book mark in the large ledger on his desk and folded it shut. "Sure Janet. Please put him through."

Stu heard a click on the phone. "Bishop Carney?"

"Yes."

Father John's Gift

"Bishop, I'm sure you don't know me. My name is Stu Pierson. I am a sports agent in the Chicago area and I represent a large number of football players on the Chicago Bears football team."

"How may I help you Mr. Pierson?"

"Is Saint Andrews Parish in your diocese?"

"Yes. We have twelve parishes, and St Andrews is one of them. Why do you ask?"

"Well Bishop, I have a favor to ask of you, but it is one which could profit both of us."

The Bishop thought Stu sounded like a used car salesman, and he was beginning to regret he had let Janet put him through. "Go on. I'm listening."

"Do you know a Bears player named, Gary Bowman?"

"Yes, I've seen him in a few games." It was true. The Bishop enjoyed watching a football game every once in a while, and he skimmed the sports page in the Tribune when he had time. He had seen the article on the Packard's game and Gary's tragic touchdown photograph which made the front page of the sports section of every major newspaper in the country. It was a sensational picture and a tragic event for the Bears, as well as for all the Bears fans. Though the Bishop was not obsessed with football, he considered himself a fan.

Stu continued, "Bishop, Gary was the best tight end that the Bears had until he broke his leg a week ago during the playoff game against Green Bay."

"Yes, I remember reading about it in the paper. What does that have to do with St Andrews?"

"Gary read the article in this morning's Chicago Tribune about your Father John and he wondered if we could persuade Father John to pay him a friendly visit."

Bishop Carney paused briefly as he processed the information Stu had just provided. He thought about where this conversation was going and whether or not he even wanted it to continue. He decided he had better put a stop to it before it got out of hand.

"Mr. Pierson, despite what you or Gary Bowman may have read in the paper, our Father John does not perform medical miracles. I'm sure he is a good and dedicated priest, but nothing more."

Gary was defensive. He didn't like the tone of the Bishop's voice, and thought if he wasn't careful, he just might lose the Bishop. Gary began again. "Bishop, please don't misunderstand me. There are no expectations of a miracle. But what could it hurt to have Father John pay Gary a visit? You must know that Gary has done well for himself, and he would be very generous to the church just to have Father John come out to his house. Do you know if Father John is a Bears fan?"

The Bishop's patience was starting to wear thin. "No, I don't know if he is a fan or is not."

"Well, let's just say he is a fan for sake of an argument. And let's just say Gary was to extend an invitation to Father John to come out to his house to watch a football game with him. And let's also say that Gary was so fond of Father John, and all the good things he is doing, that he decided he would like to make a rather large donation to Saint Andrews, you know, just to help out."

The Bishop was mildly amused. Stu was a good talker, and maybe there might be some significant money involved. It might not matter if Father John could pull off a miracle or not, and the church could always use some more money. There were always new projects to be funded, and he might even impress the Cardinal if he could get a nice chunk of change out of the deal. The Bishop was beginning to be convinced, but he needed to know more.

"I suppose it could be arranged. How large of a donation are we talking about?"

"I don't know Bishop, but I think five thousand dollars is not out of the question. Do you think you could persuade Father John to go to Gary's house to watch a football game, and accept a check for that amount, made out to St Andrews Parish?

The Bishop paused once again. He was no fool, and he now knew there was serious money on the table. He thought again about all the things he could do with an extra few thousand dollars in the coffer. The diocese cash flow could use a nice shot in the arm, and this just might be a method of doing that.

Sensing the Bishop's reluctance, Stu continued. "Bishop, as I see it, there is really no downside for you here. If we can get this done, then at the very least, Gary will have a pleasant afternoon watching a football game on TV with Father John, and St Andrews will be richer for it."

It was a proposition the Bishop could not refuse. "Mr. Pierson....ah Stu, do you think Gary could see his way to making it a ten thousand dollar donation? Saint Andrews could really use a new gymnasium just now." The Bishop hoped he had not overplayed his hand.

Stu smiled a large grin, and was glad the Bishop could not see it through the telephone. He knew he now had the Bishop in the palm of his hand. He now knew the Bishop would not reject his money. It was now a matter of negotiation. He paused briefly for effect, as if considering the Bishop's counter offer. Stu did not want to appear to give in too easily. The Bishop might sense his eagerness, and go after him for more. "Bishop, you drive a hard bargain. But I think that could be arranged. Let me see what I can do."

"OK. But I have a few conditions if we are to make this happen." The Bishop was now thinking of more bad publicity. He could just see the next article in the Chicago Tribune.

"What would that be?"

The Bishop's voice was stern. "Mr. Pierson, if we do this, I want no publicity about the visit or the donation. The press is not to be notified either before or after the visit, and as far as we are concerned, the donation will be made anonymously. Is that agreeable to you?"

Stu's answer was immediate. "Yes. That's acceptable. Thank you, Bishop. I will speak to Gary Bowman, and I will call your secretary back to let you know what he says. Can you ask her to make the final arrangements with Father John if the deal is acceptable to Gary?"

"That's fine. I will let Janet know to expect your call."

Both men hung up the phone content in the knowledge that they each got what they wanted. Neither could know what would happen next.

* * * * * * *

Chapter 18: **The Club**

Christine's mother, Helen Fitzpatrick, was part of the church community. She attended church at St Andrews, was part of the school PTA, participated in food drives for the needy members of the parish, and baked cakes for the annual church cake bingo fund raisers. St Andrews Parish now had hundreds of families. Although Helen didn't know them all, she was well connected, and most importantly, she was part of the informal women's church network, the bingo club, or "The Club" as it was called.

There was no formal organization to the Club. It had no official officers, no dues, no newsletter and no membership list. The Club never formally met to discuss business because there was no need. Club members talked constantly and informally over backyard fences, at the grocery stores, at other church functions and, if there was ever a need, there was always the telephone.

Whenever something in the church needed to be done, volunteers within the club would spontaneously form a group or subcommittee, and the task would get done. The priests and nuns at St Andrews were well aware of the Club, and they called upon various members of the Club whenever any help was needed. The Club was the heart and soul of Saint Andrews. As a group it was well connected. It functioned well, and to its credit, it was efficient. The Club performed its functions autonomously and they never asked for money from the church. What money was needed was raised by the Club largely by bake sales held at school functions and sporting events, and by Bingo

Father John's Gift

games held in the school gymnasium. All Club sponsored events were well attended by church members and their friends who gave generously for causes targeted by the Club.

News of Jeremy Wilkins's recovery had drawn considerable interest with the Club and all the members began to watch Father John more closely in the days that followed. But when news of Billy McLeary's recovery reached them, word spread like wildfire throughout the Club and the parish.

Helen Fitzpatrick got the call from her neighbor, Jenny Montgomery, on Thursday and Christine overheard just her mother's side of the phone conversation with her.

"Hello?"

"Yes, this is she."

"Oh, hi Jenny! How are you?"

"No, Fran didn't call me. What's the word Jenny?"

"No, I didn't hear anything about it."

"What? How did that happen?"

"He was in a coma at Chicago General?"

"No! Oh Sally must be scared to death!"

"He's OK now?"

"Father John was there?"

"Oh, the Club must be on fire about this!"

"Sure, I remember Jeremy Wilkins. Father John was there too! That was just last week!"

"What do you make of it Jenny?"

"I always knew Father John was special, but I never dreamed he might perform miracles!"

"Yes. I'll call her."

"OK. Thanks for calling Jenny!"

"Goodbye."

Helen hung up the phone and immediately dialed her friend, Connie Richards who was also a Club member.

Christine had hung on her mother's every word. She wished she could hear the entire conversation, but she had heard enough. "What happened Mom?"

"Just a minute Christine. I've got to tell Connie."

"Connie?"

"This is Helen."

"I'm fine. How are you?"

"Good. Connie, the Club is buzzing with news about Father John. Have you heard it yet?"

"Do you know the McLeary's?"

"Yes. They have a twelve year old daughter named Katie, and an eight year old son named Billy."

"Well, it seems Billy McLeary fell into the Des Plaines River on the way home from school and nearly drowned yesterday, but was rescued by the police and sent to Chicago General in a coma."

"I know it's awful, but the good news is that he is OK thanks to Father John!"

"No, I don't really know how it happened, but everyone thinks Father John performed a miracle and caused Billy to wake up!"

"I know it's amazing! I told Jenny I always thought our Father John was special, but this is just unbelievable!"

"I wonder what Father John will do next!"

"OK. You too."

"Bye Connie. Will you tell Janet?"

"OK. Bye Connie."

Helen hung up the phone and looked back at Christine.

"That's OK Mom. I got the gist of it."

Christine now knew she loved Father John more than life itself.

* * * * * * *

Chapter 19: **Trouble in the Rectory**

    Christine always sat in the back of the church by herself for the eight AM Saturday Mass. Her parochial schooling at St Andrews had made attending daily Mass a ritual for Christine, and if attending Mass on Saturday got you any additional points with God, Christine was going to get them. Her mother had successfully passed her devotion to the church on to Christine, and the daily routine of attending the eight o'clock Mass was so ingrained in her, that Christine could not imagine, not going. Her Catholicism defined her as a person, and at the age of fifteen, her love for Christ and his church had no real competition in her life. Most of her friends were interested in boys, and it seemed that was all they wanted to talk about. Each talked about who liked who and whether or not they had kissed yet or made it to second base. Christine couldn't care less about such boy talk, and her nonchalant attitude alienated her from many girls in her class who dismissed her and thought she was, "not cool". But the church gave her life meaning and satisfied a deeper hunger within her. Christine felt she belonged to something more important than even her own life. The church gave her life purpose; "to love Christ with all her heart".

    The Mass at 8 AM on Saturday was not well attended. Sunday was, and still is the day of worship for the vast majority of Catholics. If any did attend Mass on Saturday, it was done on Saturday evening in lieu of the Sunday attendance. Like most Saturday mornings, the church was largely empty. Those faithful who did attend the Saturday morning service sat in the front of the church, in the first five rows of pews.

    Despite Christine's devotion, she was always late for the service, and always arrived just before the sermon began. It was for this reason that she sat in the back of the church in the 35th pew, and always on the East side. Christine liked the East side because the early morning sun shone beautifully through the stained glass windows and cast a wonderful menagerie of colors on the floor and pews of the old St Andrews church. As a little girl, she imagined those colored lights were God's way of telling her that this was where she belonged.

The Saturday Mass was also not popular with the priests at St Andrews. They coveted their time off from their mandatory duties, and they looked forward to keeping Saturdays open if they could. They frequently used a relaxing Saturday visit some family or friends, watch some television or to prepare for their Sunday sermons. At the Monsignor's instruction, the priests rotated the saying of the Saturday Mass, and when they could, they took the opportunity to sleep in one day out of the week.

Because she sat by herself in the back, Christine's late arrival was noticed by all of St Andrews priests, and it had become something of a subtle joke between them. Father Bill once remarked at dinner that he could set his watch by Christine's late arrival. The remark brought smiles to the faces of all the priests. Father John agreed, and said she normally arrived just after his homily, and he could always tell if his tempo in the Mass was too fast or slow, by when Christine arrived.

Christine knew all the priests at St Andrews and liked them all, but Father John was her favorite. He had been a priest at St Andrews since she was a little girl. She had known him all her life, and for her, Father John was synonymous with St Andrews. She watched him mature from a man in his early thirties, to a handsome priest approaching forty two. Christine thought the touch of grey at his temples made him look distinguished. The fact that Father John talked frequently in his sermons about his missionary work in South America only intensified her belief that he was wise and worldly.... something that at age fifteen, she could only imagine and dream about.

As he did with so many children at St Andrews, Father John had baptized Christine and saw her grow at St Andrews over the years More than once Father John had noticed Christine noticing him. She never took her eyes off of him whenever he entered a room, and she hung on his every word during his sermons and his mini-lectures when he visited her classroom once every week or two for Catechism instruction.

Father John made a conscious effort not to encourage Christine or any of the other young girls who secretly cherished him. Still, it was difficult for him not to notice her. She was physically advanced for her age, and she had blossomed into a beautiful young woman. She had caught his eye more than once. Though John had heard Christine's intimate confessions of her love for Christ a week ago, he could not imagine how far her love for him would be expressed on this particular Saturday morning. She was obsessed with him. After hearing the miracle stories which had circulated through the parish, Father John was now, for her, the incarnation of Jesus Christ.

Christine exited the church with the other parishioners as usual when the Mass ended. It was a beautiful spring day. The sky was blue and the sun had raised just enough to peak over the top of the old St Andrews church. Father John had said the Mass and had left from the back of church to make his short walk to the Rectory as he had done a thousand times before. He did not notice that Christine watched him with great interest from the sidewalk near the corner of the church, as he entered the side door of St Andrews Rectory.

Once Father John had entered the rectory, Christine raced around to the front of the building and stood on the sidewalk twenty feet in front of the large picture window, just five feet to the left of the rectory's main entrance. She lifted a cardboard sign that she had made the night before and had hidden in the women's restroom at the front of the church before she took her seat in row thirty five. Now on the front lawn, Christine began calling out for Father John. The sign showed a large red heart, a crucifix, and the name of Father John beneath it.

"Father John!"

"Father John!"

"I love YOU Father John!"

"I want to have your baby!"

At first no one heard her passionate expressions of love. She repeated herself but shouted her testimony louder in an attempt to draw his attention.

"Father John!"

R. Allan Worrell

"Father John!"

"I love YOU Father John!"

"I want to have your baby!"   Christine began to cry.

Father Jim had just finished his breakfast of Cream of Wheat cereal when he heard Christine shouting from the front lawn. He quickly got up from the table and hurried over to the picture window in the adjacent room to see what the commotion was about. When he looked out the window, Father Jim saw Christine begin to disrobe on St Andrews front lawn. "Oh, my God!" It was all that Father Jim could say.

Christine started to disrobe just as a garbage truck was turning the corner onto Willow Street, directly in front of the St Andrews Rectory. As the truck driver started his left turn, his attention was immediately drawn to the figure of a voluptuous young, redheaded woman now stripping on the lawn of the Saint Andrews Rectory.

"What the hell!" As the words left the driver's lips he was so distracted that he failed to fully negotiate his left turn. The front right corner of his truck smashed into the rear of a car parked at the curb directly in front of the rectory sending broken glass and metal flying onto the street. The sound of the impact and breaking tail light was heard for half a block and startled everyone, particularly Christine, who spun around to face the street to see what had just happened.

"Mary Margaret!" Father Jim saw the situation was out of hand. His eyes were glued to the unbelievable scene just outside the Rectory window. He was stunned by the truck accident and by the spectacle of a naked young woman with a beautiful body crying and calling the name of Father John, not twenty five feet from the picture window.

"I'm right behind you." Margaret had rushed to the front of the rectory from the kitchen when she heard the crash. She looked past Father Jim's shoulder and saw the chaos unfolding as several people on the street came rushing to the accident.

"My God! That's Christine Fitzpatrick!" Father Jim was amazed at what a beautiful woman she had become. Having been a strong Catholic all his life, and having dedicated himself to the priesthood at age eighteen, Father Jim had seen pictures of naked women before joining the priesthood, but had never seen a completely naked woman in the flesh. The church had taught him to repress and banish such

Father John's Gift

thoughts and had labeled pornography and sex outside of marriage as a sin. But the site of Christine was nothing short of amazing. Her voluptuous body and radiant skin were flawless. Her bright red hair glistened in the morning sun and Father Jim could not take his eyes off of her.

Seeing young Christine, now standing naked on the lawn with tears streaming down her face, Margaret reached for a quilt that lay on the couch next to her. "I'll get a blanket around that girl!"

Margaret raced out the front door and down the porch steps as she unfolded the quilt. "Christine! Christine Fitzpatrick!"

Christine turned around to see Margaret rushing toward her with the outstretched quilt. Not wanting to be caught, Christine tossed her sign to the ground and ran around the small crowd of people who had come to watch the spectacle. They turned their heads as Christine ran by, followed immediately by Margaret.

Not knowing where to go, Christine ran back around the small group of people and fled up the front porch stairs and into the rectory in search of Father John. Once inside, and not wanting to be caught, Christine turned and slammed the front door of the rectory closed and locked it behind her. It was the first time Christine had ever been inside of the rectory.

Not as fast as a fifteen year old, Mary Margaret was ten to twelve feet behind Christine. She reached the front door only to have Christine slam and lock the door in her face. Caught on the rectory front porch and unable to get in, Margaret turned and started back down the steps to run to the side door. As she ran down the steps the small crowd of strangers who looked on was paralyzed in shock and just stood there and did nothing. Margaret caught the eye of a friend, Jenny Patterson, who had just run across the street from the St Andrews Elementary School office after she heard the crash. "Jenny! Gather up her clothes. She locked the front. I'm going around to the side door! I'll open up the front door for you when I get inside!"

Jenny did not yet understand what was happening but replied, "OK Margaret!"

"Father John! ..... Father John!" As Christine fled down the main hall in an unknown building, she was crying once again.

R. Allan Worrell

As Christine turned the corner toward the rectory kitchen, Monsignor Eckhart opened the door to his suite and came face to face with Christine as he stepped out into the hall. Both were stunned by the presence of the other, and both came to a complete stop and stared with disbelief at each other. The Monsignor was a virgin and tried unsuccessfully all his life not to think of naked women. Like Father Jim, he was taught and had always believed that lust for women was a sin in the eyes of God. As Christine looked into his eyes she knew the power and authority of the man now standing before her. Neither spoke a word as they each tried to make sense of their sudden encounter in the rectory hallway.

Christine turned and ran down an adjacent hall as Margaret now rounded the corner of the hall past Monsignor Eckhart, who was standing stunned and speechless by the presence of a beautiful fifteen year old girl, running naked through his rectory.

"Father John! ….. Father John!"

Christine's cries could now be heard throughout the building and three other priests came out of their rooms and started down the stairs to see what all the commotion was about. Father John stepped out of the rectory library on the first floor only to find himself enveloped in Christine's naked loving arms. "Oh Father John! Father John… I love you, Father John!" Tears of desperation flowed down Christine's cheeks.

Father John, not knowing what to do, wrapped his arms about Christine. "It's OK Christine. Shhh…. Stop crying now. It's going to be OK." At nearly six feet tall, John towered over Christine. He pulled Christine's head to his chest. "We can talk about this later."

Margaret arrived just behind Christine who was now in a full embrace of Father John. Father John looked at Margaret over top of Christine's head. Margaret returned his gaze and shook her head in disbelief and she frowned in disapproval. Margaret raised the quilt to wrap around Christine just as Jenny Patterson approached her from behind with Christine's clothes. Father John nodded briefly to Margaret, but spoke again to Christine who looked directly up at him.

"Christine, I want you to go now with Margaret, and get dressed. OK? We can talk about this after you get dressed. OK?

Father John's Gift

Christine looked up at Father John with tears in her eyes. "OK." She turned around and allowed Margaret to wrap her with the quilt and lead her back down the hall towards her small room on the first floor. Margaret didn't live full time with the priests, but she needed a room in which she could stay overnight whenever unusual situations or bad weather demanded it.

"You can get dressed in my room." Margaret understood the overwhelming affection that a young girl can have for her priest. She had those feelings herself for a priest in her own parish when she was a teen. Margaret had never married, but instead had devoted her whole life in service to the priests of Saint Andrews.

As Father John walked back to his room, he recalled the troubled confession he had heard four days ago from a confused young woman. He now knew it was Christine, and he now understood her cries for help. He knew it would be hard, but he knew he had to help her understand she needed to meet and date someone her own age. He had to redirect Christine's affection for him to someone else. It should be someone her own age who could love and appreciate Christine for herself. He knew this episode could easily turn into a scandal for Christine, and he would have to prepare her for it. He would meet privately with Christine's mother to get Christine the help, love and understanding Christine so desperately needed at home. The road ahead would be a tough one for Christine, but at least the problem had surfaced, and Father John now understood it.

As Christine and Margaret walked back down the hall in the opposite direction, Father John met the eyes of Monsignor Eckhart who had witnessed the event from the end of the hall just outside his office. The Monsignor drew a deep sigh and slowly shook his head as he looked at Father John. Not a word needed to be said between them. Father John nodded to show he agreed with the Monsignor. John turned around and reentered the library from which he had come.

* * * * * * *

Chapter 20: **The Meeting**

Father John entered the president's office a few minutes early with some trepidation. He had never met the president, and he was surprised when he received a call from the president's secretary requesting a meeting with him. Father John didn't work for the hospital. He was, after all, a volunteer who offered spiritual counseling to the sick and dying. He had been doing this work for nearly ten years at Chicago General, and this was the first time he would ever come face to face with the president.

"Father John?"

It was the president's secretary Alice Harper. Like all men of power, Dr. Robert Lieberman had a gatekeeper. Alice made all his appointments and she kept him free to conduct the business of running a major city hospital.

"Yes. Is Dr. Lieberman in?"

"Yes Father. He's expecting you. I'll let him know you are here." She pressed a button on her intercom. "Dr. Lieberman? Father John's here to see you."

"Thank you Alice, please send him in."

Father John thanked Alice and entered the president's office. It was a large room on the fifth floor of Chicago General and had a large picture window overlooking the downtown area and the Chicago River. The office was plush with fine cherry furniture, green carpet and drapes. John thought it was a fitting office of a corporate president, even if it was a hospital. He couldn't imagine what duties president

Father John's Gift

had. John concluded he must know a great deal about both business and medicine, things which he, John, knew nothing about.

As Father John entered the room, Dr. Robert Lieberman rose to greet him from behind his enormous desk. "Father John?" The president extended his hand and smiled.

Father John gladly shook his hand and looked him square in the eye. "Yes Doctor. I am glad to finally meet you."

"And I'm glad to finally meet you! I've been hearing a lot of extraordinary things about you lately, Father! Please, take a seat."

Father John selected a large comfortable chair in front of the president's desk and sat down. "Is that why you asked to see me?"

"Yes! It appears you are causing quite a stir within the hospital, particularly with our ER staff."

"Did I do something wrong?"

Both men knew what they were now talking about, but neither wanted to name it. It was clear that the surprising miracles were disruptive in some way to the hospital, and Father John sensed it as soon as Alice had called him for an appointment with the president. He felt like a school child who was in trouble and had to go to the principal's office. He was secretly glad the president did not have a large paddle behind his desk, like the principle's paddle at Saint Andrews Elementary. Although it was almost never used, it served as an ever present reminder to the students to mind their teachers, or risk suffering the consequences. Nothing was ever said to the kids about it, but they all knew it was there.

"No Father, that's not it! Please don't get the wrong idea. We are happy that you are here, and that you are contributing all you can to Chicago General. It's just that we have to be careful about how your work is perceived by the public. And frankly, I think we can and should better manage your relationship with our doctors and nurses."

"How would you like to do that?" Father John was relieved at how the conversation was going. John had given the conversation considerable thought ever since Alice called him to set up the appointment, and feared he might be asked to leave the hospital, which was something he didn't want to do. He didn't want to start over somewhere else, with a new hospital, with a new staff, a new hospital CEO, and new rules to live by.

"Well, I'd like to try to keep your work low key, you know, less visible to the public."

"So what do you propose?" Father John was intrigued. He suspected the president already had something in mind.

"As you know, we have a lot of very sick people here at Chicago General."

"Yes."

"Most of them we can help. But frankly, I think you and I both know there are many people we can't help because of the limitations of medicine. We can't cure everybody. I'm sure you have tended many of our dying patients... You have helped them find some peace in the last days or weeks of their lives."

"Yes." It was all true. But John was curious to see where the president was leading him.

"Father, you may not know it, but Chicago General is about to grow. We have a large number of cancer patients and are about to open a new oncology wing which will add over a hundred beds to our hospital".

Father John was both surprised and impressed. In his position, it was unusual for him to hear such details before they were released to the public.

The president continued. "In addition, we have plans to expand our cardiac ward and are in the process of hiring seven new heart surgeons to care for some very sick people. ... Father, I'd like to use your talent selectively. You are too important to us not to be managed properly by this hospital."

Father John made a face at the thought that his work might somehow be restricted. After all, he thought, everyone should have access to God's love and forgiveness. John now viewed his medical miracles as a part of God's love. But Father John sensed the proverbial axe was about to fall.

The president went on. "Of course, we will continue to medically help all of those we can help, and provide you with access to those

Father John's Gift

patients who we can't help, and to those who specifically request your counsel."

Father John was pleased that he would not be denied access to anyone who requested him. He did not want to, "play God". He did not want anyone to pick and choose who could or could not receive the benefits of his new gift.

"That sounds good." Father John knew he really did not have a choice in the matter as long as he wished to remain at Chicago General. His mind immediately raced to the possibility of moving to another hospital. Still, he thought, he had a history at Chicago General. He was well liked and respected by most of the staff. It would be hard to start over somewhere new, and besides, Chicago General was the largest hospital in the city had the most patients who were in need of his help.

"But Father, we need to be very careful about how your work is treated, and its relationship to the practice of medicine here at Chicago General. I must insist that you be respectful of my doctors, and of the work they are doing."

"Of course!" Father John's exclamation was genuine. He had great respect for the doctors, and his new found gift did not alter that fact.

"So Father, can I ask you to stay out of the ER, and other more public areas of the hospital?"

It was a blow to Father John. Until now he had full access to all areas of the hospital. But he could see the president was a reasonable man, and it really was not too much to ask. It might be wise to avoid the drama of the ER patients. After all, it was the McLeary family in the ER which put him at risk of exposure with the Tribune newspaper reporter. John sat back in his chair and thought about it. Doctor Lieberman was probably right. Too many questions by the wrong people might cause him trouble. "Yes." He answered.

"That's fine. I'll ask Alice to contact a lead nurse in both of our new wards to provide you a list of patients for you to visit whenever you are here."

Doctor Lieberman rose from behind his desk and walked around it to shake Father John's hand. "Believe me Father, we value your service, and I promise we will keep you busy! Thank you for stopping by today."

Father John shook the CEO's hand and nodded his head. "Thank you, Doctor."

The men ended the meeting on a high note, but both were unsure of what was to come.

* * * * * * *

Chapter 21: **The Chain of Command**

Bishop Carney, a man in his early 60's, was feeling his age as he entered his plush office the following morning. He had hurt his left knee when playing church basketball as a teen and it had plagued him on and off ever since. It now gave him pain as he slowly walked up the stairs. The fact that he suffered from a mild case of arthritis in his knees didn't help. He hated getting older, but he counted himself lucky that he was otherwise in relatively good health.

"The paper, Bishop?" His secretary, Janet Henry, handed him the city newspaper as he walked past her desk. It was a ritual they had played out a thousand times in the last eighteen years. She was a devoted and faithful servant to the Bishop, and she had watched and helped him advance his career in the church. Janet was the Bishop's administrative right arm.

"Thank you Janet." The Bishop never declined his morning news. He hung up his coat, got himself a cup of coffee from Janet's pot, walked into his office, placed the paper on his desk and still standing, he glanced at the headlines as he took his first gulp.

The front page of the Tribune was covered with local politics, and the status of a Chicago murder trial which resulted in a hung jury. The Bishop hated sensational news and he turned immediately to the religion section which was his ritualistic way to read the paper. Religion was, after all, his business and his domain.

Sam Elm's "Faith Healer" article jumped out at him from the top of the Religion page. He choked on his coffee when he read that Father

John of St Andrews parish was performing miracles in the name of religion at Chicago General Hospital. Bishop Carney pressed Janet's button on his intercom.

"Janet, get me Monsignor Eckhart at Saint Andrews please."

"Of course, Bishop." Janet pulled St Andrews number from the Rolodex on her desk. She was nothing if not organized.

"Saint Andrews Rectory. This is Margaret. How may I help you?"

"Hi Margaret, this is Janet at Bishop Carney's office. Is Monsignor Eckhart available?"

Janet caught Margaret by surprise. It was not often that Margaret got a call from the Bishop's office, and she knew it usually meant trouble.

"Yes, the Monsignor is in his office. Let me get him for you." Margaret punched the hold button and dialed the Monsignor. The Monsignor answered immediately.

"Yes Margaret."

"Monsignor? I have Bishop Carney on the line for you. Let me connect him." Margaret punched the hold button a second time. The Monsignor never refused to take a call from his boss. Margaret was under strict instructions to contact the Monsignor whenever the Bishop called. "Bishop Carney? Go ahead please. I have Monsignor Eckhart on the line for you."

"Thank you Margaret." The Bishop was polite as usual. He waited a moment for Margaret to hang up.

"Bob?"

"Yes?"

"Have you seen today's Chicago Tribune?"

"No Bishop. I haven't seen it."

"It appears your man Father John is causing quite a commotion over at Chicago General! What in the hell is going on Bob?"

"I'm sorry Bishop... I don't know what you're referring to."

"Well it's all over the paper that he is performing miracles!"

The Monsignor could tell the Bishop was agitated. This was not going to be a pleasant call.

"You have got to put a stop to it Bob! The church can't tolerate this kind of publicity! I won't have it! I don't want our parishes to get that

Father John's Gift

kind of a reputation. We are about respectable Catholicism, not some off the wall religion like the Evangelicals, doing faith healing trickery, playing with poisonous snakes, or speaking in tongues to get new converts."

"Bishop, Father John has been so busy at the hospital lately I haven't seen him all week. But I will certainly find out what's going on, and speak to Father John about it."

"Please do. And do it right away. I don't want to be a laughing stock if this gets back to the Vatican that we have a faith healer in our ranks. I just hope to God that the Cardinal doesn't read today's paper or get wind of it. If he does, I'll never hear the end of this!"

"OK Bishop. I'll speak to Father John right away."

"Thanks Bob. I know I can count on you."

The Bishop hung up the phone, and muttered to himself, "Jesus Christ, a faith healer.... that's just what I need." His day had started badly.

* * * * * * *

Chapter 22: **The Gifts**

The next day started out like any other at St Andrews and Father John was over at the church finishing up the eight o'clock Mass. But at nine AM the rectory doorbell rang and Margaret answered the rectory door to a small Mexican man dressed in heavy work clothes covered in plaster dust. He held a large fruit basket with a bright red bow tied to the handle. Behind him Margaret saw an old blue pickup truck parked at the curb with the words, "Rodriguez Drywalls" and a phone number painted in bright orange on the passenger side door.

Surprised the door was answered by a woman, the man said, "Is this St Andrews Rectory?" He spoke with a heavy Mexican accent.

"Yes it is, can I help you?"

"Do you have a Father John here that works at Chicago General?"

"Yes, but he is not here right now."

"Oh, I'm so a-sorry. My name is Jorge Rodriguez. My ten year old daughter, Lupe, fell and broke both of her-a wrists on the ice yesterday. My-a wife and I took her to Chicago General, and Father John healed her-a in the ER. I just wanted to drop off this gift to thank St Andrews for sending Father John to Chicago General Hospital." He handed the fruit basket to Margaret who was puzzled by hearing such news, and by receiving the unexpected gift from a stranger. "I wish I could do more, but we don't have much money."

Still somewhat confused, Margaret accepted the gift and looked at the bright assortment of fresh apples, pears and oranges in the basket. "Thank you Mr. Rodriguez. I will be sure Father John gets it. You

Father John's Gift

know Father John's work at the hospital is voluntary, and we really don't expect any gifts or payment for his service there."

Jorge smiled and said, "It's the least I could do. My Lupe is so happy today. She is back to her-a old self. It's a-like the accident never a-happened. Thank you again." He then turned around and left to go to work.

The basket had an envelope attached which was addressed, "To the Priests of St Andrews". Margaret opened the envelope and read the following message:

Dear St Andrews,

Please accept this basket of fruit for the wonderful work of Father John at Chicago General Hospital. Our daughter Lupe suffered two broken wrists from falling on our driveway yesterday, but she is totally healed now thanks to Father John's miracle.

We are members of St. Timothy's on Chicago's West side, but my family and I would now like to switch to your church. We will see you next Sunday, and we look forward to hearing Mass from Father John.

Muchas Gracias. God bless all of you!

Jorge & Maria Rodriguez

The gift from Jorge Rodriguez was just the first of many to arrive over the next few days, and as each gift arrived, Margaret still couldn't believe what was happening. John's patients sent gifts; baskets full of food and flowers to St Andrews with cards which thanked John again and again for having cured them or their relative at Chicago General. Some included gifts of money in envelopes; donations which were made directly to St Andrews for the wonderful work performed by Father John. All the gifts were received by Mary Margaret at the rectory front door, and all were noticed by Monsignor Eckhart when Margaret passed him the family donations of hundreds of dollars, some in cash and some in checks made out directly to St Andrews Church.

Margaret placed all the gifts in John's room and they were becoming a logistical problem for John. Measuring only ten by twelve feet, John's room was small, and there was not room enough to hold his twin bed, his desk and now the gifts which Margaret had piled up on the floor in front of his modest closet. Margaret said nothing to Monsignor Eckhart or to any of the other priests at St Andrews about what was happening. She passed the envelopes to the Monsignor in his mail and waited patiently to see what he would do.

John kept himself so busy on Thursday and Friday he arrived back at the rectory after ten o'clock each night and went straight to bed. He couldn't help but notice the gifts which Margaret had piled in his room and he made sure he was gone from the rectory each morning before the other priests and Monsignor Eckhart were up. The truth was that John was avoiding all of them, including Margaret. John didn't know what to say, or how to tell them what was happening. He didn't want to tell them the truth, but he knew he couldn't lie about it either.

John had Saturday free, and he was exhausted from all of the long hours he was keeping. He slept in until 9:00 AM and missed the Saturday morning breakfast. He got up, dressed, and retrieved an apple from the Rodriguez gift basket. He sat at his desk and read several of the cards and letters which came with his gifts. He heard a knock at his bedroom door.

"It's open."

Monsignor Eckhart opened the door and looked at John sitting at his desk with a note in one hand and a half eaten apple in the other.

"Good morning Father."

"Good morning Monsignor."

As he stood in the doorway, the Monsignor looked past John to the pile of gifts on the floor in back of him. "It looks like you have been busy the past few days. And I noticed you missed breakfast too."

John noticed the Monsignor glancing at the gifts and said nothing.

"I think we should have a talk about what's been happening, don't you Father?"

"Yes."

"Are you free this morning?"

"Yes Monsignor."

Father John's Gift

Monsignor glanced at his watch. It was already 9:15. "OK. How about you get us a small pot of coffee from the kitchen and meet me in my office in about five minutes? I'd like to ask Margaret to join us. She needs to know what's going on. Will that work for you?"

John drew a deep breath. "Yes. That will work."

John went to the kitchen to get the coffee as instructed. Father Frank was just leaving the kitchen with a cup of coffee in his hand as John arrived. "Morning John! I haven't seen you lately. Going for a cup?"

"Yes Frank... Is there any left?"

"I got the last cup, but I started a new pot. It should be done in a few minutes."

"Is it full strength?" John asked. Frank was famous for making weak coffee.

"Yes Father," he chuckled. "Its full strength... just the way you like it."

"Thanks Frank." But Frank was already out the door and five steps down the hall.

John found a small coffee pot and waited for the big caldron to finish perking. The fresh coffee smelled wonderful. With both hands on the edge of the counter, he leaned forward and stretched to relieve his tension and anxiety as he stared at the black and white tiles on the kitchen floor. "What am I going to tell the Monsignor?" When the coffee was finished he filled his small pot and retrieved a serving tray with three cups, saucers, spoons, along with a cream and sugar to carry down the hall to the Monsignor's office.

When he arrived the Monsignor and Margaret were already there, waiting for John to join them. As he walked into the room Margaret said, "Good morning Father!"

John looked at her and he could not help but notice she was looking at him as she never had before, with large eyes. He set the tray down on top a large, waist-high chest of drawers where each could get a cup.

Margaret stood up to get coffee. "Coffee Monsignor?"

"Yes, thank you Margaret." She approached John who just began to pour himself a cup.

Father John couldn't help but notice her unusual, cautious behavior as she approached him. John whispered, "Margaret, settle down. It's just me. ... Here, let me pour."

Margaret allowed John to pour the coffee, but she was so nervous she almost dropped a cup as she carried it over to the Monsignor's desk. All three were now seated and started sipping their coffees, each wondering how to begin the conversation. Monsignor Eckhart spoke first.

"Father, Margaret showed me all the gifts and cards you received. She accepted all the gifts at our front door and I accepted all the money and checks which came with the gifts. The checks were made out to St Andrews, and I want you to know they totaled about four thousand dollars."

John didn't know about the money. He was surprised and raised his eyebrows but didn't reply.

The Monsignor continued, "Father, do you want to tell me what has been going on?"

"Monsignor, I really don't know what to tell you except that I have been helping out in Chicago General's ER this week."

"It seems so! But all the cards and notes said you cured the sick! Did you know you made the Friday newspaper?"

"No Monsignor, I didn't."

"I don't have a copy of it, but I got a call from Bishop Carney who was quite upset about the publicity. He doesn't want... that is, we don't want to hear any more about it. It could cause all of us trouble with the media and even trouble within the church."

It was clear the Monsignor didn't want to ask John how he could perform miracles. He didn't know what to think. The Monsignor couldn't believe that one of his own could perform miracles. He had known Father John for nearly ten years, and John had never shown any special ability before. For him, John was a regular priest, no different than himself or any of the other priests Monsignor Eckhart had ever known.

No one said anything for a moment as they all contemplated why or how John's miracles could cause a problem for the church. None of

Father John's Gift

them understood it, least of all Margaret who sat quietly and said nothing.

"What do you suggest I do Monsignor?"

"Well, whatever you do, you can't go back to Chicago General. The Bishop forbids it. Can I tell him you will stop going?"

It was a devastating blow to John. Just when he thought he had everything under control the rug had been pulled out from under him by the church.

"Yes. If that is what the church wishes."

Monsignor Eckhart could see John was disappointed about having to give up something he obviously loved to do.

"I'm sorry Father. I can see you don't want to give it up, but it's for the best."

All three accepted the verdict, but all of them, including Monsignor Eckhart wondered who it would be the best for. All of them suspected it was not the best for Father John or for the patients he would not heal.

* * * * * *

Chapter 23: **The Super Bowl**

"Welcome back from the break, Ladies and Gentleman! My name is Brad Martin, and I am your commentator along with my partner, Mike O'Manski. You are watching live coverage of Super Bowl X from Minneapolis, Minnesota, shown exclusively on STN, the Sports Television Network."

"It has been one heck of a game hasn't it Mike?"

"That's for sure! These two teams are so equally matched, both in offense and defense."

"You're right about that Mike! The Steelers had the edge with a score of 35 to 30 going into the second half. We now stand at 47 to 50 with the Bears in the lead. But despite the high scoring game, the defense on both sides has made the game an emotional rollercoaster. With only five minutes left on the clock, the game could still go either way."

"It has been just an unbelievable game. We've seen five turnovers in the passing game alone! The Bears intercepted the ball three times, and the Steelers intercepted it twice. I don't know about you, but with all these turnovers, this game has been hard for me to watch!"

Brad looked down at the statistics written on the sheets before him. "I know what you mean Mike. You would think that with all those turnovers the teams would have switched to a running game in the second half, but with the weather so bad, the running game has been bad too. Both teams have fumbled the ball four times in the second half resulting in turnovers about half the time."

Father John's Gift

Shaking his head and looking straight into the camera, Mike remarked, "No doubt about it Brad. This game has been all about the weather. I don't know how any of those guys can keep their hands on the ball. Its twenty five degrees out there and it has been snowing nonstop since the beginning of the game. The players are sliding all over the field!"

Brad agreed. "The Refs had to call a time out due to blizzard-like conditions three times in the last hour. I've never seen a Super Bowl like this one! It's got to be one for the record books. The snow just will not stop!"

Brad turned to Mike and said, "Well, we've had snow before... but it's anybody's guess how this will turn out. I spoke to our affiliate weatherman Hank Delrose, at WNRJ-TV during the break. Hank told me he expects a total of ten inches tonight. With six inches on the ground now, we still have four more to go! With all that ice and snow I just don't know how the players can keep their hands on the ball."

The camera turned to the field revealing the Bears lined up in a 'V' formation on a snow covered field, ready to kick off to the Steelers.

"The Bears scored the last touchdown before the break. Here comes the kick to the Steelers."

"The kick is good.... high and long. It was caught by Number 33, Don Metery on the twenty who ran it to the left side of the field, gaining fifteen yards before being brought down by the Bears tackle Number 12, Shawn Stern."

"Shawn has had a great game tonight. He sure knows how to read a run-back. That was his fourth take-down tonight on a kick return."

The Steelers ran the ball repeatedly achieving one first down after another as they marched the ball down the field. They then scored a touchdown on a reverse play which put them into the lead 53 to 50, but they then failed to get the extra point when the wind caused the ball to bounce off the left upright.

With only two minutes left in the game, it looked like it was all over for the Bears.

The Steelers kick was short, and the Bears had recovered the ball on their own forty five yard line. The clock was stopped, but the Bears would have enough time for one or maybe, two more plays. They would have to take to the air to win the game.

Ted Reiner called the play in the huddle. His receiver Jeff McCarthy would have to catch the ball long, and run out of bounds to stop the clock to gain a final play. The snap was good and Jeff was off and running long and left of the field. The pass was near perfect and Jeff caught it, but he came down hard on his left foot twisting his ankle badly in the snow before stepping out of bounds at the Bears twenty three yard line. He got the clock stopped, but Jeff was hurt.

Brad Martin commented, "Looks like Jeff McCarthy got hurt on that play!" With only ten seconds left in the game, this isn't good for the Bears."

Mike chimed in, "Brad, Jeff got the clock stopped, but the Bears have no more timeouts." The camera switched back to the field. Mike continued, "Jeff is now being helped off the field by two teammates." Instant replay showed Jeff twisting his ankle badly when he landed on the side of his foot after catching the long pass. "Wow, that's got to hurt. He's clearly out of the game tonight. Jeff put the Bears in good position, and he got the clock stopped, but it might just be in vain if the Bears can't pull off another good play."

Brad changed the subject, "Look Mike! Can it be? The Bears Coach Winder has just sent in Number 15, Gary Bowman, to replace Jeff McCarthy! This is totally unexpected! Gary was on the Questionable List for today's game, but I've not seen him on the bench during the entire game! ..... For those fans who don't know, Gary broke his leg just two weeks ago in the playoff game against the Green Bay Packers. I don't see how he is able to walk without crutches, much less play football tonight!"

Mike added, "It's a mystery to me too Brad! Gary must have been hiding in the Bears locker room, keeping warm until now. Putting in Gary Bowman is an amazing turn of events! There may be hope for the Bears after all!"

Brad looked up from the monitor and straight into the camera. "Folks, this is just incredible. It looks like the introduction of Gary Bowman has thrown the Steelers for a loop! They have called for their last timeout!"

Father John's Gift

Both teams regrouped into their huddles. The Steelers coach instructed their defensive line not to worry about Gary Bowman. He believed Gary's introduction in the game was a bluff, meant to draw attention away from a run.

Ted Reiner knew differently. He told Gary to execute the same play that worked so well against the Packers. "The Steelers would never expect them to repeat it. "

Gary laughed. "Yeah Ted, but didn't I brake my leg last time we ran this play?"

"Sure Gary." Ted answered. "But just run faster this time!" Ted grinned through his helmet. "Remember, you're warm and fresh, and the Packard's are cold and tired. You'll be way ahead of them on this play." Ted knew he was right, and he knew his remark would give Gary the psychological edge he needed.

"OK. You got it Ted. Just put it in my hands." Gary smiled back at Ted who gave him a nod. Gary was ready for the play of his life.

"OK Guys, This is it. It's just like downtown. We go on twenty five." Ted placed his clenched fist in the middle of the huddle and everyone put a hand on top of his. As Ted raised and lowered his fist the team yelled, "Go Bears!" to end the huddle as they had done a thousand times before. They were now united as a team in what was probably the last play of the night. They all knew it was now or never.

The Bears lined up in the snow at the twenty three year line, and Ted began his count.

"Fifteen! …. Thirty two! …..Seventy four! …… Twenty five!"

The ball was snapped and Ted fell back to the thirty yard line. He turned and looked for Gary.

Pumped up with adrenaline, Gary had shot off the line of scrimmage like a bolt of lightning. He was in the Bears end-zone, running free and clear of all the Steelers' defensive ends in no time. Ted's pass was perfect, and the ball was in Gary's hands just as Ted had promised. The crowd went wild as Ted held the ball high above his head and jumped up and down in the end-zone for all to see. The touchdown put the score in the Bears favor at 56 to 53 with no time remaining. The entire Bears team rushed to the end of the field to join Ted in his jubilation at having won the game, but the referees blue their whistles to restore a modicum of order. Though it was moot, the Bears still had to kick the ball in one last play to finish the game.

Both teams lined up for the kick though none of the Steelers even moved when the ball was snapped. The extra point was good as the Bears kicked the ball through the uprights, just for the record books.

Bears fans all over the world were ecstatic. All of Chicago rejoiced, and Gary Bowman was their new hero!

* * * * * * *

Chapter 24: **The Interview**

The victorious Chicago Bears carried their star quarterback, Ted Reiner and their star wide receiver, Gary Bowman on their shoulders across the snowy field into the Bears locker room. On the way off the field, the team repeatedly chanted "Go Bears! Go Bears! Go Bears, GRRRR!" The "Victory Chant" as they called it, was started by Ted Reiner's four year old daughter, Catherine, one day after a successful Bear's practice. All the players adored "Little Catherine", and they loved her Victory Chant. They chanted it repeatedly wherever and whenever they won a game. They had done it so often it soon became part of the Bears culture, and it was echoed by Bears fans everywhere, both before and after the games.

Winning the Super Bowl was a dream-come-true for all the players, but for no one more than it was for Gary. The press, with TV cameras rolling, followed the team into the locker room. Everyone, it seemed, wanted to talk to Gary Bowman. Commentator Brad Martin announced, "We take you now to the Bears locker room where we have Tom Molan standing by. Tom?"

"Thank you, Brad. As Brad said, I'm now in the Chicago Bears locker room, standing next to the star wide receiver, Gary Bowman, who just minutes ago made the winning touchdown catch for the Bears. How does it feel Gary?" Tom pointed the microphone towards Gary.

Gary looked at Tom and then the camera as sweat poured down his face. "It feels great Tom! This is a dream come true. I've been dreaming about this moment all my life! But remember, the coach put me in the game at the tail end of it. You gotta give credit to all the other guys for doing a great job tonight, particularly Ted Reiner who led the team through the game, and Jeff McCarthy who got hurt before

R. Allan Worrell

I went in, as I'm sure you know. Everyone played a great game, particularly considering the terrible weather out there." Gary had watched the entire game on television from the locker room.

"Gary, you are absolutely right. The weather was awful during the whole game, and the entire team is to be congratulated." Tom changed his voice to a more serious tone. "However, we all know you broke your right leg just two weeks ago in the playoff game against Green Bay, and we were all amazed when you took to the field tonight. Gary, how did you do it? Wasn't your leg broken? How did you mend your leg so quickly?"

Gary put his right leg up on the bench and rubbed it with his hand. Looking down at his leg Gary said, "Tom, I have to tell you that after I broke my leg, I thought the season was over for me. I thought I blew my one chance and I might never get to play in the Super Bowl." Gary looked up straight into the TV camera. "But all that changed after I met with Father John from St. Andrews Parish at my house just last week. I mean, Father John blessed my leg, and it was healed! Tom, I'm here to tell you it was an honest-to-God miracle! You can see it for yourself!" Gary looked back down at his leg. "I'm as good as new. It's like I never broke my leg."

Tom was amazed. He never expected Gary would answer him this way. Tom looked skeptically at Gary. "Gary, let me make sure I understand you. Are you saying a Catholic priest healed your broken leg just last week?" Tom pointed the microphone back to Gary.

"Well, after the accident I went to the hospital and my leg was set in a cast as you might expect. It hurt like hell, and it itched and started to slowly heal, of course. But Tom, I am telling you that I owe this Super Bowl win to Father John at St. Andrews Parish who blessed my leg last week." Gary shook his head and looked again directly into the camera. "I never would have been able to play tonight if it wasn't for Father John. And that's the fuckin' truth!" Gary smiled large for the TV camera revealing a beautiful set of pearly white teeth.

Gary was never one for mincing words, and he knew his language would enhance his reputation with most football fans. Football was a game, but he also knew it was showmanship; entertainment both on and off the field. His fans loved his tough language. He knew, after all,

Father John's Gift

that most of the pro-football fans were rough men like him, and their families, who loved the macho game with its macho players. Besides, he was now a rich man, and he really didn't give a damn if someone didn't like the way he talked off the field.

Tom Molan didn't blink at Gary's explicative. He had been around professional football players enough to expect foul language as part of the culture, and of the game. Moreover, Tom knew the word was automatically censored by the station.

Tom thought of another question. "We didn't see you at the Bears practice session this last week in preparation for today's game. Were you there?"

Gary nodded and smiled again. "Oh yeah, well... That was the coach's idea. He didn't want the Steelers to know that I might play today. So, I've been working out in private.... you know, with my physical therapist and a sports trainer, separate from the team. The coach said I could play if I was ready, and if he needed me bad enough...and so I got ready. .... And it looks like he needed me!" Gary laughed out loud with a twinkle in his eye.

"Gary, that's quite a story! Congratulations once again to you and to your entire team for tonight's Super Bowl win. It was an amazing game with a fabulous ending!"

"Thanks Tom!" Gary beamed into the camera as a player in back of him yelled out, "Go Bears! GRRRR!" and two other players shook up champagne bottles and popped the corks spraying champagne over the crowd of jubilant Bears players towards the sportscaster, Tom Molan. With the champagne flying all over them, the team answered with a loud roar in the background and all started laughing when the Bears coach was drenched in the bubbly.

Tom instinctively put up one elbow to try to shield him from the champagne spray as he made his concluding remarks. "Whoa! There you have it Brad.... From the Chicago Bears locker room in full celebration after Super Bowl X. I'm Tom Molan.... Back to you Brad!"

On cue, the camera switched back to Brad Martin in the TV news box. Fans could be seen leaving the stadium out the news box window in the background. "Thank you Tom! For those of you who may have just signed on, Super Bowl X from Minneapolis, Minnesota goes to the Chicago Bears, with a final score of 57 to 53 over the Pittsburg Steelers! And what a game it was! This is Brad Martin, Mike O'Manski and Tom Molan from the Sports Television Network, signing off for the night.... Good night everyone!"

The station then broke for a commercial.

* * * * * * *

Chapter 25: "Cardinal Gino"

It was past 11 PM in Rome, Italy, but Cardinal Ricardo Benna saw the live locker room interview with the Bears' star receiver, Gary Bowman. Noting the late hour, Ricardo reluctantly picked up the phone and dialed his friend and mentor, Cardinal Alessandro Pescanni.

"Ciao Alessandro."

"Ciao Ricardo."

"Alessandro, I'm sorry to have to call you at such a late hour, but I thought it was important. Did you watch the Super Bowl tonight?"

"Yes. I saw it. It was a great game! But you did not call me about the game."

"Yes Alessandro, that's correct. Did you see the Gary Bowman interview broadcast right after the game?"

"Yes. I saw that too Ricardo, and you were right to call me about it. I think the Father John situation could quickly get out of control." He thought more about the interview and then continued his thought. "In fact, it is probably out of control already. We need to put out this fire as fast as we can. The Super Bowl international TV exposure could be a big problem for us. Do you know who the bishop is at St Andrew's Parish in Chicago?"

Ricardo was now glad he had called his old friend. "No. But I will find out first thing tomorrow."

"OK good. Please call me after you find out. This situation could become a political matter within the church. I have a special relationship with Cardinal Gino, who I would like to help us handle this matter quietly. Do you understand?"

Ricardo was shocked. "Gino" was not invoked or spoken of often within the church. "Gino" was the church code word for the Tambino family, named after Gaspar Tambino who was the head of the Costa

Nostra, the Italian Mafia. The Tambino family had operations which extended all the way to America, and was particularly strong in New York and Chicago.

Mafia members were all Catholics. The Italian priests knew who they were, and knew a great deal about their activities. The priests heard stories of Mafia activity during confessions, or whenever one priest confided in another to ask advice about how to handle a morally questionable situation that often rose during a Mafia confession. Names were never mentioned; they were not necessary.

The relationship between the Mafia and the church had evolved over the years. The two organizations had been adversaries long ago, but each found a way to peacefully coexist with the other for the past hundred years. They had grown to depend on each other from time to time, and each new generation of Mafia was introduced to their respective Catholic counterpart as they advanced in their ranks in the family.

Though they rarely understood why the introduction was made, the Mafia rank and file knew they had achieved real status in the family if they were formally introduced to a Catholic contact. And although they would not admit it, the Bishops and Cardinals at the Vatican felt the same way about meeting members of the Mafia family. The two organizations found it in their best interest to see each other as mutually beneficial friends, rather than as enemies. There was considerable cooperation between the two organizations, particularly when both had something to gain. Large sums of money were always exchanged from one to the other, and it was always earned tax free.

All of the Costa Nostra activities were illegal in both Italy and the USA. The activities were extremely profitable, and included prostitution, gambling, distribution of illegal drugs, and racketeering… which occasionally ended in murder. The Italian authorities believed the church hierarchy had a long standing relationship with the Italian Mafia, and that they were somehow involved in the Mafia activities. But the police could never prove it. Besides, tying the church to the Mob would not look good to the public, and the predominately Catholic Italian voters would not be pleased to have the church's good name smeared in the press. Though never expressed, all the Italian politicians instinctively knew it would be political suicide to tie the church to the Mafia's criminal activities.

Mafia leaders knew they could count on the church to forgive their henchmen their most egregious sins. Mob bosses trusted the church not to leak any information to the authorities since the church might implicate itself, or even worse, anger the Mob. The secrets were the bond between the church and the family. The church helped the Mafia leaders to maintain control of the organization. Members could always reconcile their brutality by knowing they could, "Come home to Jesus", confess their sins, and start again the next day with a clean slate. Knowing they could always be forgiven gave the men the courage to do the dirty work of the Mob. Seeing the family bosses rub elbows with the clergy didn't hurt either. After all, if what they were doing was ok with the church, who were they to argue? It was the ultimate rationalization, and besides…it was great money.

Ricardo asked his old friend for clarification. "Alessandro… are you referring to the Cardinal Gino?"

Alessandro immediately understood Ricardo was asking if Father John should be killed. "No, I'm sorry Ricardo. I really do know a Cardinal Gino. His name is unfortunate, and I'm sure it has caused him a lot of trouble in the church. I didn't mean for you to take it the wrong way. Alessandro paused and then added, "I think that Father John should take a vacation, don't you?"

Ricardo was relieved. "Alessandro, I hope that a vacation will be sufficient." Ricardo knew "vacation" was a code word which meant a permanent church reassignment. He was afraid the Father John problem might be shifted to another church, only to resurface there.

"Don't worry Ricardo. We can take additional steps if we must, but I don't think it will be needed. Let's take one step at a time and see what happens. I think our Father John will get the message."

"I understand. Grazie Alessandro."

"Buena nota Ricardo."

"Ciao Alessandro."

"Ciao Ricardo."

* * * * * * *

Chapter 26: **The Call from Rome**

Bishop Carney got the call from Rome at 2 AM the night of the game. A new employee in Cardinal Gino's office failed to realize he had placed a call to Chicago, Illinois, and he had not taken the seven hour time difference into consideration. It was already 9 AM in Rome, and Cardinal Gino's office workers had already been hard at work for over an hour.

Bishop Carney had seen the game, but he didn't stay up to watch the Bowman interview. The Bishop was startled from his sleep when the phone rang in his bedroom. Still groggy, the Bishop reached for his phone after a few rings.

"Hello?"

"Bishop Carney?"

"Yes? Ah, this is Bishop Carney. Who is this please?"

Cardinal Gino sensed that the Bishop was still sleeping. "Bishopa, I'ma sorry, did I awaka you?"

"Yes. What time is it? Who is this please?"

"Bishopa. My namea isa Cardinal Gino. I'm callin you from the Vatican. The Cardinal was not used to speaking in English. He spoke slowly and deliberately, carefully selecting his words as he spoke them. "Ima sorry for a wakin you ata this hour. My staffa did notta realize thata you are ina Chicago. I willa call you back tomorrow...that is in abouta seven hours ifa that isa OK with youa."

Bishop Carney was so surprised to receive a call from Rome, he was now fully awake. He sat straight up in bed and reached for a glass of water on his night stand. "No Cardinal, I'm OK. I am awake now. Please, tell me what this call is about."

"Bishopa, dida you see the Super Bowl tonighta?"

"Yes. I saw it." Greenly wondered where this was going. Why would he get a call from Rome about the Super Bowl?"

"Dida you see the interview with Gary Bowman after the game?"

"No Cardinal. I did not see it. I went to bed right after the game ended."

"Wella, it seems that Gary Bowman said your Father Johna performed a miracle and healed Gary's lega." The Cardinal stopped briefly to let that sink in, and then said, "This could be a big problem for a you and the church. It affects all of us."

"I see." Only Bishop Carney really did not see. He couldn't know just how big the problem would become. The Bishop had seen the newspaper articles about Father John. He had negotiated the "deal" with the agent, Stu Pierson for Father John to visit Gary Bowman just over a week ago, and now with a phone call from Rome, he was beginning to believe the Father John miracle stories might actually be true. The Bishop took the opportunity to ask a pointed question.

"Cardinal, do you believe it is true? Did Father John perform a miracle?"

"Bishopa. I would like to tell you a story. The church will officially deny it, of course. But it may help you to understand what we are dealing with and why this is so importanta."

"OK Cardinal. Go on."

"Bishopa, do you believe in UFO's?"

The question surprised the Bishop but he answered it, wondering what the Cardinal was about to tell him. He tried his best to respect the Cardinal's question and answer it in an intelligent way. "I believe that some people have seen things in the night sky that they do not understand, yes. But I do not think there are visitors here... from other planets... do you?"

"Yes. I do."

The Bishop was shocked. It was not the answer he expected, and he could hardly believe the Cardinal had said it. He said nothing and waited for Cardinal Gino to continue.

"We know they come to visit us from time to time, and your Father John's miracle is proof of their existence. Of course, the church cannot let the secret out, or it would hurt us badly. We know every once in a while, the aliens empower a human with the ability to heala. We don't know awhy they do this, but they do. We musta stop Father John from exercising this extraordinary power."

Now overloaded with information, the Bishop could not believe what he was hearing at two AM in his bedroom. It was like a bad dream he could not stop, even if he wanted to stop it. But he didn't want to stop it. He wanted …he needed to see where the conversation was going.

"Why Cardinal? If Father John can heal, why do we have to stop him?"

"Bishopa, you musta stop Father Johna, because Jesus Christ was the first human in history that the aliens so empowereda. If the public comes to understand this, it would cause panic throughout the worlda, and of course, Christianity, as we know it, could come to an enda. It woulda change everything."

"I see." Bishop Carney really did see this time. "What do you want me to do?"

Cardinal Gino laid out a plan for Bishop Carney. The Bishop did not sleep the rest of the night.

* * * * * * * *

Chapter 27: **The News Media**

Thanks to recent advances in satellite television, over two hundred and thirty five million people around the world had watched the snowy Super Bowl game with its spectacular ending, and over ninety five million of them had stayed up to watch the Gary Bowman locker room interview which immediately followed it. Gary Bowman was now famous throughout the sports world, and as a result, so was Father John of Chicago's St. Andrews Parish.

Word of the Chicago Bears Super Bowl victory and Gary Bowman's interview was spread by the Associated Press and syndicated sports journalists, and it was spread by word of mouth the next day by those who saw it live on television the night before. Steeler's fans were unhappy about the Super Bowl outcome, but fans from both teams everywhere were talking about Gary Bowman's dramatic catch and his remarkable recovery, all made possible by a miracle from Father John. Everyone wondered, "Was his leg really broken in the playoff game? Could the miracle be true?"

As the miracle story was told and retold by news reporters around the world, it became bigger news than the Super Bowl win itself. After all, lots of people around the world don't understand or care about American football, but everyone was fascinated by the news of a miracle which apparently had determined its outcome.

Mary Margaret was one of those rare people in the USA who did not care about football, and she did not watch the game. Though she had spoken to him once briefly on the phone, she didn't know about

Gary Bowman's super bowl touchdown, his dramatic recovery, or his post-game interview. Once more, Margaret didn't care about any sports, and she really couldn't care less. Ironically she was, perhaps, the last person in all of Chicago to know her Father John, at St Andrews Parish, was now famous throughout the civilized world.

Margaret arrived at St. Andrews at six AM and picked up the copy of the Tribune left at the front door of the rectory by the newspaper boy at five. She couldn't help but see the four inch headline which read, "Bears Win!" on the Tribune's front page with a four by four inch picture of Gary Bowman catching the winning touchdown pass. But Margaret didn't care, and she didn't take time to read the article. However, when Margaret stepped through the rectory door, she was alarmed because the rectory phone was already ringing. She thought it was surprisingly early for a call at the rectory, but without removing her coat, she put down the newspaper and her purse on the foyer table and answered the phone.

"Good morning, St. Andrew's Rectory."

"Good morning. Who is this please?"

"My name is Margaret Winkle. I am the rectory housekeeper. Can I help you?"

"Mrs. Winkle, My name is Bill Thompson. I am a CBS News reporter for Channel 2 Television WBNS out of New York City. Can you tell me please, do you have a priest there named, "Father John?"

Margaret immediately recognized the man's strong New York accent, and she believed the call was genuine despite the fact she had never received a call at the rectory from New York before. "Yes, we do have a Father John, but it's a little early, and I'm afraid he is not up yet. Can I ask what this is concerning?"

"I'm calling to speak with Father John about the Bear's football player, Gary Bowman's, allegation that Father John cured his broken leg. Can you confirm Gary's story?"

Margaret was not pleased. The call sounded remarkably like the one she had taken from Gary Bowman a few weeks ago, and she had received numerous gifts from grateful patients seen by Father John at Chicago General. But true or not, she was not about to confirm a miracle with a CBS news reporter over the phone.

Father John's Gift

Margaret's voice was emphatic. "No, I can't confirm it. But if you call back after eight, you might speak personally to Father John about it."

"Well OK. I will call back in an hour. But if you see him before that, would you please let Father John know I called, and please tell him that CBS would be willing to fly him to New York City for a live exclusive interview? In addition, I'm sure the station would pay him handsomely for it, and make it worth his time. Would you tell him that for me please?"

"Yes, Mr. Thompson, I'll tell him." At least the caller was polite.

As soon as she hung up the receiver, the phone rang again and again, each time with a call from some other reporter or network from somewhere else in the country. It seemed to Margaret that every newspaper, magazine, and television personality in the country suddenly wanted to interview Father John. All promised to grant Father John an exclusive interview, and all said they would pay Father John or the church a lot of money for it.

Margaret was stunned. Never in her life had she be so inundated with press attention. What was going on here? Did Father John really cure Gary Bowman's leg? She didn't know anything about the deal made by Bishop Carney, or Father John's visit to Gary Bowman's house.

Unable to get through by telephone, the Chicago Tribune sent two reporters and three photographers to St. Andrews to cover all the exits at the rectory. Samuel Elms was there. His boss, GlennReddy had called Sam immediately after seeing the Gary Bowman interview, live on television, and he had instructed Sam to get to St. Andrews bright and early with a photographer.

After her fifth phone call, there was a knock at the front door. Margaret opened the door to Sam Elms. With pen and paper in hand, Sam spoke up before Margaret had a chance to say anything.

"Hello Ma'am, I'm Samuel Elms from the Chicago Tribune. Is Father John here?"

Margaret could stand no more. It was all she could do to blurt out, "I'm sorry, but the church has no comment. Now please go away." Afraid the reporter would not take, "no comment" for an answer,

R. Allan Worrell

Margaret slammed the door in Sam's face and twisted the heavy dead bold closed.

Margaret raced into the living room and peeked behind the closed curtain at the corner of the front picture window. Television crews from every major station in Chicago and were now parked in the street in front of the St. Andrews Rectory, and more were arriving as she watched! All hoped to get a shot of Father John on camera to broadcast on the morning news. Crews poured out of the trucks and began setting up their equipment on the sidewalk and the lawn in front of the rectory. As soon as they realized they would be unable to speak with anyone from the church, they began to interview each other on camera, and they replayed the Gary Bowman interview over and over again. Each interview always ended with a shot of a reporter standing in front of the St. Andrew's Church or Rectory. Though they never said so directly, it was a now a foregone conclusion by the Associated Press that Father John was responsible for curing Gary Bowman's broken leg and the subsequent Bear's win of Super Bowl X.

It didn't take long for the television station news rooms to dig up Sam Elm's newspaper articles on the previous Father John miracles, and Sam found himself to be a target of the news media insatiable appetite for any information related to Father John. Sam held his ground, told what he knew about the events he had covered. Sam stated that although he had made inquiries, he had not received any official word from the church regarding the validity of any of Father John's "alleged miracles".

At promptly six thirty AM, Monsignor Eckhart entered the hall from his quarters at the far end of the rectory as he had done every day for the past nine years. As he walked down the hall towards Margaret, the rectory phone rang once again, and he saw Margaret answer it. She picked up the receiver, held it to her ear and just listened. He noticed she did not say, "Hello".

"I'm sorry, we have no comment." Margaret slammed the phone receiver back on the hook, and without missing a beat, the phone rang again. Margaret started to walk away from the phone.

"Aren't you going to answer that?" Although the Monsignor had seen the Super Bowl, he didn't stay up to see the Bowman interview,

Father John's Gift

and because he had spent the early morning in his back office, he was oblivious to what was happening in the front of the rectory.

Margaret's answer was indignant. "No Monsignor, all the calls are the same. Apparently everyone thinks Father John performed a miracle on a Chicago Bear's football player, and now they all want to interview Father John about it."

Another knock came at the rectory door.

"And I'm not going to answer that either!" Margaret had now been battling the press for more than an hour, and she was not happy. Until this morning she had nothing but good thoughts for the news media, but she had no idea dealing with the press could be such a nightmare. It seemed they never gave up, and she was amazed at how many of them there were.

Monsignor Eckhart was alarmed by her indignation. "Margaret, who is it at the door?"

"It's the Tribune, or the Daily Herald, or the Times, or Channel Seven, or Channel Nine, or Channel Twenty! I don't know who it is, and I have to tell you at this point, I don't care! They all want the same thing, and they won't take, "no comment", for an answer!" Monsignor Eckhart stood motionless and just looked at Margaret without saying anything. It was obvious he didn't believe her. Margaret pointed at the front door. "Monsignor, if you don't believe me, just look outside at all the news media trucks parked in front of the rectory!"

"OK Margaret, please settle down. I'll take a look."

The Monsignor turned left from the hall and entered the front living room. He reached for the curtain ropes and pulled open the drapes on the large picture window. With the drapes now open, he stepped in the center of the large window to see the mayhem taking place at six thirty AM on the street and front lawn of his rectory. It was still dark out, but he could see the truck headlights and all the lights the camera crews had already set up not twenty feet from his window. As he looked outside, he was nearly blinded by the flash of cameras. He was immediately photographed by six news photographers and numerous TV cameras, all of which had been waiting for the main drapes to open so they might get a shot of anyone inside the rectory. Shocked by the photographers and by the presence of now ten camera trucks which clogged the street in front of St Andrews, the Monsignor said, "Oh my God!" and he reached for the curtain ropes and yanked the drapes back shut.

"Margaret, call the police. Tell them what is going on over here, and ask them to send over a few squad cars to control the traffic." The rectory phone rang again. "And take the phone off the hook so we won't receive any more calls. Then please find Father John and send him to my office right away."

"You got it Monsignor!" Margaret was happy the Monsignor understood the gravity of the situation and was now on her side.

The Monsignor turned around and headed back down the hall to his office.

Across town, Bishop Carney was glued to the large black and white television in his office. He saw the Channel 7 interview of Sam Elms standing in front of the St. Andrews Rectory.

"Damnation! I knew this would get out of hand. Janet! Get me Monsignor Eckhart at St. Andrews!"

Unlike Margaret, Janet was a huge sports fan. She had watched the entire game and stayed awake to see the Gary Bowman locker room interview. Janet was smart enough to surmise what was happening at St. Andrews. She kept her composure, looked back at the Bishop and replied immediately. "I'm sorry Bishop. I've been trying all of their numbers for the last half hour, but I can't get through. All the lines are busy. My guess is that Margaret has taken all the rectory phones off the hook. That's what I would do."

Though she didn't say it, Janet had seen the Chicago news media go crazy six months ago over a murder trial, and she was secretly glad that she was not in Margaret's position. The media response to the trial verdict was so intense the news frenzy itself became news and got national attention when the reporters erupted into a brawl on the steps of the Chicago Courthouse. One reporter was taken to the Chicago General ER after he was struck in the face with a TV camera.

The Bishop regained his poise and said, "OK, I'm sorry for yelling Janet. Thank you for trying." He turned and grabbed his black winter coat off the hook in his office. He started for the stairs he said, "Janet, please cancel all my appointments for the day. I will have to go over there and deal with this crisis in person."

Bishop Carney was caught by surprise when Cardinal Gino called him in the middle of the night, and he had been given his marching orders. He now knew what had to be done, and he knew it would be a long day.

* * * * * * * *

Chapter 28: **Father Mark**

Ten years had passed since the snowy Super Bowl X football game.

At half past noon, Father Mark Harrington stepped up to the vestibule of the St. Josephina Catholic Rectory in the state of Chihuahua, Mexico. He was dressed appropriately for the hot Mexican weather and wore his collar, identifying him as a Catholic priest. He knocked at the front door of the rectory and heard a small dog bark somewhere inside. A middle aged, petite Mexican house keeper came to the door dressed plainly. She wore a simple white apron over her plain brown dress which went past her knees. She wiped her hands on her apron as if she had been cooking something and had just come from the kitchen. At only four feet five inches tall she looked up at Father Mark who was five feet nine. "Hola Padre. ?Le puedo ayudar en algo?" (Hello Father. Can I help you?)

Father Mark did not speak much Spanish, but he knew a few words. "Buenos días Señora. Father John, por favor?"

The house keeper immediately realized he was not from Mexico, and gave him a look of understanding. She nodded her head and said, "Si, si Padre. Yo comprendo. Usted tiene Padre Juan. Nuestros Padre Juan esta' alli'." (I understand. You want Father John. Our Father John is over there.) She pointed to the church in the lot adjacent to the rectory and added, "Él está escuchando las confesiones de esta mañana." ("He is hearing confessions this morning.") Father Mark recognized the word, "confessions", in her sentence. He smiled, and he nodded to show he understood her.

Father John's Gift

"Gracias Señora. Audios." Mark walked down the rectory steps and over to the St Josephina church.

Mark pulled the handle old wooden door of the modest church. It was warm from the sun and appeared to be stuck. Mark tugged harder on the handle and he managed to open the heavy door. The noon day sun was so bright that Mark had to squint and wait for his eyes to adjust to the dim light once he was inside and the door was closed. With his eyes adjusted, Mark saw the church was lit only by a small stain glass window in the back of the church and a few candles lit near the front. The church was empty of patrons, and it smelled old and musty, but having only one window, the church maintained the coolness from the previous desert night. He was immediately relieved to get out of the hot Mexican sun. He spotted just one confessional on the right side where he believed Father John to be.

Mark entered the confessional and Father John slid open the confessional window.

Mark surprised Father John by speaking first. "Father John?"

"Si?" I mean, "Yes?"

John didn't recognize the voice, but because the parish congregation was small, it was not unusual for a parishioner to call him by name, even in the confessional. But John was taken aback by someone calling him, "Father" and not, "Padre". He had not been called, "Father" by a parishioner in over ten years.

"Are you Father John Danek from St Andrews Parish in Chicago, Illinois?" Mark had to make sure he had the right man.

"Yes. I am Father Danek."

"Father, you don't know me. My name is Father Mark Harrington, and I came all the way from up-state New York to find you."

Father John was alarmed. His transfer from St. Andrews was sudden, and was done with no fanfare. Few knew his whereabouts, and he was under strict orders from the church not to contact anyone from St. Andrews. Wishing to remain a priest, John had accepted the transfer to Mexico without question. After all he had been through in Chicago, he believed in the wisdom of his superiors and, at the time with the Super Bowl trouble, he thought they knew best. But outside of the small town of Tarahumara, Mexico, Father John lived in relative obscurity. After life in prosperous the 1960's Chicago, John now felt banished by the church.

John replied to Mark, "What can I do for you Father Mark? Do you wish to make a confession?"

"No Father. It took me nearly a year to find you. Can you please listen to what I have to say?"

"Yes, go on."

"I read about you in the New York Times in 1960. I read about all the miracles you performed."

Father John said nothing. He waited for Mark to continue.

"Of course, I was naturally skeptical about it, but I was curious too. You made quite an impression on all of us at St. Anthony's, and we followed your story for quite a while."

"All of us?" John asked.

"All the priests at St Anthony's Parish in Albany. I suspected there might be some truth to the stories when our local bishop issued an edict for us to "down-play" your miracles in our weekly sermons. Then, after a few weeks, the stories in the newspaper stopped. It was as if you had just disappeared. We all wondered what happened to you." Mark corrected himself. "At least I wondered what happened to you."

John was mildly amused. He was amused that the church had down-played or spun the stories of his miracles in an attempt to discredit him, and he was impressed that Father Mark would see this as an indication that there was some truth to the miracles. John was now curious to see what Mark would say next.

John said, "And then?"

"And then life went on and we all forgot about you... or at least, I forgot about you... until ...."

John interrupted, "Until what?"

"Until it happened to me."

John was surprised. "What do you mean Father Mark? What happened to you?"

"Father, I'm not exactly sure what happened, but I believe, that like you, I can cure the sick with the touch of my hand."

John felt immediate surprise and self-pity. He had never considered the possibility there might be others like him who possessed a power to

Father John's Gift

heal. How could he have been so selfish, so self-centered not to consider the possibility there might be others like him. He should have thought about it years ago. "Go on Father Mark, I'm listening."

Mark sighed deeply but went on to explain. "About a year ago, I began to suffer a crisis in my faith. I needed a break from my church duties so I went to stay for a week with my brother Peter. Peter has a large farm near Albany. It was a way for me to get away from my church responsibilities, and I hoped to gain some perspective on my life and my calling. I had been on the farm with Peter and his family for just a day, and was still so troubled with doubt I could not sleep."

Mark continued with his story, "Being early risers on their farm, Peter and his family always go to bed early. It was just after eight PM and I quietly stepped out of the house after they went to bed. I thought a short walk on a country road might clear my head and help me sleep. It was about nine PM on a beautiful summer night.... the sky was clear, the sun had just set, and the stars were all out. It was beautiful. I remember thinking I could see stars there I could never see in the city. I started down Pete's long driveway toward the road when I saw a bright flash of light in the sky. I thought it was a meteor, but I honestly don't know what it was. That's really all I remember. The sun woke me up before six the next morning. And when I woke up, I was flat on my back in the grass next to Peter's driveway. Fortunately, it was before anyone in the house woke up and I was able to step back inside and no one was the wiser. I say "fortunately", because I didn't want to alarm anyone, and frankly I didn't know what to tell them, other than I had slept outside all night."

"I didn't think more of it in the following weeks but it wasn't too long after... that strange things began to happen to me."

It sounded all too familiar to John, but he didn't want to let Mark know. After all, he didn't really know this man who found him more than ten years after his own UFO experience.

"What strange things, Father?"

"A few days after I returned to the church, I witnessed a bicycle accident." Mark relived the event in his mind, and then continued. "I had just said Mass on a Sunday afternoon and was walking across the street to return to the rectory. A young boy, about ten years old, got hit by a car as the car made a right hand turn on the corner near my rectory. I heard the car slam on its brakes and then heard the car hit the bicycle. I saw it happen from a distance of about fifty feet, and I knew it was bad. The boy was thrown from his bike and he must have landed hard on the pavement. He didn't get up. I ran to the child to see what I could do. I could see the boy had a bad head bruise and was knocked unconscious. I asked a parishioner who had witnessed the accident, to run to the rectory and call for an ambulance. I laid the boy flat on his back and straightened out his body. I covered him with my jacket to keep him from going into shock."

Mark continued, "Not knowing what else to do, I touched the boy's head with my left hand and blessed him with my right. I felt a wave of energy go through me. I can't explain it. The boy opened his eyes and began to cry. I didn't want to say it at the time, but it felt like a miracle, and everyone who witnessed the event was shocked by what I had done. No one spoke a word, but everyone was staring at me strangely after the blessing. I stayed with the boy and kept him down and quiet until the ambulance arrived."

Mark paused again, allowing Father John to think about what he had said.

John said, "Were there other events like this one?"

"Yes. There were several other events which occurred over the next few months. I stopped helping out at my local hospital, because I was afraid of what was happening to me. I didn't understand it. The more I thought more about it, the more I became convinced that I was like you. I remembered the articles I had read about you, and I was afraid I might draw too much attention to myself, and I might disappear… just as you did." Mark paused briefly. "I had to find you, Father John."

John could not help but notice that Mark sounded desperate, and perhaps depressed. He was convinced that Mark's UFO experience and concerns were real. "Have you told anyone else this story besides me?"

"No."

"Have you heard about or met any other healers besides me?" John was curious to know if there were others besides Mark. He needed to know the extent of Mark's knowledge.

"No. As far as I know we are the only ones. It's why I had to find you."

"Mark, you must know that what you are saying is sacrilege to the church."

"Yes... I believe that's true."

John sensed that Mark's words were sincere, and that they troubled him. John continued. "You must also know the church hicrarchy cannot exist if there is evidence of intelligent life on other planets, particularly if the aliens are intellectually superior to man."

"But why Father? What would be so wrong with other life forms on other planets? Isn't there room for all of us in God's universe?"

"No. Not according to the Bible. The Bible says we were made in the image and likeness of God. Mark, think of what would it mean if we had proof that there are other, more intelligent species in the universe. We would not be like God. We would be reduced to an inferior species, like mere ants on planet Earth. The universe could be teeming with intelligent life far more advanced than us, and we would lose our high place in the order of things."

John continued. "And, if people such as you and me can perform medical miracles, just as Jesus did, what is the church to conclude? What would normal lay people think of us? What would they then conclude about Jesus and what's written about him in the Bible? What would the church do with us? Well, you found out what happened to me."

Mark said nothing as he pondered all John's questions.

John continued, "How old are you Father Mark?"

"I'm thirty five."

"You are still a young man. There is still much good you can do in your life, as a priest or otherwise. Do you want to continue to be a priest?"

"Yes. I like being a priest. I like helping people, but I'm not sure I believe in God anymore." Mark had softened his lack of belief. He was now an atheist, but he couldn't bring himself to say it out loud.

"Father, how can I go on if there is no God? How can any of us go on living if there is no God, no heaven, or no afterlife?" Mark's voice softened. "I would feel lost without my faith."

John thought about Mark's loss of faith and the fact that he had lost his own faith years ago. John had struggled with the same issues and had asked himself the same questions at the time.

"Mark, I do understand the crisis that you feel. I struggled with those same questions years ago. I don't have all the answers, but I'm sure you know from the Seminary each of us must decide the meaning of life for ourselves. I can tell you only what I have found to be true for me. Would you like to hear it?"

It was just what Mark had come for. He wanted to hear how Father John had solved his own philosophical problem. "Yes Father, please go on."

"After struggling for months with my own loss of faith, I concluded we exist to help each other... I know it sounds simplistic, but allow me to explain." John leaned closer to the window which separated him from Father Mark and whispered, "If you reject mystical ideas and conclude there is no God, and no soul, then you must also conclude that life and our consciousness is nothing short of amazing. How life happened, or how it started, no one knows. But Mark, think about it. We are here, you and me. We are two conscious beings, made of matter; of minerals and molecules of water, contemplating the fact we are alive, and trying our best to understand what it means to be alive and to be conscious of ourselves, of our surroundings, and of one another."

John continued. "In addition, the fact that we grow old and die makes life all the more precious. Think of it. We are here for such a brief period of time, and if there is no afterlife, then when we die we lose our consciousness, and we are gone forever. So whatever we decide to do with our time, with our lives while we are here and alive… is everything. Each of us changes the world every day with everything we do. We can change the world by teaching what we know and influence others with our kindness. All we can do is to try to leave a good legacy for ourselves by helping others every way we can. The message of Jesus Christ was right about that. There is so much disease, death, and suffering of people all over the world. We can only try our best to love one another, to see each of us as a miracle of life, and to try to make life as easy as possible for everyone."

Father John's Gift

John waited before continuing. He wanted to let Mark absorb his ideas.

"Mark, I cannot tell you what to do regarding the church. I cannot help you with that decision. It is one which you must make for yourself. But you need to know that you could be in great danger. The church is powerful, and they will do whatever is necessary to maintain the status quo. They must keep our secret quiet. I hate to say it, but they might even have you killed." As it left his lips John immediately regretted his last sentence. It revealed too much of his own bitterness towards the church, and he thought Father Mark might think he was crazy. But John went on. "You risked a great deal just by coming to see me."

Mark did not reply.

"Does anyone know you are here?"

"No. No one knows I am here. I took a leave of absence. My Monsignor believes I am staying with my brother again."

"Then how did you find me?"

"I tried all the normal channels to find you, and was stone-walled by the church. I got nowhere by asking church officials. First I was told you were transferred to Rome. Then when I pressed for more information, they told me in confidence you left the church in a scandal. They said that you were mentally unbalanced after all the attention you had received, but I didn't believe it. Or, I didn't want to believe it. After much frustration, I finally went to your old St. Andrew's Rectory and I spoke directly with the housekeeper, Margaret Winkle. I lied and told her that I was your older brother, Steve, and that it was vital that I contact you regarding the health of our... that is, your mother. Margaret told me that she was not supposed to let anyone know, but under the circumstances, she told me you were here. It was obvious that she loves you, Father John, and she misses you."

John felt a stab of pain at Mark's last remark. John had a great life at St. Andrews, and he missed all his friends and colleagues terribly, particularly Mary Margaret. Leaving St. Andrews was the hardest thing he had ever done. He was not given the opportunity to say goodbye, and he often wondered what they and the parishioners at St. Andrews had been told about his departure.

"How is she Mark?"

"Well, I had traveled all day from New York to Chicago so it was past six o'clock when I saw her. She was tired, and I suspect she is not well." Mark smiled softly as he recalled his meeting with Margaret. "But I saw a spark in her eye when she spoke of you."

John's tone turned serious. "Father Mark, I do understand your dilemma, and I understand your need to find me. But this should be our one and only meeting. I am concerned for your safety, as well as my own. You should not try to contact me again."

Mark replied, "I understand."

"Do you think you were you followed? Did anyone follow you here?

"I'm not sure, but I don't think so. I didn't notice anyone following me, but then, I wasn't looking for anyone."

"Well, we can't be too careful. Did you park in front of the church?"

"No Father. I parked in front of your rectory and walked over to the church."

"OK. That's good. We can use that to our advantage. Most people don't know it, but there is a tunnel that runs from the church sacristy to the rectory. My confession time is up. I will escort you through the tunnel to the rectory. So, with a little luck you can leave here without being detected, or at least it should give you a head start on anyone who might be following you. Is there anything more you want to ask me before we go?"

Mark hesitated, sighed deeply and replied, "No, I guess not. Thank you for your help and for your words of wisdom. I'm glad I found you, Father."

"Think nothing of it Father Mark. I'm glad you found me too. Let's go."

Both priests exited the confessional and saw each other for the first time. Mark was surprised at how tall John was, and how much he had aged from the pictures which were published in the New York Times Mark had saved and memorized so many years ago.

Father John's Gift

John looked around and was pleased they were alone in the church. He then looked at Mark and said in a low voice, "It was nice to meet you Father Mark. Follow me. The sacristy is this way."

John grabbed the lit candle on the side of the church and Mark followed Father John through a door to the sacristy room located at the front of the church behind the altar and crucifix wall. Built to accommodate only two priests, the sacristy was small. John motioned to Mark to step aside and then he moved a bench located in the middle of the room a few feet to one side revealing a hinged door built into the center of the floor. John pulled on a rope to open the door and propped it up against the bench. Under the door were a series of steps leading down to a narrow tunnel to the rectory. The tunnel was just wide enough for one person to enter at a time. John then reached for a switch on the wall and clicked on the tunnel lights and said, "OK. Follow me."

As they stepped down into the tunnel, John explained, "The eldest priest told me the story of the tunnel soon after I arrived here ten years ago. As you might imagine, the church builder created this tunnel so the priests could stay out of the weather when going to and from the church. The church and rectory were built at about the same time, but the tunnel between them was added last."

"Unfortunately, the builder found digging the tunnel was difficult due to the rocky soil conditions. It was originally planned to connect the church to the main hallway in the rectory, but like so many construction jobs, the builder was over budget, and the parish ran short of money before the tunnel was completed. The builder solved the problem by connecting the tunnel to the rectory bedroom located closest to the church. The connection between the two buildings works, but the priest who inhabits the bedroom has no real privacy whenever the weather is bad, and the tunnel gets used."

The priests arrived at the end of the tunnel, and after climbing a few steps John opened the tunnel door to the bedroom. As they entered the sparsely appointed room, John turned to Mark, smiled and said softly, "Welcome to my bedroom." Both men laughed at John's revelation.

"I will show you the way out. You said you parked in front of the rectory?

"Yes."

"Did anyone see you here at the church today?"

Mark thought about John's question for a moment and replied, "Your house keeper was the only person I had contact with. She answered the door when I first arrived, and she told me in Spanish you were saying confessions in the church when I asked for you."

"That's Jolina. I'm sure she is OK. But I think we should be on the safe side. I don't want you to be seen by anyone else. I will lead you to a side door, and you should walk along the side of the building towards your car in the front. I think it's best if you are not seen leaving the rectory by anyone, including Jolina, if you can avoid it."

"I understand."

Before they left the room John stopped at the door, extended his hand and whispered, "I will show you the way out, but I will say my good bye to you now. Good luck to you Father Mark."

"Thank you Father John."

When he opened his bedroom door for Father Mark, the house dog, a small brown terrier mutt ran into John's bedroom which surprised them both. John turned to Mark and said, "That's Benito! Don't worry about him, he's harmless."

Mark reached down and gave Benito a friendly pet. "I love dogs. He's really cute!" Benito looked up at Mark and wagged his tail.

John reached down, picked up the small dog and tossed him on his bed and, with an exaggerated hand motion, John said, "Benito. Stay boy! Stay!" Now panting, Benito lay down on John's bed and wagged his tail.

John then turned to Mark and said, "OK, let's go. Good bye, Mark."

The two priests shook hands again and parted as friends. Both knew it was unlikely they would ever meet again. John re-opened the door, and after he was sure the coast was clear, he escorted Mark through a narrow hallway to an exit on the opposite side of the building.

On his trip back home Father Mark thought a great deal about what he would do when he arrived at St Anthony's back in New York. When he left Father John, he had a renewed sense of purpose. Mark was an idealist. He would no longer label human suffering as a virtue,

Father John's Gift

or an offering to God for the redemption of sins of the souls in Purgatory. No, the church was wrong to preach such ideas. Mark decided he would do what he could to eliminate the pain and suffering of others with his new-found gift. It no longer mattered to Mark how he got the gift, or where it came from. He knew Father John's warning of imminent danger was probably right, but now Mark didn't care about his own safety. He would play his part regardless of the views of the church, or his impact on it. His new outlook was a simple one, and Father John had made it all too clear: he had a gift, and he would use it to help people. Helping others was what he always did. It was why he was a priest. No, Mark concluded he would not let the church, or anyone keep him from his renewed purpose in life.

After two days of driving, Mark returned to St Anthony's Parish in Up-State New York and told no one of his travels to Mexico. When he got back to his private room in the rectory, his first call was to his brother Peter.

"Hello, Pete?"

"Yes." Mark did not call often. Peter was always surprised to hear from Mark.

"Pete? It's Mark!"

"Hi Mark! How you doin?"

"Pete, I'm OK, but listen. Do you have a few minutes? This is important. I had to call you."

"Sure Mark, but what's going on? Are you in trouble with the church? " Pete already knew Mark was suffering a crisis of faith. Pete had talked with him about it before.

Mark replied, "No... At least not yet, but I might be forced to leave the church, for all the wrong reasons."

"What do you mean Mark? Do you want to tell me about it?" Pete knew Mark would tell him when he was ready, but Pete didn't want to pry.

"No Pete. But I want you to know that I lied to my Monsignor and told him I was with you this past week."

"Why, where did you go?"

"Pete I think you and your family will be safer if you not know the details. I just want you to know that I was searching for the truth, and I found it. I feel better now than I have in a long time because I now know what I have to do. Pete, I hate to ask you this, but can I ask you to say I was with you if anyone calls?" Telling a lie was one thing. Asking his brother to lie on his behalf was quite another.

"Yeah, OK Mark. I'm not happy about it, but I'm sure you have your reasons. Do you really think we are in danger?"

"I hope not, but I really don't know for sure. It's possible. You may hear some strange things about me soon which the church will not like. I know it sounds weird, and believe me, it is. It's... complicated." Mark thought about the understatement he had just made.

"OK Mark. You do what you have to do. Just know that Betsy and I are here for you if you need us. Call me back if you want to talk. And feel free to come here if you need a place to stay. You know I can always use your help around the farm."

Mark smiled at the thought. Pete had a strong independent streak. Organic farming was Pete's way to reject the modern world and to connect to the soil. In many ways Mark and Pete were the same... but they had chosen radically different paths in life. By becoming a priest Mark had embraced people, and by being a farmer Pete had isolated himself from them. Peter was proud in the knowledge that he could provide for his family and live entirely off the farm if he had to.

"Thanks Pete. I know I can always count on you. Give my best to Betsy and Cathy." Mark hung up the phone and was glad he made the call. He loved his brother.

The next day Father Mark drove into town and stopped in to the Ever-Life Insurance Company. He took $10,000 of his $12,000 savings and bought a million dollar term life insurance policy against himself to be paid to Peter and Betsy Harrington. Once back at the church rectory Mark wrote the following letter to his brother and sister-in-law.

Dear Pete and Betsy,
If you are reading this letter it is because something has happened to me, and I have died. I want you to know that I was

Father John's Gift

given a special gift to heal others, and I am now determined to use that gift. As bizarre as it sounds, it is my belief that the church will not tolerate my activity, and they may kill me to stop me from using my gift. I have taken out a $1,000,000 life insurance contract against my life to be paid to the both of you in the event of my death. (See the instructions below.)

Peter,

First, I know your life on the farm has been hard for you, and your family. Please take $500,000 of the life insurance money and do what you can to enjoy your life with your family while you can. I suggest that you invest some of the money in USA Government bonds to provide for Cathy's college education, and save some to protect yourself and Betsy against future crop failures. Pay off the mortgage on the farm. Tell Cathy her college education was a gift from me after she graduates from high school.

Secondly Pete, I would like you to send the remaining $500,000 to a priest I met in Tarahumara, Mexico. His name is Father John Danek and he is at St Josephina's Church. I know he is a good and decent man, and he helped me in my time of need. I will provide you with a stamped addressed envelope for you to send a check to Father John, and I will include a brief note to Father John in that envelope as well. Pete, if you should ever need help and don't know where to turn, I know you could trust Father John with your life. Thank you for sending this money to John for me. I don't trust the church to give it to him.

Finally, please do not attempt to investigate my death, or go after the church for any kind of retribution. I now believe the church is much too powerful and corrupt, and you will waste every penny I am sending to you. The church has political connections, lawyers, and almost unlimited resources.

R. Allan Worrell

If you try to fight them in court, you will spend all the money I am giving to you now and you will lose. You will undo all the good that I am now trying to do. The church does not know about the insurance policy, and I suggest that you not tell anyone about the money (except Father John as I have instructed above).

Also Pete, I recommend that you not get flashy with the money, or people may get wise to it, and it could cause you some trouble. Spend it slowly and sensibly, as I'm sure you will.

You were my only family. I love you all, and wish you every future happiness.

Your Brother,
Mark

Mark then marked the envelope, "To Be Opened ONLY Upon My Death", and sealed it. He placed it and the letter to Father John he had already written into a large manila envelope. He addressed the large envelope to Peter, and dropped it in a mailbox located at the curb in front of the St Anthony church.

Mark did nothing to draw attention over the next several days. He placed a call Mercy Hospital in Albany to let them know he would be back as a volunteer the following Monday. On that day Mark showed up bright and early and resumed his cycle of healing in earnest. It took only a few weeks before the hospital, the press, and the church all took note of Mark's unusual activities. Mark knew the attention was inevitable. It was an unavoidable consequence of doing what he knew he must.

Two months later, "The New York Times" acquired a story from the Associated Press and reported Mark's death as an accident on the bottom of their front page:

Faith Healer, Killed in Car Accident
Albany, New York: Father Mark Harrington from St Anthony's Parish was found dead in his

car as a result of an apparent car accident. Albany police reported the Catholic priest's car apparently slid on an icy road into the side of a concrete bridge crushing the front of the vehicle and killing the priest instantly. Albany police stated Father Mark was not wearing a seat belt, and there were no other occupants in the car at the time of the crash.

Father Mark was best known as a Catholic priest who did good works at Mercy Hospital in downtown Albany. The Albany Times Union Newspaper reported Father Mark had healed many seriously ill patients at the hospital in the two months prior to his death. A spokesman for St Anthony's Church stated Father Mark was on his way to Mercy Hospital when the apparent auto accident occurred.

Father Mark was preceded in death by his parents George and Anna Harrington, but is survived by his brother Peter Harrington also of Albany, New York. A funeral Mass will be held in honor of Father Mark on Wednesday, March 3rd at St Anthony's Church in downtown Albany. He will be buried in the St Anthony Cemetery next to the church immediately following the service.

The New York Times editor determined the story was front page news because of Mark's status as a miracle worker. The Times had run a Father Mark "Miracle Story" on the religion page of the Sunday paper every week in the two months leading up to his death. The Times could not help but notice circulation was up twenty seven percent in all the Sunday papers which included stories about Father Mark's medical miracles. Father Mark had become a New York Times' celebrity. It was clear Mark's miracles sold newspapers; lots of them.

Since Mark was a priest, the police did not suspect foul play in the accident, and no investigation of the car was performed. Had they checked, they would have found both his power steering and brake lines had been slit and were slowly leaking hydraulic fluid on every trip. His car was a ticking time bomb; an accident waiting to happen. But why would anyone want to harm a priest, particularly one who performed daily miracles at the local hospital? Everybody, so they thought ... loved Father Mark.... and nearly everyone did.

Father John read the Times article about Mark's death, but he did not subscribe to the "Albany Times Union ", and therefore he did not see the small Obituary regarding a relatively unknown hit-man named, Timothy Vanuchi, who was only thirty five. The minor obit was not news worthy. It did not make the Associated Press, and was not published in the New York Times.

Oddly enough, Timothy Vanuchi died in a car crash in exactly the same way as Father Mark Harrington. He wasn't wearing a seat belt, and the police reported he died instantly when his car hit a tree and he went through the windshield of his car. Timothy had no family, and was survived by no one. The obit was placed and paid for by an anonymous source. The coroner's report stated his blood alcohol level was twice the legal limit of 0.1% and there was an empty bottle of vodka in the front seat of his car. No one could have guessed his blood alcohol level, the empty bottle of vodka, and the car crash itself were all the work of aliens seeking retribution for the death of one of their chosen few, Father Mark Harrington.

****

Chapter 29: **The Check**

Although the St. Josephina Church was located on the edge of town, it was the center of life for the people of Tarahumara, Mexico. Nearly all were Catholic, and though most were relatively poor, they took great pride in their church and financially supported it with all that they could. The church thrived, and by the early 1970's Father John was one of seven priests at St. Josephina's supporting a congregation approaching 8,000 parishioners.

Now in his fifties, Father John was well known, and he was loved in the community. He had performed so many baptisms, marriages and funerals over the last ten years that he had lost count of them long ago. Though he should have been made a Monsignor by his age, the Bishop was under strict orders from Rome to keep John a lowly parish priest.

The day after Father Mark left his church, John renewed his subscription to the New York Times. He didn't know what Father Mark might do, but he believed the newspaper would enable him to keep tabs on Father Mark. When John began reading the miracle stories about Mark over the next few weeks, he knew Mark was headed for trouble. John's fears were confirmed when he read the Times article about Mark's car accident and death. It sickened John to think the church had anything to do with it, but he was convinced there was a connection. He knew in his heart that Mark's death was no mishap.

Two weeks after the Times article appeared, John received the letter from Mark which read:

Dear Father John,

By now you must know that I have died. Please don't blame yourself. I was determined to use my gift in spite of the church. I took out a large life insurance policy on myself and asked my brother Peter to send you a check for $500,000 from the proceeds in the event of my death. The church knows nothing about it. Use the money as you see fit. I hope it can help you in some way.

Thank you for helping me in my time of need.

Your friend,

Father Mark Harrington

Mark's letter made Father John feel terribly guilty. Unlike Mark, John had allowed the church to suppress his gift. He had cured no one in the ten years since his transfer to St. Josephina. The people of Tarahumara were poor and there was, as yet, no hospital in town. John realized he had allowed himself to be bullied and intimidated by the church. Mark's death shocked John into believing that he, John, was a coward.

John stared at the check in his hands. It was more money than John had ever held or even seen at one time. It was twenty five times his annual salary of $20,000, and it was made out directly to him. What would he do with the money? Spending it could be a problem. Even if he were to use it for a good cause, or donate it to the church, it could cause suspicion. He didn't want the check to connect him back to Father Mark. He didn't want to have to answer questions about it from his superiors. No one gives a gift of $500,000, unless they were a millionaire, and there were no millionaires in Tarahumara. The church also knew John did not have any rich relatives. No, he would deposit the money into a new bank account in the nearby town of Batopilas and worry about what to do with the money later.

Father John's Gift

The next day was a Friday. John's Sunday sermons were already completed, and he had no appointments scheduled. Depositing the money in a bank in Tarahumara might draw attention to him. His reputation in town was beyond reproach, and he wanted to keep it that way. John was well known, and he was worried word about the money could raise suspicions. He made an excuse to the Monsignor to take the day off, and the next day he put on casual street clothes and a collar, and drove forty five miles to the prosperous town of Batopilas. Once there, John stopped at the first bank he found on the edge of town to deposit the money; The First National Bank of Batopilas. John thought one bank was as good as any other, and for his purposes, any bank would do. He parked his car on the street, walked into the bank and was pleased to see it was not crowded. There were only a few patrons waiting in line for a single teller at the counter. He went over to a ledge along the wall and filled out a new checking account application he found lying in a neat stack on the counter. After waiting his turn, John approached the bank teller, an attractive young lady wearing a white nametag pinned to her bright pink blouse. The nametag said simply, "Maria".

"Hello Maria, can I open a new checking account with you?"

"Certainly Father! Did you fill out a form yet?" Maria's English was very good, and she was always happy to be able to use it, particularly with a new English speaking customer. When waiting on another customer, Maria had seen Father John writing something on the counter from across the room and she had noticed his collar.

"Yes. I think I've entered everything correctly. I have just this one check." Father John signed the back of his check and slid the check and the completed form across the counter to Maria.

Maria looked over the form and her eyes grew large when she saw the deposit amount. She then looked at the check and noticed that it was written against a United States bank. Since she had only worked at the bank for a few months, she was relatively new at her job. John's check was the largest deposit she handled to date, and it was written in US dollars.

"Excuse me Father; this is an unusually large transaction. I will have to get my manager to approve the deposit into your new account.

I will be right back." Maria took the check, turned around and walked about twenty five feet and disappeared behind a closed door into her manager's office.

After a short minute, Maria returned with her manager, a tall man dressed in a dark suit. He looked at Father John and said, "Hello Father. My name is Senior Sanchez. Maria showed me your deposit. I'm afraid the return on our checking accounts is not very good, and your deposit is quite large. Would you like me to place these funds into a savings account for you where you can earn more interest?"

Father John didn't know when he would need to move the money from the savings account to a checking account, and he didn't want to have to drive back to the bank from Tarahumara to move the money.

"Can I transfer the funds from the savings to a checking account over the phone?"

"No, I'm sorry Father. We require a signature to transfer funds from one account to another. Therefore you would have to do that in person."

John replied, "Then my answer is no. Please put the money into a checking account for me. I don't know how soon I will need the funds, and I'm not sure when I can come back here."

Maria looked at the application form and noticed the St. Josephina Rectory address in Tarahumara. She didn't say anything.

The manager looked at Father John and replied, "Very well Father. I will have Maria place the funds into a new checking account for you. We will have to place a five business day hold on the money until the check clears the bank in the United States… and the exchange rate is ten pesos for every dollar." The manager took the application from Maria, initialed the bottom of the form and handed it back to her. He then looked at Father John and said, "Thank you for your business Father, we are happy to have you." He turned to Maria. "Maria, please deposit the check into the new account and get the good Father started with a checkbook."

"Yes Sir, I will be happy to do that. Thank you."

Father John echoed her sentiment. "Thank you Señor Sanchez."

Father John had forgotten about the exchange rate. He walked out of the bank with a new checkbook in hand, and a bank receipt showing

Father John's Gift

a tentative balance of five million pesos in his checking account. He now had a new problem. What would he do with all that money?

****

Chapter 30: **The Project**

Over the next few days Father John found it difficult to perform his normal duties. He could not stop thinking about the money. He didn't want to divide it up on small projects. He was determined to put it to good use to make Father Mark's death mean something. Five million pesos could go a long way in Mexico, and the town of Tarahumara needed a hospital. He thought the money was not enough for a large facility, but he felt sure he could use it to secure a loan to construct a decent size building; one large enough to attract a reputable health care provider.

John knew a hospital project was more than he could handle by himself. He wanted the hospital to be a non-profit venture to provide affordable care, and he thought it should be associated with the church. He knew the hospital would survive him and the church would oversee the operations and expenses of the hospital administrators. However, John was a priest; not a business man. He had taken a vow of poverty and knew the church legally owned all of his wealth and possessions. He believed his Monsignor was a fair man, and he thought the Monsignor would let him start the project as long as John gave up control of it to the church. After more thought, John concluded he would tell his Monsignor about the money, and what he wanted to do. He now believed he had to be "above board" about the money with his superiors, even if it did tie him to Father Mark.

But John had connections in the community. He knew the honest construction companies in town and knew who he could trust, and who

Father John's Gift

was unscrupulous. Lastly, he knew honest bankers and real estate people who knew how to make things happen quickly. Ten years of hearing confessions got you people knowledge, and John knew such knowledge was powerful. He would put it to good use; he would get others to build and run the hospital.

Father John called Jose Gomez, a local architect to draw up plans for the new hospital. He told Jose it would be built on the vacant property next to the St. Josephina Church. Jose had designed several small hospitals in nearby towns and could give him a good ballpark figure for the cost. With the cost known, he called Alberto Gonzalez, a Banco de Mexico executive to see how much he could borrow to finance the project. Finally, John called a representative with the Mexican Health Systems, Inc. to see if he could attract them to set up shop in Tarahumara.

Excited by the project, John could not wait to get started. He knew he would need a front person, a general contractor….someone he could trust to hire good people, handle the money and attend to the thousands of details a new hospital would require. He called Enrique Hernandez, a contractor who lived in Tarahumara, who was a member of the St. Josephina church and was his longtime personal friend.

"Enrique?"

"Yes, speaking." John immediately recognized Enrique's distinctive gruff voice. Enrique didn't smoke, but John always thought he sounded like a long time smoker.

"Enrique, this is Father John from St. Josephina's."

"Oh… Hello Father! How are you?"

"Very well Enrique. I called because I have a special project in mind and I need your help. How would you like to build me a small hospital next to our church?"

"Wow! I would love to Father. That sounds wonderful! How big of a hospital are you talking about?"

"Oh, I don't really know. I expect the final size will depend on the cost. I think it should be a relatively small hospital…. one with perhaps one hundred beds. I have already contacted Mexico Health Systems to set up shop in our new hospital, and I think they will do it.

It will be a nonprofit hospital and will be associated with the church. Can you build me a hospital for the cost of the labor and materials?"

"Sure Father, I can do it for cost. It has been a good year for us and most of my ongoing work will be completed this month. I have two projects which are just starting, but they are small ones, and I think we could take on one more. When would you want to start it?"

"I want to start as soon as possible. Do you think you could start sometime in the next six months?"

I'll have to check my schedule, but I think we could break ground in three or four months. How does that sound?" Enrique thought about it some more. "Do you have the plans yet?"

John was encouraged and was now glad he called Enrique. "Three or four months sounds great Enrique! I talked to Jose Gomez who has agreed to create the drawings, and I already spoke to Alberto Gonzalez at Banco de Mexico about the financing. But Enrique, I have a special favor to ask of you. I need someone to spearhead this project. I would like for you to take over this project and just report back to me with a monthly status until it is completed. Will you do that for me?"

Yes, of course Father. I would be happy to manage this project for you. I have worked with Jose Gomez on several projects. He is a good architect, and I know we will work well together. You don't need to worry about anything."

The conversation was going just as he had hoped. John was pleased to offload the responsibility for the project to someone he trusted. "Enrique, when do you think we should talk next?"

Enrique looked again at his schedule. "Well, my next two weeks are booked solid, but I will call Jose Gomez tomorrow and meet with him to go over the plans as soon as he has them ready. I will call you after we talk to let you know our next steps.

"Thank you Enrique. How much money do you need to get started?" John knew he should send some money to start the relationship.

"We usually start a project with ten thousand pesos to retain the company. Later I will let you know when we need to order materials and more money is needed."

Father John's Gift

"That's sounds fine Enrique. I just deposited a check in a new bank account three days ago, but it will take another few days for the check to clear the bank in the United States and the funds to become available to me. I will send you a check in the mail tomorrow. You should get it by Friday, but can I ask you wait until next Thursday to cash it? I just want to make sure there is enough time for the funds to be transferred and deposited in my bank account in Batopilas."

"Of course, Father!"

"Thank you again Enrique. I know I can trust you to do a good job."

"Thank you Father! I'm sure we will build you a hospital you will be proud of. And you know the people of Tarahumara will love you for this!"

Father John was excited to build a hospital for the people of Tarahumara, and he was confident he had picked the right man for the job.

* * * * * * *

Chapter 31: **Tina**

Father John was about to finish his homily in his Thursday morning eight o'clock Mass when he looked up from the church podium and saw the back door to the church open. He paused in his remarks and watched a tall woman enter the church and take a seat in the back on the left hand side. The rear of the church had no windows, and was not well lit, so although he could tell the person was a woman, he could only see her silhouette. He thought it strange someone should enter at that time, because the St. Josephina parishioners were rarely if ever late for Mass, particularly for the eight o'clock service on a Thursday morning.

Could it be Christine? The situation was too reminiscent of the old days at St. Andrews. He tried his best to ignore the strange woman for the rest of the Mass, but found himself distracted by the knowledge of her presence. John couldn't help himself. During the Mass he glanced often at the back corner of the church to see if she was still there. She sat in a pew next to a church pillar which cast a shadow over her and prevented John from seeing her face.

After the Mass, John greeted several of the parishioners exiting the rear of the church and though he hoped to meet the mystery woman, she did not exit that door, or he thought she must have slipped out before the end of the Mass when he wasn't looking. But if that was the case, then why was she so secretive? And who was she? She was too tall to be from Tarahumara. All of the local women were short; very few were over five feet tall, and though he did not see her well, he thought she was Caucasian. She must be a transient. Was she a traveler who was just passing through? No, it just didn't make sense. He sometimes got tourists on a Sunday service, but never at an eight o'clock Mass on a Thursday morning.

As usual at this time of year, John was scheduled to hear Confessions on the next day from three to five o'clock in the afternoon.

Father John's Gift

If the woman was Christine, as he suspected, she might contact him in the confessional. John asked Juanita, the St Josephina housekeeper, if there had been any phone calls or inquiries about his confession schedule, and Juanita had said, "No". There was only one confessional in the small church, so if the mystery woman was to contact him via the confessional, John believed it would happen tomorrow.

The Friday confessions were the same few people, with their usual sins. Though he knew almost all his St Josephina parishioners by name, John was always true to his vow of secrecy, and he kept the confessions strictly confidential; that is, he never revealed anything about the sins he heard to anyone. He never let anyone know he even knew any of his confessors.

John lamented the fact that he knew his confessors and most of their sins by heart. It was not hard to do. Either their sins were fabricated, so they could have something to confess, or his confessors rarely took his council seriously, and committed the same sins over and over again. Moreover, it did not speak well of his confessors. He tired of hearing confessions since he rarely heard a confession which he had not heard before, or one which was even the slightest bit challenging. He chuckled at the thought and considered himself lucky not to have heard any horrendous confessions. It was ironic he should consider them in any way entertaining, though he was sure he could write a book based on the confessions he had heard in his life. He almost laughed out loud at that idea. He could only imagine what the Bishop would say if he was to author such a book. He was sure he would be expelled from the priesthood, and maybe even excommunicated from the church.

His two hour Confession window was nearly up, and there had been no confessors for more than half an hour. John almost gave up and was about to call it quits for the day when she arrived. He heard the confessional door close and saw the indicator light turn on signaling someone had knelt down in the chamber next to him to begin the sacrament. He slid open the confessional window and started to make the traditional sign of the cross when she interrupted him.

"Father John?"

"Yes?" John did not recognize her voice, but he knew it was her. He had expected Spanish, "Bendíceme padre, porque he pecado".

(Bless me father, for I have sinned). No one ever spoke English in Tarahumara. Even if he had been addressed by name, everyone from St. Josephina addressed him with his Spanish name, "Padre Juan".

"It's Christine."

"Christine O'Roark?"

"Yes."

John was nearly in shock. Though he had suspected it was Christine when he saw her in the church, he hadn't thought about what he would say if and when they met. He didn't know what to say, and so he said nothing. After a few awkward seconds, Christine broke the silence.

"Father, is there someplace we can meet... privately? I need to see you." She did want to see him, but more importantly, Christine wanted Father John to see her. Father John said the first thing that came to his mind.

"Where are you staying Christine?"

"I have a room at the Hotel Grande in Batopilas. It is about forty minutes from here."

John was relieved. He had thought of how to meet her ahead of time, and he concluded he didn't want to meet her in Tarahumara. The town was too small, and everyone there knew him. If he were to meet Christine there, he might start a rumor which could cause him trouble with the church. As a priest, John knew local rumors and gossips were sometimes vicious and they circulated quickly in the small town. The last thing he needed was a scandal, or even the appearance of one. John thought about the location of the Hotel Grande.

"I know where it is. Let's meet in the lobby at your hotel tomorrow morning at ten o'clock. Then we can go to a small coffee shop nearby. Will that work for you?"

"Yes. I will see you tomorrow."

And then she left. There was no confession for Christine, or even the pretense of one.

John tried to understand his own emotional reaction to Christine's presence, but he didn't understand it. He knew only he was excited to see her.

The next morning Father John was so eager to get his day started he woke up an hour earlier than usual. He put on his normal street clothes and he wore his collar, but decided he would remove it once he was in Batopilas. Except for a few bank employees, he was unknown in Batopilas, and he didn't want to draw attention to himself, or let anyone there know he was a priest.

He ate breakfast with four other St. Josephina priests who were also up early, and he excused himself from their normal Saturday morning chatter. It was always fun to regroup with the other priests at the Saturday breakfast, but he didn't have time for it this morning. John left the rectory dining room and stopped by his room to grab his wallet and car keys before exiting at the rear of the building. He rarely carried more than two hundred pesos (twenty dollars) and he would stop by his bank as soon as they opened to get some more cash. His gas tank was almost empty. He would need gas for the Batopilas trip, and he also wanted a little extra money to spend at the coffee shop.

Since it was still early and a Saturday, there was virtually no traffic on the two lane highway between Tarahumara and Batopilas and he made good time. He arrived at the Hotel Grande about twenty minutes early and parked his car in back of the hotel. He removed his collar and put it in the glove box as planned, exited the car, and walked around to the front of the building. He pushed through a revolving glass door and saw Christine. She was standing just inside the lobby with her back to the door reading a newspaper; waiting for him. When she heard the distinctive swoosh of the revolving door, she turned around and looked directly at him.

Though he had not seen her in ten years, John recognized her instantly. Christine was beyond beautiful. She was tall, thin, and stunning. She wore a black knee length dress which, if it had been much longer, could have been mistaken for an evening gown. It had a plunging neckline which revealed her beautiful cleavage, and a small number of light freckles on her chest. The back of the dress was sheer; almost like it wasn't there and showed off her feminine frail tapered back. Her hair, which had been more orange as a child, was now a striking immodest red. Though it was still long, Christine wore it up in a bun at the back of her head off of her long slender neck and radiant flawless, white Irish skin. She had been an attractive girl at age fifteen, but now, at age twenty five, Christine was a virtual Irish goddess. She wore no makeup, but then, John saw she didn't need to. He could hardly believe the sight of her. Could this beautiful, confident, striking woman really be the same young girl he had helped over ten years ago?

"Christine?"

Christine ran towards him and almost leapt into John's arms. "Father John!"

She gave him a hello hug that surprised them both. Christine clung tightly to him and did not let go. John embraced her, but after a few moments he began to feel uncomfortable, and he had to nudge her back, as if he had held her for too long. They were, after all, old friends; not a reunited married couple. John smiled at her and was the first to speak.

"Christine, look at you! You look great!" He smiled at her. "Let's go get some coffee."

"Thanks Father, you look good too." She smiled at his remark. "OK. How far is the coffee shop?"

"I think it's a short block from here. We should be able to walk there."

"That sounds good. I could use a bit of exercise." Christine had on short black pumps; not heels. The morning sun was bright, but the temperature was not yet too hot for a short walk. Christine put down her newspaper on an end table in front of the main desk and they exited the hotel onto the sidewalk. It was a Saturday, and there were few walkers on the street.

"Hang on Christine. I know its close, but I'm not sure which direction it is from the hotel." John looked up and down the street to get his bearings. He spotted a large red sign which read, "Tolito's Coffee Stop" about a block away. "There it is." John pointed to the sign. "It's that big red sign down there. It's called, 'Tolito's Coffee Stop'."

Christine turned and looked down the street. "Oh, I see it." She said matter-of-factly.

They began their short trek to the next block. John started the conversation as they walked.

"Christine, when did you get here?"

"Last week."

Father John's Gift

"I thought I saw you in church last Thursday morning, at the eight o'clock Mass."

"Yes, that was me."

"You were late as usual." John looked at her and smiled.

"I'm sorry Father. Old habits are hard to break. I have always found it hard to get up early for an eight o'clock Mass". She smiled back at him.

"Are you traveling on a business trip? Or are you on vacation?" John had almost said a "pleasure trip" but thought "vacation" sounded better. Oh God, he realized, he was analyzing and censoring his own words!

"Well, it is sort of a vacation, and I have seen some of the local sights. But I really came to Mexico to see you, Father." Christine was to the point, and John was not shocked. He had expected as much.

"Christine?"

"Yes?"

"Did you notice I am not wearing my collar?"

"Yes. I noticed you are out of uniform." She snickered. "Why is that?" Her remark was sarcastic, and she turned and smiled at him almost with a laugh.

"It is because I am out of town, and I don't want to be recognized as a priest. Can you please just call me 'John' when we are out of the church?"

"OK. John it is." Christine liked the sound if it. The significance of the name change was not lost on her, and she accepted it. She felt in her heart she was already making progress with him. They walked to the next block and were almost to the coffee shop.

"Christine, I'm happy to see you of course, but why did you need to see me?" Father John was almost afraid to ask the question, but he had to ask it. The question was important to both of them so they could understand their new relationship as adults. Christine's answer was immediate.

"Because I have been married and divorced twice!" John was grateful there was no one else on the sidewalk to overhear her answer, though John realized immediately it was a moot point. They were speaking English, and in Batopilas, there was no one on the street who would have understood them.

"Oh, Christine!" John's exclamation was genuine. It no longer mattered to him that the church did not recognize divorce, but John understood the emotional pain and trauma divorce always caused, and he now knew Christine had experienced it, not once, but twice!

"Well, I learned a lot." Her tone was frank.

She finished her short sentence just as they arrived at the coffee shop. John opened the door for Christine, and they entered the attractive eatery to a wonderful aroma of strong coffee and fresh cinnamon Mexican pastries which were baked earlier that morning. The pastries were displayed in a large glass case near the front of the store, and they all looked delicious.

"Let's order some coffee and cinnamon pasteles. I have them here whenever I come to Batopilas, and they are always very good. It's my treat."

"Thank you John."

They looked at each other and smiled over her use of his name.

"How do you take your coffee?"

"Just black is fine."

"Well, be careful Christine. The coffee here is flavorful, but it is also quite strong."

Christine laughed, "Yes, I found that out the hard way when I arrived last week. I made the mistake of drinking some local coffee after I got to the hotel at about midnight, and it kept me up most of the night, despite my long trip, and my arrival at such a late hour. I was a wreck the next day. But I like the coffee, and I think I'm getting used to it now."

John said nothing in response but placed the order in Spanish with the young girl across the counter who got them some coffee and cinnamon rolls. John paid for the drinks and pastries in pesos. They walked past several seated patrons to the rear of eatery to find a small private table out of the glare of the morning sun which now shone brightly through the windows at the front of the shop. Each sipped the hot strong black coffee and stared silently at the other from across the

Father John's Gift

table. John could hardly believe he was looking at Christine, now sitting across the table from him after so many years.

Christine put down her drink and was the first to speak.

"Your Spanish is very good! I didn't know you spoke it so well."

"Well, I first learned to speak it over twenty years ago in Costa Rica, but I've had a lot of practice in the ten years since I moved here from Chicago. Do you speak any Spanish?"

"Oh, I know a little. I studied it in High School and liked it a lot. I got an 'A' in the class." Christine laughed at the thought that her High School grade would impress John. "Of course, I forgot a lot of what I learned, but it's coming back. My Spanish is getting better every day I'm here. But I'm still a long way from being fluent."

Christine changed the subject. "John, why did you not want to be recognized as a priest? Haven't you been a priest all your life?"

"Yes I have... Well, there are a few reasons." He hesitated to tell Christine.

"Such as?" Christine sensed his hesitation to tell her.

"To be honest, I didn't want anyone to get any ideas about you and me. If anyone recognized me as a priest, it could start a bad rumor which might hurt St. Josephina in Tarahumara, and could impact my career with the church. Though it has grown, the parish is still very tight knit, and I have to be careful about appearances." Christine smiled at the thought she could cause a scandal.

"I understand." She changed the subject again. "But what happened to you in Chicago, John? Why did they send you here? You never even said goodbye to me, or anyone at St. Andrews as far as I know." There was so much that was left unsaid about John's departure from St. Andrews, Christine was full of questions about why he left, even ten years after the fact.

He gave her a serious look. "Christine, it's complicated. I don't think you would believe me if I told you."

"But I want to understand. Try me, John."

Looking straight into her eyes, John paused and thought about what he should tell her. She was no longer the fifteen year old girl he knew in Chicago. She was a beautiful adult woman who knew much of his past and had already expressed real affection and concern for him. She had traveled to Mexico to see him!

Except for Father Mark, John had not talked to anyone about his miracles; either before or since his move to Mexico, and he was reluctant to say too much to Christine now. Despite his reluctance, he wanted to tell her as much as he could. He had been carrying it around inside him for years, and he wanted and needed to finally share it with someone who knew him, and someone he could trust. Besides, he thought he owed her a good explanation; she had trusted him with so much of her early life. Could he tell her the full truth? He felt she hardly knew him; particularly now since they had not seen each other in over ten years. He wanted to tell Christine, but did he really know her? Could he trust her with his life? He concluded it was only fair to trust her now.

"Christine, can you keep a secret?"

"Of course, John. You know, you can tell me anything. Besides, who would I tell? You are the only person in Mexico I really know, my Spanish is not very good, and I no longer have any real connections with the church back in Chicago."

John looked surprised at her last remark, but it made it easier for him to tell her his secret. "Christine, I want to be honest with you of all people. You always shared so much of yourself with me." He leaned closer to her, lowered his voice and whispered, "You may find it shocking to hear, but I have lost my faith."

She knew he was sincere. She said nothing, but looked at him intently, and tried hard to understand why he would say such a thing. She knew from the expression on his face there was more to come. John went on.

"Although there are many reasons for that, let me just say I found out the leaders of the church are devious and ruthless. It took me a long time to understand, but I now believe they see me as a threat, not only to them, but also to the church. It was why they forced me to leave Chicago, and I believe it is why they sent me here.

"Then why don't you just leave the priesthood?"

"Believe me Christine; I have thought a lot about doing that. However I am now over fifty, and I think I am too old to start over."

Father John's Gift

"But John, fifty is not old! Surely you know life is too short to be unhappy at any age with what you do."

John felt as if the tables had turned. Christine was now offering him advice. "Well, I'm not unhappy. I do like being a priest, and I love the Mexican people. It is only the church hierarchy that I believe is corrupt. And frankly, I no longer believe in the liturgy." John shook his head as he continued. "I know that makes me something of a hypocrite to keep practicing the Catholic faith, but at least I know I'm safe here, and the people need me. They also need something to believe in. I know as long as I remain a priest at St Josephina, the church will leave me alone. If I were to leave the church, they might have me killed." It was as deep a confession as John had ever made to anyone.

Christine looked at him with shock and disbelief. She had her own doubts about the church, but never thought they would do anyone harm, particularly to one of their own. "Why? Why would the church want to kill you? Why would they do that?"

"You might find it hard to believe, and I could never prove it, but I feel sure they were instrumental in the death of a friend of mine."

"The church killed your friend? I can't believe it! Why, John, why?"

"Christine, it's complicated. Let me just say that my friend was a priest who knew too much. And I believe I'm also a threat to the church, because I know what he knew." Christine looked confused and concerned for John's safety. She never expected his answer, and she was afraid to ask what it was he knew.

"Did it have something to do with the miracles you performed?"

John looked back at her with surprise. "Christine, what do you know about the miracles?" He was curious to see what she remembered after so many years, and what his legacy was back in Chicago.

Christine began her story. "Oh, it was so long ago, and I was pretty young then. I'm sure I didn't hear everything, or even understand all of it at the time. I don't remember a lot of details. I only know the entire parish was focused on the healings you did. And I know you caused quite a commotion at St. Andrews when you left so suddenly. My mother was a part of the Club, and she said most of Chicago was looking for you after you left. I'm sure that was an exaggeration. The Monsignor told us all at Mass you were promoted, and that you had to leave quickly for Rome. And, after all the publicity about you in the newspapers, everyone in the church believed him."

Christine continued, "I understand a journalist at the Tribune tried hard to find you in Italy. My mother showed me a newspaper article he wrote which discussed his search and it asked what happened to you. It took a long time, about six months to a year, for all the fanfare to finally die down. But were the healings real? Did they get you in trouble with the church? How did they happen?" Christine had been asking herself these questions for years.

"I can't tell you how it happened, because I really don't understand it myself, but yes, somehow I did get the power to heal. I healed several people in Chicago the month before I left. You were right. The miracles got me in trouble with the church after it all exploded in the press and I gained sudden notoriety from the Super Bowl story. Do you remember that?"

Christine gave John a solemn nod and said, "Yes. I wasn't a sports fan, and I didn't see the game, but I heard all about it. It was all I heard about for so long after the game."

Father John's sudden fame and departure was all the Club members would talk about for months after the Super Bowl. After John left, Christine got tired of hearing her mother talk about it with Club members on the phone, and with just about everyone else, everywhere they went. Christine was devastated when John left without so much as a "goodbye", and she hated to be continually reminded of it by her mother and all her mother's friends. The fact that Father John had been elevated to a miracle worker only made it worse for her.

John continued. "I know it sounds weird, but the church could not tolerate the healings I did. Oh, they do acknowledge "medical miracles" after the fact; that is, sometime after the healer dies, and only then are they willing to declare him or her a Saint. The "Saint" scenario fits nicely into the biblical teachings. But don't let them catch you in the act, or they will come down hard on you, as they did on me."

John shook his head. "I've thought a lot about it, Christine. It really is simple. The church had to put a stop to my miracles, because they couldn't explain them. It was why they forced me to leave Chicago, and I have to say, it worked. I have not healed anyone since I came to Mexico over ten years ago." John started to feel uncomfortable with what he had revealed, and thought he had said enough. He changed the subject.

"Let's talk about you. I have not seen you since I left. What happened to you, Christine?" Christine began.

"My story is far less dramatic than yours. After high school I couldn't wait to get out on my own. I suffered greatly by my episode with you when I was in High School, just like you said I would. Knowing it would happen made it understandable, but not less painful for me. I left Chicago and got a job as a waitress at a restaurant in the new suburb of Deerfield where I worked for about five years before I married for the first time. My first husband, Jim, was a handsome construction worker who was working in the area. We met in the restaurant, and I waited on him almost every day at lunch.

There was a tremendous amount of building going on in the area, and he made a lot of money and we got to know each other. Of course, I now know the attraction between us was largely physical." Christine looked down at the table and blushed at what she had just exposed. "We got married and loved each other for about a year, but there was an insurmountable problem which I didn't recognize or even fully understand until after I divorced my second husband."

It was now John's turn to show concern. "What was that Christine?"

"I realized he wasn't you, John. They weren't you." Christine looked up at him and was saddened by what she had just revealed.

"Christine..."

She raised her hand and got a serious look on her face. "No, don't stop me John. I have waited years to say this to you, and I need to say it. It is why I came to Mexico to see you." She looked directly into his eyes. "I love you now, and I have always loved you. It doesn't matter to me that you are twice my age, or that you have lost your faith and no longer want to be a priest. Actually, I'm glad it happened to you because after my divorces, and after much reflection; I lost my faith as well. There were just too many problems with the church doctrine, which I could no longer believe when I thought more seriously about them. Nevertheless, I realized my problem was how I felt about you. I loved you when I was fifteen, and I still love you. I have never stopped loving you, John. Even when I was married, I realized my husband's traits I loved the most, were those traits which reminded me of you. My second husband sensed it. Oh, I never told him about you, but I knew he could tell I loved someone else. That someone else was you, John. I don't know if you could or will ever stop being a priest and be able to love me. Maybe it doesn't matter now. I had to find you John, and I had to tell you these things. I realized long ago that it was, and is important for me to tell you how I feel."

John had sat quietly looking directly at Christine throughout her speech. At the end of it they both looked down at the table and realized they were holding each other's hands. Christine's speech was the most honest and striking statement of love John had ever heard in all his years as a priest.

They heard the clatter of dishes from a young bus boy clearing a table next to them. He dropped a dish which shattered on the hard wood floor. John looked straight into Christine eyes and said, "Christina, let's get out of here."

She smiled back knowingly, and he stood and tossed their cinnamon rolls back into the small paper bag. They grabbed their Styrofoam coffee cups and quickly left the restaurant to head back to the hotel.

What they did not know was their entire visit to the coffee shop had been observed by a young man who was waiting for his waitress girlfriend to get off work at the shop. He was seated at a table on the opposite side of the coffee shop, directly across from John and Christine. Although he understood almost no English, it didn't matter. He couldn't help but notice the unusual tall Caucasian couple when they entered the store, and he had watched them with great interest the entire time they were there. He understood their body language perfectly, and he thought how lucky John was to have such a beautiful young woman who appeared to be half his age. The young man's name was Carlos Martinez.

* * * * * * *

Chapter 32: **Maria Lopez**

Maria Lopez was the twenty two year old daughter of Jaime Lopez, who was the Batopilas Mafia ring leader. Jaime had a constant need to launder his drug and extortion money, and his daughter, Maria, was good at math and had completed her Associate degree in accounting at the Chihuahua Community College. Jaime pulled a few strings and was able to get Maria a teller position at The First National Bank in Batopilas. Nobody in Batopilas dared to deny a request from Jaime, particularly for such a small favor.

The truth was Jaime could get Maria a job at any number of businesses in town, but he liked the idea of her working at the largest bank, and she liked it too. He hoped she might someday be able to help him with his money laundering problems. Besides, he thought, having a set of eyes and ears at the local bank would enable him to keep tabs on all the local businesses. Money was the pulse of business, and all of it eventually flowed through the banks. Having Maria there just made good business sense.

One morning Maria overheard her father on the phone discussing Carlos Martinez who she knew from her secondary school days. Though Carlos was not a close friend, Maria could tell from her father's conversation that Carlos was in trouble, and it was clear he owed her father two hundred thousand pesos ($20,000) in gambling debts. Carlos had made one bad bet after another, and in a final act of desperation, he had borrowed even more money, and threw it all away at the race track on a "hot tip" he heard from a friend.

Maria walked out onto the back patio of their sprawling brick ranch to bring her father a fresh cup of espresso to complete a wonderful lunch of salad and beef tostadas. Jaime was enjoying a pleasant Saturday afternoon, sitting at his covered patio table reading the local daily paper. As Maria set down the coffee, she cautiously approached her father on the subject of Carlos.

"Papa?"

"Yes Maria."

"I heard you talking about Carlos Martinez on the phone before lunch."

"It is not your concern Maria."

Jaime was careful not to involve his family in his business. Jaime believed the less they knew about his Mafia dealings, the better for all of them, himself included. His reputation and influence were widely known by all except by members of his immediate family, particularly Maria. She knew better than to ask her father questions about his business, and she knew she was now treading into dangerous territory. Not speaking of her father's business was an idea that never had to be taught to her, but one she quickly learned from her mother and older brothers at a young age. She knew certain subjects were off limits, but she was older now, and she felt confident she could handle the conversation and possibly help both Carlos and her father.

"I know Papa. But I may know a way that Carlos might be able to repay the money he owes you."

Maria now had her father's attention. He put down his paper and looked up at her curiously, anxious to hear what she would say next. Maria never spoke to her father this way before, and she had been quiet about her bank activities since she was hired six months earlier. It occurred to Jaime that her job at the bank may start to pay some dividends after all.

"Go on Maria... Tell me what you know."

Maria set down her now empty tray on the table and pulled up a chair next to her father and began.

"A few days ago a Catholic priest deposited five million pesos into a new checking account at my branch. I helped him open the account."

Father John's Gift

She smiled at the thought she might impress her father by telling him she could handle such a large amount of money.

"Do you know this priest?"

"No, I don't know him personally, but his name is Father John Danek, and I know he is a priest at St. Josephina's Church in Tarahumara."

Maria then told her father everything she knew about the transaction. She concluded, "I just thought that maybe Carlos could go to this priest and ask him for help with the debt."

Jaime took one more sip of his espresso and carefully placed the small cup back on its saucer. He looked up at her graciously. "Thank you Maria. That might be very helpful." Even a monster in the Mexican Mafia could be polite to his daughter.

Later that day, Jaime Lopez entered his home office and called Bishop Hernandez who was the head of Archdiocese of Chihuahua. Unless it was an emergency, Jaime always called the Bishop's residence number early in the evening. His relationship with the Bishop was not public knowledge, and both he and Bishop wanted it to remain that way.

"Bishop?"

"Yes, this is Bishop Hernandez. Jaime? Is that you?" Jaime's voice was unusual enough that the Bishop always recognized it, but Jaime called so infrequently the call was always a surprise to the Bishop. Jaime's calls were usually friendly in tone but were never social. A call from Jaime almost always meant trouble.

"Yes Bishop. Do you know a Father John Danek at St. Josephina Church?" Jaime always came right to the point. He was not one for making small talk, and the Bishop knew it. Although they were not friends, the two had been doing "business" together for more than fifteen years and they knew each other well.

"Yes, I know Father John."

"I understand from a reliable source that Father John made a rather large deposit at a bank in Batopilas a few days ago. Do you know about this?"

"No. I know nothing about it. How much money are we talking about?"

"My source said it was five million pesos."

The Bishop raised his eyebrows in surprise and his answer was immediate. "That is a lot of money for anyone, particularly for a priest in my parish! I don't know where or how Father John got that much money. Do you know the source of his funds?"

Jaime scratched his head as he recalled what Maria had told him. "My source tells me the check was written against a bank account in Albany, New York. The person who wrote the check is named, "Peter Harrington". Do you know him, or what the money was for?"

"No Jaime, I don't know, but I will look into it. Can I ask you to stay clear of Father John? How about I call you back in a few days?"

"That will be OK. But Bishop, remember…

"I called you first about it."

"I understand. Thank you Jaime." The Bishop hung up his phone.

The Bishop despised Jaime and he hated dealing with him, but the Bishop always showed Jaime respect. One did not get on the bad side of anyone in the Mafia, particularly not with Jaime. The Bishop understood that with Jaime, everything was business. After fifteen years of doing business with him the Bishop knew Jaime was a maniac who would not hesitate to have him killed if it suited some business need. The Mafia violence and killings were horrific and widely known by those members in the church who heard Mafia confessions. The local stories always made their way to the Bishop in one way or another, and virtually all of them pointed back to Jaime as the instigator or ring leader. After all, executing ruthless business was how Jaime had reached his position in the Mob.

The Bishop's position enabled him to know far more about the local and regional crimes than the newspaper reporters who covered them, or even the police detectives who investigated them. The priests never spoke of it, but they all knew they were often in a unique position to know the guilty party, and it sometimes bothered many of them. It was always a perplexing dilemma to the priests when the police got it wrong: that they had an innocent suspect in custody and had charged him with a crime the priests knew he did not commit. Troubled as they were, the priests could never say anything to anyone about what they knew. To tell anyone would not only violate their sacred oath as priests, but it could also get them killed by members of the local Mafia for ratting on one of their own.

The Bishop then called Monsignor Santos Rodriguez at St. Josephina who answered without so much as a ring.

"Santos? This is Miguel." The Monsignor and the Bishop spoke about once a week and were on a first name basis. "Santos, how's everything going?"

"Pretty good Miguel, what's up?"

"I understand your Father John has deposited five million pesos in a bank account in a Batopilas. Do you know about it?"

"Oh Yes. John told me about it. He said he received the money from a friend who just died in the States. John wants to donate the money to the church to build a nonprofit hospital for the people of Tarahumara. I was going to speak to you about it at our quarterly meeting next week. Is there a problem?"

"I hope not. I just heard about the money from a round-about source and I wanted to make sure you were on top of it. I'm glad Father John is transparent with you about the money. Santos, that's all I needed to know for now. Thanks for the information."

Despite his rank in the church, Bishop Hernandez was not the kind of man who made decisions easily. He was under strict orders from Rome not to promote Father John, and he thought Rome should be informed in any matters related to John. The Bishop sent the following fax from his residence in his rectory to his contact in Rome:

To the Vatican Consulate General

Father John Danek at St. Josephina in Tarahumara, Mexico received five million pesos from a Mr. Peter Harrington on or about 22-05-1971.

Monsignor Santos Rodriguez reports Father John intent to use the funds to build a non-profit hospital for the church in Tarahumara.

Requesting recommended action from the Vatican on behalf of the church.

Sincerely,
Bishop Miguel Hernandez
Archdiocese of Chihuahua, Mexico

The Bishop got up the next morning at his usual five fifteen AM and checked his fax machine. He was surprised to find he had already received a reply from Rome. The reply read:

(For your eyes only. Please dispose properly after you read this note.)

Stato della Città del Vaticano
Tell Monsignor Rodriguez to proceed with Tarahumara Hospital.
Contact Gino regarding Father John.
Inform Gino double normal rates apply, but the Peter Harrington family is off limits.
Tell Gino payment will be made to his bank account in Rome when the task is complete.

There was no signature, but the message was clear. Father John was to be killed. Bishop Hernandez was shocked. Why would they do that? He sat down on the edge of his bed and stared out into space as he contemplated the message. He had done shady deals with Jaime before. There was coercion, intimidation, and even bribery, but there was never murder. To make matters worse, the victim was a priest, one of his own! The Bishop shook his head, "No, no, Oh God no!" He shook his head as he stared at the fax in his hands and read it again and again. He rationalized it. He told himself it was not his decision to make. He was only a Lieutenant following orders from above and he had no choice.

Sickened by what he was about to do he muttered to himself, "God help me!"

Bishop Hernandez swallowed his pride, and despite the early hour he picked up the phone and dialed Jaime.

* * * * * * *

Chapter 33: **Carlos Martinez**

At age twenty three, Carlos Martinez went to Mass every Sunday, and though he was far from perfect, he tried his best to be a good person. But now Carlos was in serious trouble, and he knew it. He had called the St. Josephina Rectory and made an appointment to see Father John. He told the Juanita only that he was in trouble, and he needed to see Father John as soon as possible. Juanita knew all the priests kept every Thursday evening open for special appointments. She checked the rectory appointment book and saw Father John was still free the following Thursday, so she made an eight o'clock PM appointment for Carlos.

Carlos arrived at the St. Josephina Rectory promptly at the appointed time on Thursday night. He walked up the steps and knocked on the large wooden rectory door. The knock was answered by Father John who was expecting him. Though he had changed his clothes, Father John still wore his priest collar for the meeting.

"Carlos Martinez?"

"Yes."

John opened the door and said, "Come in please."

Carlos entered the vestibule and John extended his hand and said, "I am Father John." Carlos' eyes got large when he looked at John and knew instantly he had seen him somewhere before, but where? His mind was at first overloaded as he struggled to remember, and then he recalled seeing John in Batopilas with Christine the previous week in the coffee shop. Was this man really a priest? What was he doing with the beautiful red headed woman? How could this be?

Carlos said nothing about the coffee shop or Christine, but instead he shook Father John's hand and said, "Thank you for meeting me Father."

"Let's meet in here." John turned and opened one half of a set of French doors to an anteroom just inside the rectory. He reached around the door and clicked a switch on the wall to turn on a light. The room was small, but had a few nice blue velvet high back Queen Anne chairs separated by a round end table with a lamp on it. Behind the chairs was a wall of built-in shelves which held frequently used volumes from the rectory library. The room was cozy, and quiet, and one could sit and read undisturbed for hours.

As they entered the room Father John started to close the door but stopped short. He turned to Carlos and said, "Carlos, please have a seat. Would you like some coffee? I just started a pot." John could see the young man was nervous about being there. He wanted Carlos to relax and to feel comfortable in the rectory surroundings.

Carlos did not really want a drink, but he didn't want to be a bad guest. "Sure Father, coffee would be nice."

John smiled at Carlos, "Do you take anything in your coffee?"

"One sugar and a little milk, if you have it."

John nodded at Carlos and said, "OK. The coffee is almost done. I'll be back in a minute."

Carlos waited nervously for Father John who returned with a serving tray containing two cups of coffee, a sugar bowl, and a small creamer. John set the tray down on a coffee table in front of Carlos and closed the door giving them some privacy in the small room. He sat down next to Carlos and said, "Please Carlos, help yourself."

As John stirred his coffee he said, "Carlos, I really don't know what this meeting is about. Juanita didn't tell me. How can I help you?"

Carlos looked down at his coffee on the table and said, "Father... I'm in trouble." He picked up his coffee and his hands were visibly shaking. The spoon rattled in his cup and Carlos sipped the drink, afraid that the coffee would spill.

John could see Carlos was scared and reluctant to talk. "What kind of trouble Carlos?"

Father John's Gift

Carlos put down his drink. He looked up at Father John and said, "I owe a lot of money to some very bad people."

Father John wanted to get Carlos talking. He could see the young man needed to tell his side of the story.

"Carlos, why don't you just tell me what happened. Start at the beginning. I won't judge you. Just give me the facts as you know them, and I will listen."

Carlos put down his cup, stared down at the floor and began. "It started when I borrowed some money from a friend to buy a used car. I bought the car because I needed transportation and…. I wanted to impress my girlfriend. The car was only fifteen thousand pesos ($1500), but it was more money than I had, so I borrowed most of it from a guy who lived down the street from me named Sergio. I grew up with Sergio, and although we were not close, I thought he was my friend. My next paycheck was for five thousand pesos that I knew I would get the following week, and I figured I would pay off the loan over the next few months. I was late for work a few times in the following weeks when the car wouldn't start, and my boss got so mad he fired me. I didn't know Sergio was working for a local drug dealer, and the money I borrowed came from the Mexican Mafia." Tears welled up in Carlos' eyes.

John leaned toward Carlos and touched his arm. "It's OK Carlos. Go on. Tell me what happened."

Carlos said, "After I missed my second payment, Sergio showed up with a partner, a big guy named Victor who I didn't know. Victor told me the interest rate was going up. He said it was because I was now a bad risk. I knew it was bad but I had no choice. I worked whatever small jobs I could find, but my earnings were never enough to pay down the loan."

John kept his eyes on Carlos. He could see Carlos was relieved just to be able to tell someone…anyone who would listen and understand his troubles.

"The problem only got worse over the next five months. The amount of interest grew because I could never get caught up in my payments. I was desperate. I thought if I could win the money at the race track I could be done with the Mafia, so I borrowed even more money from Sergio at a higher rate. Of course, my sure bet was a loser. Now they say I owe them two hundred thousand pesos, and I don't know how I will ever be able to repay them." Carlos took a deep breath before he continued. "Father, they say if I don't get the money by next Saturday, they will kill me."

John had read about such stories before, and he believed all of it. The Mafia could be ruthless, and Carlos's life might be in danger. John thought about the money he had sent to Enrique a few days ago. It was too late to get that money back, and even if he could get it back, John didn't want to jeopardize the hospital project and loose Enrique's trust. No, there had to be another way.

"Carlos, how much money do you have now?"

"I have only five thousand pesos."

"Is there no one you can go to? Have you talked with your parents or a close relative about the money?"

"No Father. My father died when I was only four, and my mother is poor. She cleans houses and hotel rooms for a living, and she has very little savings. I am an only child, and I don't have any close relatives."

Father John thought about the situation. The Mob boss might listen to a priest eager to help, and he thought he might be able to negotiate a deal with them. He couldn't let Carlos go to the meeting alone. The mob would be reluctant to kill Carlos if he was there, and he would tell them how they could get their money. Even Mafia thugs would trust a priest.

"Do you have a time and place you will meet these people tomorrow?"

"Yes. It is the Hacienda Restaurant on Canal Street in Batopilas. I am to meet them at three o'clock next Saturday afternoon."

John did not make the connection that he had deposited his money from Father Mark in Batopilas a week earlier. "Carlos, I don't have much money. But I have five thousand pesos to loan you, and you can pay me back whenever you can. I know some businessmen in town, and I will be happy to talk with them on your behalf to help you find better paying work. I will go with you on Saturday and try to negotiate a deal with these people so you can repay them. Don't worry Carlos.

Father John's Gift

They don't really want to kill you. They want their money. They want you to keep paying them."

Father John sounded upbeat and convincing. Relieved, Carlos looked up at Father John and said, "Thank you Father."

As soon as Carlos left St Andrews, he got in his car and drove down the street to the Pemex gas station on the corner to use a pay phone. Carlos now knew Father John had a girlfriend, and he knew the Mafia had a large interest in John, one that Carlos did not understand. Still, he thought if he was forthcoming to the Mafia with what he knew, they might see him as valuable and give him more time to repay his loan.

Carlos picked up the phone and dialed Sergio.

"Sergio?"

"Yes."

"It's Carlos. I just met with Father John at St Andrews in Tarahumara."

"That's good. Is he coming with you next Saturday?"

"Yes. But Sergio, I thought there was something you might like to know about Father John."

"Yeah? What's that?"

"He has a girlfriend."

Sergio chuckled to himself at the thought of a Catholic priest with a girlfriend. Sergio was not Catholic, and he didn't like priests. He had heard too many Mafia stories over the years about the hypocrisy of priests to trust them, and Carlos had just added one more story to his list. "Well, our priest is human after all! That could be useful. Do you know who she is?"

"No, but she is a tall beautiful gringo with red head in her mid-twenties. I saw her with Father John at Tolito's Coffee Cafe in Batopilas last week. You can't miss her. My girlfriend, Lola, works at the shop tells me she has been back to Tolito's for coffee and cinnamon pasteles every day since then. She told me last Friday the red headed woman always comes for coffee and a cinnamon roll at eight AM."

"Thanks Carlos. I'll let the boss know. I can't give you any promises, but maybe he will give you a break after all." Carlos had been told to bring the money AND Father John.

R. Allan Worrell

Carlos hung up the phone, left the station, and walked slowly back to his car mulling over his conversation with Sergio in his head. He felt sick about what he had just done, and he knew he could not undo it. Father John had offered to help him with his troubles, and he had repaid his help by getting both Father John and his girlfriend in real trouble with the mob. When he reached the car, Carlos opened the door but abruptly stopped and repeatedly beat the roof of his car with his fist.

"Damn it! Damn it! Damn this car!"

He leaned his head in his arms up against the vehicle and cried, "Oh God, what have I done now?" Carlos slammed the car door closed and turned around to walk back into the gas station. He had to warn Father John.

"St. Josephina Rectory. How may I help you?" It was Juanita.

"My name is Carlos Martinez. I met with Father John tonight, just ten or fifteen minutes ago. Is he still there?"

"I think so. Let me get him for you."

"Thank you." Carlos turned and looked around the interior of the small gas station. A tired young attendant opened a glass door at the other end of the room and walked in from the garage wiping his black greasy hands with a white cotton towel. He threw the towel on a chair in the corner of the room and looked for his cigarettes behind the cluttered counter near the cash register. He found them and tamped the package upside down on the counter and extracted a cigarette from the pack. With the cigarette in his mouth, he patted himself down trying to find a matches or a lighter. He looked at Carlos who was still on the pay phone in the opposite corner of the room and gestured at him for a light. Carlos didn't smoke and wanted to have a private conversation with Father John. With the phone receiver still held to his ear, Carlos shot him a mean look, a frown, and shook his head at the attendant. The young mechanic got the message, turned around, and disappeared back into the garage.

"This is Father John."

"Father, this is Carlos."

Father John's Gift

"Carlos? Where are you? Are you OK?" Father John could not believe he was hearing back so soon from Carlos. After all, Carlos had left him not fifteen minutes ago. Was he having car problems?

"Father, I just did a bad thing, and I believe I may have got you into a lot of trouble."

"Why? What did you do, Carlos?"

"I told Sergio about you, and your girlfriend."

"My girlfriend?" Father John was speechless.

"Yes Father. I saw you both in the coffee shop in Batopilas over a week ago. I thought if I told the Mafia about you and her, that it might make them go easier on me. But I realized it was a terrible mistake as soon as I told Sergio tonight. I'm very sorry Father. I don't know what to do now."

John was stunned. He held the phone to his ear and said nothing as he tried to process the information.

"Father John? Are you there? Did you hear what I just said?"

"Yes Carlos. I'm here. You did the right thing by calling me and telling me about what you did." John paused as he thought more about the situation. "What did Sergio say when you told him?"

Carlos replayed his conversation with Sergio in his mind. "He thanked me and said it could be useful. He said he would tell his boss. But Father, I don't understand. Why are they interested in you?"

"I'm not sure Carlos, but I have an idea." John was now thinking of the money. "How did you get my name and number? Did Sergio tell you to come to see me tonight and to ask for my help?"

"Yes."

John now understood the Mafia would try to get to him and his money by threatening to harm or kill Christina. But how did they know about the money? Father John dismissed the thought. It really didn't matter how they knew. It mattered only that they knew, and he now needed to protect Christina. He would have to warn her.

"That's OK Carlos. I'm glad you came to see me tonight and that you told me about your conversation with Sergio. Is there anything else I need to know? Did Sergio say anything else?"

"No. That's all Father. I'm so sorry for all of this. I can't seem to do anything right."

"It's OK Carlos. I understand. I'm just glad you called and told me what happened. Now that I know about it, I can deal with it. Is your meeting still scheduled for next Saturday at three o'clock?"

"Yes Father."

"OK. Remember to arrive about ten minutes early, and meet me just outside the restaurant as we planned, and Carlos, don't forget to bring your money."

"I won't forget."

"OK. Goodnight Carlos."

"Goodnight Father."

Although he was still concerned for Carlos, John hung up the phone thinking only of Christine.

* * * * * * *

Chapter 34: **Sergio's Call**

Still at his house, Sergio just got off the phone with Carlos. He decided the information from Carlos was too good to keep to himself. He had to tell Jaime right away. He pressed the switch hook on his phone to get a dial tone and dialed Jaime at his home office. Jaime was eating a late dinner with his family in the kitchen when he heard his phone ring in his office. Never concerned about missing a call, Jaime got up from the table and leisurely walked into his office closing the glass French doors behind him. Sergio heard him pick up the receiver.

"Jaime?"

"Yes."

"This is Sergio."

"What's up Sergio?" Jaime was annoyed to receive the call, but he also knew Sergio would not call him at home unless it was important.

"I just got off the phone with Carlos, and he told me something which I thought might be useful." Sergio paused for effect. "I think you're going to like it, boss."

"Sergio, just tell me. What is it?" Jaime had had long day and he just wanted it to be over. He wanted to kick back and relax in front of some mindless television. He thought there might be a soccer game starting in a few minutes, and he didn't want to miss the start of it.

"Carlos told me Father John has a girlfriend." Carlos waited for a response before divulging more.

Jaime smiled as he processed the information. "That is good news! Good work Sergio. Did he tell you who she is or how to find her?"

"No, he didn't know her name, but we should be able to find her easily enough. He said she is a gringo with red hair from the States, and goes to Tolito's Coffee Cafe" on Larned Street for breakfast every morning. You know, it's that place we went to for our monthly meeting last month. I remember you liked their apple fritters." Sergio smiled. He thought the apple fritter remark was a nice touch.

"Yeah, I remember it. It's down the street from the Hotel Grande. Maybe the girlfriend is staying there. She certainly will not be staying at the rectory with Father John", he said sarcastically. Both men laughed at his stupid joke. "Sergio, take Raul and pick her up tomorrow morning and bring her to my office on the South side. And Sergio, don't hurt her. There is no need for violence here. We just want to scare her a little bit and put some pressure on Father John. Remember, she is out of her element. ... We will show her how we do things here in Mexico. Do you understand?"

"Sure. You got it boss."

Jaime hung up the phone and smiled. The day ended on a positive note after all. The Mafia was now in a win-win position which just might get even sweeter.

* * * * * * *

Chapter 35: **The Warning**

    John hung up the phone in the foyer from the conversation he had with Carlos and walked to the kitchen at rear of the rectory. It was after eight PM, and although the kitchen was not off limits to the priests, it was closed for the evening. Father John wanted to use the kitchen phone which afforded him some measure of privacy. He clicked on a small light in the kitchen, closed the swing door which had been propped open, and dialed the Hotel Grande. The phone rang once and was answered by the hotel operator.

"Buenos Tardes. (Good Evening.) Hotel Grande!"

"Room 210 please."

"Gracias."

"Hello?" It was Christine. After what he just learned from Carlos, John was relieved to hear her voice, and to know she was still OK.

"Hello, Christine?"

"Yes. John? Is that you?" John's greeting had such a serious tone Christine didn't recognize him.

"Yes Tina, it's me. I need to talk to you in person... tonight. Can you wait for me in your hotel room?"

"Of course. But why? Are you OK?"

"Yes, I'm OK, but it's a long story. I will explain it all when I see you. Something bad has happened, and I am afraid for your safety. I want you to lock your door and not open it for anyone but me. Will you do that?"

"Yes, but you are scaring me."

"I'm sorry Christine. It may not be as bad as I think, but we can't afford to take any chances. I'll explain everything when I see you."

    "OK. I'll wait for you. Drive carefully sweetheart." Christine was worried. She expected to see him on Saturday afternoon and had no idea what could have prompted John's call on a Thursday evening. It was unlike him.

"OK Christine. I will see you in about an hour." John hung up the phone and exited the kitchen. He hurried back to his bedroom and grabbed his keys, his priest bag and a coat. On his way out he stuck his head into the small office to let Juanita know he would be out for the evening and not to expect him back until midnight.

The ride to Batopilas was uneventful. The traffic was light and the summertime sun was setting on the Sierra Nevada Mountains and reflected a beautiful orange color off of a stream of wispy clouds high in the atmosphere. It was more beautiful than John had remembered seeing it before. He marveled at nature's beauty, as he thought about what he would say to Christine when he saw her.

When he got to the hotel he parked in the rear as usual, entered the back door, and climbed the stairs to the second floor. Relieved he was alone in the long hall John wasted no time and went straight to Christine's room.

When she heard him knock, she looked through the peep hole in the door to see who it was. Tina opened the door with a look of consternation. She was shocked to see John standing in front of her in his priest gown. It was the first time she had seen him in his black priest gown outside of a Mass. In his rush to see her, John had not taken the time to change. John stepped inside of the room, turned and locked the door.

They said nothing, looked at each other, embraced and kissed.

Christine backed off from him and looked down his long black gown. "I have to tell you, John. I feel funny kissing a priest." She smiled at him.

John looked down at himself and laughed at her comment. "I'm sorry Tina. I didn't take the time to change. I thought it was too important that I see you right away."

"What is it John? What's happened? What's so important that it couldn't wait?" Christine had been driving herself crazy in the last hour as she tried to understand John's urgent call and his need to see her.

Father John's Gift

John sat down on a small loveseat at the front of her room. He patted the cushion next to him and said, "Tina, please sit down." Worried, she said nothing but sat down next to him. She expected him to say something terrible.

"I don't know how to tell you this, but I believe you are in some real danger from the Mexican Mafia. It was why I didn't want you to open the door to anyone but me."

Tina looked at him with shock and disbelief. "The Mexican Mafia?" It was the last thing she expected him to say, and she knew he was serious. "Oh my God! What does the Mafia want with me?"

"Tina, please let me tell you the whole story, and I'm sure you will understand." John leaned back in the love seat and stared for a moment at the ceiling as he collected his thoughts. "I have been helping a young man named, "Carlos" who is in trouble with the Mafia. He owes them a lot of money and is unable to repay them."

"What has that got to do with me?"

"Let me explain. Do you remember me telling you in the coffee shop that first day about my friend who died?"

"Yes."

"Well, his name was Father Mark Harrington. He was a priest from upstate New York; St Anthony's Parish. But that's not important. Mark took out an insurance policy on himself and he wrote me in as a beneficiary. After he died in an automobile accident, Mark's brother sent me a cashier's check for five hundred thousand dollars, which I deposited into a bank here in Batopilas."

Christine raised her eyebrows when she heard the amount. "I see. And you think the Mafia knows about the money?"

"Yes. I'm sure of it. There can be no other reason why they would have an interest in me."

"Then you are not safe either, John."

"Well, they don't know I've already spent the money. I plan to build a small hospital here in Tarahumara. And, I know it sounds funny, but the Mafia doesn't know that I know that they know about the money." John and Tina both smiled at what he had just said. She loved him for his wit and for his ability to laugh at himself, even in the face of real danger.

Tina answered him with her usual sarcasm. "And that protects you how?"

"Well, I thought about that on the way here tonight. I have an advantage, because I know they won't believe me if I try to pretend the money doesn't exist, so I won't deny it. However, if I can show them I've already spent the money, then they will have to give up on extorting it from me. I can't give them money I no longer have."

John paused before changing the subject, and he lowered his voice. "But Tina, my real concern is you." She looked up at him and waited for his explanation. "As hard as it is for me to say it, you must leave Mexico as soon as possible. You and I both know the Mafia will use you against me for as long as you are here." He leaned forward and stared at the floor as he continued his thought. "I'm sure they will rightfully conclude I would do anything to keep you safe, and of course, it's a given they will try to blackmail me by threatening you or revealing our relationship to the church. Tina, I'm sure they will stop at nothing to profit from my relationship with you. And they will do it, however they can. It could get ugly, and you could get hurt."

Tina reached over and touched his shoulder. "I'm sure you're right. I just hate the thought of leaving you now. I knew I would have to leave eventually, but the past few weeks have been so wonderful, and time has gone so fast, it feels like I just got here." Tina leaned forward and gave John a kiss on his cheek and grabbed hold of his hand. "I'll go back to Chicago tomorrow if I have to, but I want you to come back with me."

John looked her in her eyes. "Tina, sweetheart... I want to. I really do. But I can't leave Mexico just yet. I want to make sure the new hospital gets built. The people of Tarahumara need it badly, and I've just started it for them. I've found good people to do the design and construction, but please, can you give me six months or a year to make sure the project gets going, and then I will return to you in Chicago?"

"Will you promise me that? Can I hold you to a year?"

"Yes, you can hold me to a year. I love you Tina. If I can't do it in a year, then I will know it probably won't ever get done. I may be able to return to Chicago sooner if all goes well... once this Mafia problem is resolved, and once the hospital construction is underway."

Father John's Gift

John looked seriously at Christina. "Tina, when I come back to Chicago, I promise you I will leave the church for good. I don't know what I will do, but I will find something. I know now I don't want to live without you."

Tina said no more but looked at him silently with love in her eyes. His commitment to her was everything she ever wanted from him.

John stood up and started to pace the small room. "Check out of here first thing tomorrow morning, and take the first flight you can get back to Chicago."

"John, I can't." His look told her he didn't understand. She continued. "I already know all the Chicago flights are full. I tried to reschedule my return flight a few days ago and found out I had to postpone it for a month! Not that I am complaining, I have enjoyed my time with you." She smiled at him and then continued, "There is just one flight a week back to Chicago, and it fills up quickly. It might take me a few weeks to get a flight to Chicago out of the Culiacan Airport."

"Then fly to Dallas, or Houston, or San Antonio.... Tina, just get out of Mexico as soon as you can. If you have to wait a day or two for a flight, then get a hotel room at the airport, but I want you to check in under a different name. Use a Spanish name so the hotel staff won't tell the Mafia you are there if they call the airport hotel and ask for you."

"OK, what name should I use?" She laughed at him and at the whole idea of having to pretend to be someone else. Tina was beginning to feel like a character in a spy novel.

"Oh, I don't know. How about using Carmen Morales?" The name had just popped into John's head. Carmen Morales was a precocious fourth grader John knew at St Josephina grade school.

"What if they ask for some ID? I don't have anything with the name "Carmen Morales" on it. And there's no way I can get a passport with that name."

"You will have to use your passport and driver's license to fly back home. If the hotel asks you for ID, tell them your last purse was stolen and that you lost all your IDs. Tell them you had to buy a new purse and you are now waiting for new cards to be sent to you. Make sure you put all your cards in your pocket. Pay for your room with cash from your purse. It will be easy for anyone at the hotel to believe a robbery story here in Mexico. There are so many pickpockets here. Just make sure you have enough cash to cover the cost of the hotel and your meals for a few days." John had heard too many confessions over the years, and he knew theft and purse snatching from tourists was common when young men got desperate for money.

"OK John." she said, "Carmen Morales it is!"

"And Tina, I hate to suggest this, but do you think you could buy a black wig? It's that beautiful red hair of yours! You don't want to make it easy for the Mafia to find you. You must know you look conspicuous with that red hair around here." He laughed at what he just said.

"You think? ... And I thought you never noticed!" she said sarcastically. She smiled and looked at herself in the mirror. She pulled her long bright red hair back into a ponytail and put a rubber band around it.

John approached her from behind, placed his hands on her fragile shoulders and slowly turned her around to face him. He looked at her sternly. "Tina, please. Listen to me. These Mafia guys don't mess around. We have to be careful, or we could both end up dead.... And I'm not kidding."

"OK. I'm sorry. I know you are right. I promise to be careful, and I'll do everything you asked."

"There is one more thing. I need to ask you to do a big favor for me when you get back to Chicago."

"What do you want me to do?"

"Before I left Chicago ten years ago, I went to the State Penitentiary to hear a last confession from a young man about to be executed. His name was Lamar Johnson." John reached beside his chair and grabbed his black bag. He opened the bag and retrieved Lamar's ten year old letter. It was unopened, slightly bent, and the envelope had turned brown around the edges. "Lamar gave me this letter to deliver to his mother, in person. He asked me to tell her that he loved her, and that he was sorry for everything. But with all that happened to me after that, I never had a chance to get it to her. Lamar was afraid she would just throw it away if he mailed it to her, so I didn't want to mail it. I have been carrying it around with me all this time, and of course, I have not been back to Chicago since I left."

"You want me to deliver it to her?"

"Yes. I know it is a lot to ask, but I feel bad about it, and it would mean a lot to me. I don't even know if she is still alive, but I know I, or we, at least need to make the effort to find her. I'm sure it will change how she feels about her son, and maybe even herself. Will you do that for me?"

"Of course." Christine reached for the letter, and John handed it to her.

"Thank you sweetheart. Please let me know what happens."

Christine looked at John, nodded, flipped the letter over to read the address on the back of the envelope, got up and placed it in her purse.

John thought about her trip and her need for cash. "Christina, we have never talked about money. Do you have enough cash to get home?

Tina smiled at him. "Yes, I'm OK. You don't need to worry about me."

Not satisfied with her answer, John asked, "Tina, you never told me. How is it you can afford to stay over a month here in Mexico? Don't you have to get back to work in Chicago?"

"No, I got a large inheritance from my mother when she died a few years ago."

"Oh, I'm so sorry, Tina, I didn't know you lost your mother."

John knew her mother, and he knew she didn't have much money and struggled financially to raise Christine by herself. "I knew your mother fairly well, and I know she didn't have a lot of money. How could she have left you much of anything?" Tina looked back at him with a look of sadness and disappointment. She really did not want to relive her mother's death. "Please tell me Tina. I want to understand."

Christine turned and sat down on a comfortable chair. She looked at John and matter-of-factly started her story. "My mother died of a stroke on Christmas Eve, two years ago. It was the strangest thing. We had a good meal together, and we talked about silly things late into the evening. She was fine when I went to bed at about 10 o'clock, but she said she didn't want to go to bed just yet. She stayed up to watch the eleven o'clock news on television. So I said goodnight and went upstairs to bed. When I came back downstairs the next morning, I found her dead in her favorite chair in front of the television. The TV was still on. I didn't know what else to do, so I called the police. They said her death was not suspicious, but they were required to order an autopsy in such circumstances. They said it was police policy. They called me a week later and told me the Coroner report stated mother had a massive stroke and had died quickly. She was only fifty two." Christine tried hard not to cry, but John saw her wipe a tear from her eye.

Christine continued. "But you asked about the money. Well, it turned out my mother had a great aunt named, June, who was quite wealthy and left her entire estate to my mother. For some reason I don't understand, June's lawyer failed to find my mother to tell her about it. Unfortunately, Aunt June had been estranged from her immediate family for years, and when they found out they were cut out of her will, they were so upset about not getting the money, they never bothered to tell my mother about the June's death, or her estate. I guess they figured if they couldn't get it, they wouldn't let anyone have it, or it may have satisfied some deep resentment against Aunt June to not honor her final wishes. Whatever the reason, my poor mother never knew about her inheritance, and as you said, she worked hard her whole life to raise me. Then, after she died, I found out about the inheritance.

Christine paused and took a drink of her coffee. She shook her head as she recalled a memory. "I have to say when I learned about the money, it was quite a day! My mother died with a few thousand dollars in the bank and I was shocked to find out she was worth several million dollars. She never even knew it, and she never got to enjoy her life. She worked hard her whole life for my benefit."

John was amazed. "Well, it was a choice your mother made. I know she loved you Tina, and I'm sure she would be proud of the woman you have become." John was sincere. "And, I have to say, I'm happy you got the money. Life is so strange sometimes. You never know what will happen next." John stood up. It was obvious he had to leave. "Tina, I know that was hard for you. Thank you for telling me."

Father John's Gift

She looked at him with sadness in her eyes. "There is one more thing I wanted to ask you before you go."

"What's that?"

"Well, it was something you said to me in the Batopilas coffee shop on the first day we met which has been bothering me. You said you knew something Father Mark knew, and you believed it got him killed, and it could get you killed. I wondered what you meant, but I didn't want to ask you about it at the time, because I was scared, and thought it could get me killed too. But I think considering the position we are in, it might not make a difference now. Can you tell me now? What did you mean? What was it you couldn't or didn't want to tell me?"

John looked at her and said, "Did you ever wonder how I was able to cure those people in Chicago?"

"Yes. I guess I thought it was something spiritual, like a gift from God."

"It's a gift, Christine, but it's more complicated than that."

"What do you mean?"

"Do you believe in UFOs?"

Christine looked at him with surprise. "You mean, like from outer space?"

"Yes."

"To be honest, I never thought about it that much. Why? Did you see a UFO?" she said sarcastically.

"Yes, Christine. You may not believe it, but I had an encounter with a UFO out side of Chicago. Somehow, and I still don't understand how or why, the UFO gave me the power to heal people."

"Oh my God." Tina sat down as she began to absorb what he just told her. She believed him. "Do you see them often?"

"No. That was the one and only time I ever encountered them. I am sure my healing ability came from them, and I believe they gave it to Father Mark also. Why they picked two Catholic priests, I don't know. But I'm sure it's why the church had to get me out of the public spotlight in Chicago. It was why they sent me here, and I believe it was why they had Father Mark killed. He was determined to use his healing power for good, and the church must have concluded he was out of their control."

"I see." Christine stared ahead at the wall. She was in shock with John's explanation.

John looked at his watch. "Christine, it's getting late. It's almost eleven. I have to go now before I am missed at the rectory. I told Juanita I would be back by midnight, so I have to leave now." He noticed her blank stare. "Are you OK?"

She looked up at him. "Yes. I'm OK, and I believe you. It's just such a surprise. It's lot for me to absorb."

"I totally understand. It took me a long time to come to grips with it as well. Christine, I wish I could stay longer, but I have to go." With that she stood up and he gave her a big kiss.

"Don't forget your coat!" She picked up his coat he had slung over a chair and handed it to him at the door. She looked at him from head to toe again and said, "Priest or not, miracles or not, UFOs or not ... I still love you John." She laughed, kissed him again and smiled.

John knew she was an amazing person. He looked at her eyes and smiled back at her. "I love you too, Tina. Please be careful tomorrow, and call me when you are back safety in the United States, OK?"

"OK. I will. I promise."

The next morning Christine got up early and ordered room service. She ate a small breakfast of toast and coffee and quickly left to run errands. She stopped at a bank to cash her remaining Traveler's checks for $2,000, and then she went shopping for a black wig at a boutique within walking distance from the hotel.

Jaime had sent Sergio and one of Sergio's thugs, Raul, to the coffee shop early Saturday morning. Raul was short in stature and suffered from a severe Napoleon complex. He had been teased for his size as a child, and had turned into a mean person as a result. It didn't help matters that Raul had no conscious, no sense of right and wrong, a trait which made Raul a perfect fit for the Mafia. Raul was a man of few words. He had learned early in childhood to keep his mouth shut because he found whenever he said anything, it always got him in trouble. Jaime had seen his share of men like Raul in the Mob and had wisely assigned him to Sergio and instructed Sergio to keep Raul on a short leash, least Raul get himself, Sergio, and the Mob all in trouble with the police.

Father John's Gift

Jaime had much of the Batopilas police force in his pocket, but ever conscious of public opinion, he used his police influence sparingly. It was better to avoid trouble than try to get out of it once it happened. Jaime's mantra was, "An ounce of prevention...". He had learned the lesson the hard way, and he would never let his men forget it. He drilled the expression into his men the way those in legitimate businesses talked about safety. In Jaime's gang, the consequences of police trouble almost always meant someone would have to die unnecessarily.

Sergio and Raul's assignment was to quietly apprehend Christine when she came to the Coffee Shop for her daily morning breakfast of black coffee and a pastry. They arrived at the shop at seven thirty, early enough to catch Christine at eight, and to give themselves some margin of error if she arrived a few minutes early. Sergio and Raul didn't look like Mafia. They looked like ordinary, law abiding, hardworking citizens, and they blended in well with the regular customers.

Sergio looked at his watch as they entered the shop. He turned to Raul. "We are right on-time. First, we need to make sure she is not already here. Then, if she is not here, we can get some coffee and wait for her." Raul nodded his head and went to the left of the shop and Sergio went to the right. Both looked at the seated customers on their side and met at the far end of the coffee shop. "See anything?" Raul shook his head and followed Sergio back around to the front of the shop. "Get us a table. I'll get us some coffee and a bite to eat." Raul sat down near the front of the shop where they could watch the front door and Sergio ordered some coffee and pastels.

As he enjoyed his roll and coffee, Sergio checked his watch every five minutes. When Christine didn't show up by eight thirty, Sergio looked at Raul and said, "She's not coming Raul. Let's get out of here and try to find her."

When they exited the shop Sergio looked up and down the street.

"You cross here and look in all the shop windows for her on the other side of the street. Remember, she is a tall gringo with red hair. Just whistle at me if you spot her. Whatever you do, don't try and take her alone." Sergio pointed to the next block. "We will both go that way towards the hotel. The boss thinks she may be staying in the Hotel

Grande about a block from here. When I get to the hotel you should wait for me. I will go inside and see if she ever checked in and see if the hotel clerk knows where she is. If she is there, I will come back out to the street to get you. But stay on that side of the street unless I motion for you to come into the hotel with me. We need to cover at least a few blocks on both sides of the street within walking distance from the hotel. Got it?"

Raul nodded at Sergio and quickly crossed the street when there was an opening in the traffic. He thought Sergio was smart and he liked the explicit instructions Sergio always gave him. Raul liked to think he was an army soldier, and Sergio was his drill sergeant who always told him what to do, and how to do it.

Sergio and Raul each methodically peered in one shop window after another as they made their way down the street towards the hotel. When Sergio reached the hotel he looked at Raul across the street and signaled for him to wait. Raul stopped and waited for Sergio who disappeared into the hotel as planned.

Sergio approached the front desk and waited patiently for the clerk, named Alejandro to check out a guest who was leaving.

"Excuse me. Do you have a tall red headed gringo woman staying at this hotel?"

"I'm sorry sir. I'm not allowed to give out that information."

Sergio opened his light coat jacket and flashed a revolver which was seated under his arm in a shoulder holster. "Oh, I think you can make an exception to that rule, don't you?"

"Yes... I'm sorry sir. ... We do have a guest who fits that description, but she is not here."

"Do you know where she went?"

"No, I don't know, but I can tell you she left the hotel about eight o'clock this morning."

Sergio checked his watch. It was now eight fifty five. "Thank you for your help. If you see her, don't tell her anything about our little talk or there will be trouble. Do you understand me?" He patted his gun on the outside of his jacket.

Father John's Gift

Alejandro just nodded to him, but Sergio was not satisfied. He wanted to make sure Alejandro was sufficiently intimidated. "Say it! Say you understand!"

"Yes. I understand."

Sergio turned and quickly left the hotel. He looked across the street at Raul and shook his head and signaled that they should continue the store search to the next block.

After they reached the next block the sidewalk traffic picked up as the shops finally opened for waiting customers. Sergio glanced in one window after another without results when he finally reached, "The Wig Boutique". However, Sergio was standing directly in front of the store window, and he couldn't see the sign which hung a few feet above him. When he looked through the front window, he saw a several attractive women milling about and fussing with the hair of others seated in what looked like barber's chairs. Sergio didn't realize the shop sold wigs and he mistakenly thought the store was a hair salon. As Sergio gazed into the window, Christine exited the store onto the busy sidewalk with her new black wig and dark sunglasses on, and a shopping bag in each hand. She quickly turned to the right to walk back to the hotel.

Just as Christine was leaving, a well-to-do middle aged woman with two little adorable Shih Tzu puppies on leashes passed by Sergio on the sidewalk, and a few other attractive women shoppers who encountered them bent over to pet the little dogs and made a fuss about how cute they were and asked the owner about their age. It didn't help Sergio that the two making a fuss over the puppies were young women in their twenties with large breasts wearing clingy tops with low necklines. Sergio was so distracted by the dogs, the young women with large breasts, and with all the confusion on the sidewalk, that he didn't see Christine leave.

Raul looked across the street at Sergio, the women, and the dogs. He saw Christine leave, but he dismissed her since Sergio had told him to look for a tall red-headed woman. And although he had read the sign above the door and he did see the word, "Wig", Raul did not understand the word, "Boutique", and he did not put two and two together. It was not Raul's finest hour; but then, Raul was not the brightest candle in the Mob.

Christine quickly walked the block and a half and returned to the Grand Hotel and went straight to her room to retrieve the four suitcases she had packed the night before. She picked up the phone in her room and dialed the front desk.

"This is the Front Desk. Alejandro speaking, how may I help you?"

"Hi Alejandro! This is Christine O'Roark in room 215. I will be checking out this morning to return home in the United States. Can you send up a porter to help me with my bags?"

"Certainly Ms. O'Roark. I will be happy to send up Edwardo to help you. But I want you to know there was a bad man with a gun looking for you here about ten minutes ago. I think you should avoid him if at all possible. He threatened me, and he told me not to tell you about him, but I think we can keep this conversation between the two of us, don't you?"

Christine was alarmed. "Yes. Of course! Thank you for telling me, Alejandro. Can I exit out the back of the hotel?"

"Yes. I think that's a good idea. Would you like for me to ask our concierge, Luis, to call a taxi for you?"

"Yes. Please tell him I will need a ride to the Batopilas train station, and to have the cab meet me around back."

"Very good ma'am. It has been a pleasure serving you Ms. O'Roark. I will give your final bill to Edwardo to bring to your room. You can just sign it and leave it there for the maid to collect. I hope you have a safe journey home.

"Alejandro?"

"Yes Ma'am?"

"Thank you so much for all your help. Please give yourself and Luis a nice big thank you tip from me, will you? I will look for it on my bill when I get it."

"You are so kind Ms. O'Roark, but that won't be necessary. We are always happy to serve our best guests." It was true. Christine was a joy to be around. She was completely happy for the first time in her life, and it showed. She lit up every room she entered.

Father John's Gift

"Well, thank you again Alejandro. I have enjoyed my stay here, and I hope I didn't get you in any trouble."

"It was no trouble at all Ms. O'Roark. Thank you again."

Despite his protest, Christine added a nice tip for both Alejandro and Luis. She also gave the bell hop, Edwardo, and the taxi driver each a big tip and asked them all not to tell anyone about her. All were taken with Christine and were more than happy to comply.

Although the return train ride to the Culiacan International Airport was over five hours long, the morning trip through the mountains was scenic, and Christine enjoyed the trip. Once at the airport, she paid cash for a next-day direct flight to Dallas, and then she checked into a hotel at the airport under the pseudonym, Carmen Morales.

* * * * * *

Chapter 36: **Lamar's Mother**

It took two days for Christine to arrive back home in Chicago and once back, she was exhausted from the trip. On the following Friday she retrieved Lamar's letter from her purse and looked at the address. She had told John she would try to deliver the letter and the message to Lamar's mother, and she thought she would have the best chance of catching his mother at home on Saturday morning. She was curious to know if she would be able to find her, and even more curious to know how Lamar's mother would react to receiving a letter from her son, ten years after his death.

Before she left her house the next morning, Christine had no idea where to find Lamar's mother's house at 235 East 133 Place in Riverdale, so she called the US Post office and was given directions to the Riverdale suburb on the South side of Chicago. After a thirty minute drive in moderately heavy traffic, she found an attractive but modest neighborhood of town houses, but there were no immediate parking spaces available. She circled the block and parked her car on the opposite side of the street half a block away from the address. It was a bright Saturday morning, and Christine took a large breath for courage before she knocked on the door. A small grey haired black woman came to the door and looked at Christine through the glass pane in the door. Suspicious at the sight of Christine, she cracked the door but did not unlock her security chain.

"May I help you?" She asked.

"Mrs. Johnson?"

"Yes."

"My name is Christine O'Roark. I need to talk to you about your son, Lamar... May I come in?"

Father John's Gift

Mrs. Johnson's eyes grew large. She could not imagine what Lamar could have in common with a red headed Irish woman, or why anyone would want to talk to her about him ten years after he died in prison. She didn't want to talk to a stranger who approached her without warning, but her curiosity got the better of her.

"Yes. I suppose it will be all right." She unlocked the chain and opened the door for Christine to step inside. Christine entered foyer of the small town house and spoke immediately.

"Mrs. Johnson, I know this may come as a shock to you, but before Lamar died, your son met with a friend of mine, a Catholic priest named, Father John."

"What does that have to do with me?"

"Father John asked me to tell you Lamar wanted you to know he was sorry, and that he loved you."

"Lady, I don't know you. It has been ten years since Lamar was put to death in prison. I have had to live with that all this time. I think it is best that you just go, and leave me alone. If you will excuse me, I have house work to do."

"I'm sorry Mrs. Johnson, but I promised Father John I would give you this letter from Lamar." Christine extended the letter to her and Mrs. Johnson just looked at the envelope with her name and address written in Lamar's handwriting.

Mrs. Johnson was indignant. "Why didn't Father John give me the letter ten years ago? Or better yet, why didn't Lamar just mail it to me?"

"Father John was unexpectedly sent to Mexico, and he said Lamar was afraid you wouldn't read it if he just mailed it to you."

Mrs. Johnson took the letter from Christine and said, "Lamar was right. I'm sorry you took the trouble to bring it to me. I gave up crying for Lamar ten years ago. I don't want to think about Lamar anymore. He gave me nothing but trouble." She tossed the letter into a small wicker trashcan near the entrance and then held the door open for Christine to leave.

* * * * * * *

Chapter 37: **The Hacienda**

The same Saturday Christine met Lamar's mother, Father John met with Carlos outside of the restaurant at fifteen minutes till three as planned. John gave Carlos the five thousand pesos he had promised him and they entered the restaurant to wait for Jaime.

The restaurant owner was himself indebted to the Mob and Jaime frequently did his business there. Jaime always selected three PM as a meeting time because Jaime knew the restaurant was almost always empty at that hour. By three, the lunch hour was over, and the dinner hour had not yet begun. Father John and Carlos sat down and each ordered a Coke to ease their nerves and quench their thirst from the hot afternoon.

Jaime Lopez and Pedro Garcia approached the restaurant promptly at three PM as planned. Jaime had recently promoted Pedro Garcia to be his personal bodyguard and hit man after his last bodyguard failed to show up once too often and had to be, "let go". Proud of his new assignment, Pedro was motivated to do well in his new position, and he wanted to show his dedication and loyalty to Jaime, who had always been good to him. Poor from birth, Pedro had failed at school and all his attempts at normal jobs before he, "found himself" in the Mafia. He had no living parents, no brothers or sisters, and no relatives. In short, he did not have a family, or a life. He had nothing to lose by being in the Mafia, and he could hardly believe he could make so much money by intimidating people unfriendly to Jaime. As yet, Pedro had never killed anyone, but he had no problem with the idea. If the truth be told, Pedro was excited by the fact that he might have to kill someone today.

Jaime grabbed the door handle but stopped short of entering the restaurant. He turned to Pedro and said, "If we get the money from the kid and he is alone, we will let him go. If the priest is here, kill them both if I give you the nod. You got that?"

Pedro's response was immediate. He nodded, cracked a wry smile and said, "You got it boss."

Jaime and Pedro entered the restaurant. When the few seated patrons saw Jaime, they got up and left the restaurant leaving their unfinished meals behind. They did not need a request to leave, and they did not need an introduction to Jaime. His position in the Mafia and control of Batopilas was well known: his reputation always preceded him. Everyone knew of Jaime, and knew he had the local police in his pocket and that he could get away with murder.

Father John and Carlos were now alone at a table on the right side of the restaurant. Jaime and Pedro approached them and Jaime said, "Let's go to the back room." Pedro drew the revolver he had hidden in a shoulder harness beneath his suit coat, and they all went into the stock room at the rear of the restaurant. Jaime reached just inside the door and clicked on a ceiling light. The room was large and well kept, with shelves of large jars of banana and jalapeno peppers and countless sixty four ounce cans of diced tomatoes and refried beans stacked on the shelves from the floor to the ceiling.

Jaime wasted no time coming to the point. He looked at Carlos and asked, "Do you have my money?"

Carlos was so nervous he could not speak. He looked at Father John who turned to Jaime and said, "We have ten thousand pesos for you today. I would like to help Carlos earn the money for you, that is, if we can negotiate a better deal."

Jaime threw a cold stare back at Father John and replied, "Fuck you priest. I already have a better deal."

Jaime then nodded at Pedro who shot Carlos and then John. Though ruthless, Pedro was new at killing. He had shot each of them in the gut, rather than the head or the chest. John and Carlos each fell to the floor and now lay motionless, and both started bleeding badly. Satisfied they were as good as dead, Jaime turned to Pedro and said, "OK Pedro, let's go."

The two men turned and walked through the door back into the eating area and left the restaurant way they had come. They strolled casually out of the restaurant as if nothing had happened. For them it was just another day at the office.

Both Carlos and John were still alive, but both were critically wounded. Holding his wound with one hand Father John slid himself over to Carlos along the floor with the other and said, "I'm sorry Carlos. I didn't think it would end this way."

John placed his now bloody left hand over Carlos's wound. John sat up and started to bless Carlos with his right hand, but John suddenly felt a great rush of energy he had not experienced in the ten years since he had moved to Mexico. The bullet had passed clear through Carlos, and Father John healed him. However, John's gunshot wound and his healing of Carlos were too much for him. Father John collapsed back on the floor next to Carlos and now lay unconscious.

With his wounds healed, Carlos got up slowly. He looked at Father John and thought he was dead. He looked at himself and the blood stain on his shirt. He pulled his shirt tails out of his pants and looked for the gunshot wound on his naked abdomen. There was no gunshot! Visibly shaken, Carlos looked back at Father John. There was a pool of dark red blood growing from underneath John's body. Not knowing what to do, Carlos pulled back his tears and raised his bloodied hands to his forehead. As he did, he cursed in Spanish under his breath,

"Dios Mio!" (My God!)

"Dios Mio!" (My God!)

"What have I done now?"

Carlos was terrified. Afraid of what would happen next and unable to explain the events which had just occurred, Carlos knew he didn't want to be there when the police arrived. He turned, cracked open the store room door, and peeked into the dining room. He was relieved to see the restaurant was empty, and that Jaime and Pedro were gone.

Father John's Gift

Carlos turned to John who was now unconscious and said, "I'm sorry Father." With ten thousand pesos in his pocket, Carlos wasted no time. He exited the restaurant, left town, and never looked back.

When Jaime returned to his home, he had Pedro call the restaurant owner to tell him the police had been notified, and the police would stop by the restaurant soon, but wouldn't ask any questions. The bodies would be taken to the Batopilas Funeral Home and the restaurant owner need not worry: it would be business as usual.

But Jaime was shocked when Pedro returned to report the owner had found no bodies in the back room of the restaurant. Hidden behind a closed door in his office, the Hacienda owner did not see Carlos or John leave the building. The owner reported he found a fair amount of blood on the store room floor, and the police had already come and gone. However, the police said they could do nothing without bodies. As far as they were concerned, the presence of blood meant nothing: it was just as likely some employee accidentally cut himself and went home. With no bodies present, there was no crime... or so the police said.

The aliens had monitored the communications between Rome and the Mafia, and they knew Jaime was instructed to kill Father John. They knew the time and location of the meeting at the Hacienda Restaurant, and they would not let John die if it could be prevented. They almost failed, but luckily, they had intervened in time.

Strangely, no one saw the alien ship come or go. The aliens used a time dilation device which froze time for a millionth of a second for the entire city of Batopilas after Carlos left the restaurant. The device allowed the aliens to land, enter the Hacienda restaurant, and rescue John; all without detection. If anyone had been looking directly at Father John at the time, they would not have seen the aliens come or go. It would have appeared to them as if John had just vanished into thin air. They would be both astonished and confounded by what they observed. One moment he was there, and the next moment he was gone. What would anyone have made of that?

Jaime was alarmed when Pedro did not call in, and did not show up for work the next day. Jaime picked up the phone at his office and called Sergio. The phone rang only once.

"Sergio?"

"Yes."

"This is Jaime. Have you heard from Pedro? He did not show up for work today."

"No boss. I haven't seen him here, but that doesn't sound like Pedro. I know he likes his job."

"That's true." Jaime leaned forward in his chair as he spoke to Sergio on the phone. "Listen Sergio, can you go over to Pedro's house? I am a little worried about him. He never missed a day before without calling me. I'm a little concerned. It just doesn't make any sense."

"Sure boss. He doesn't live too far from me."

"Let me know what you find out, OK?"

"Sure boss."

Sergio was surprised to see three police cars and an ambulance at Pedro's apartment when he arrived. He stopped one of the cops who were walking back to the squad car.

"Excuse me, officer?"

"Yes?"

"Can you tell me what happened here?"

The officer looked at him strangely and wondered why Sergio was so curious to stop and ask him anything. He asked Sergio, "Do you know the man who lives here?"

"Yes. His name is Pedro Garcia. Is he OK?"

"When did you see him last?" The policeman was not forthcoming but wanted answers himself.

"Well, I'm just a friend. It has been a few days since I saw him."

The officer took out his pen and paper. "Can I have your name please? I might need to contact you later."

Sergio was alarmed. "Why officer? What's happened? Is Pedro OK?"

"Your name please?" The officer was insistent.

Sergio relented. "My name is Sergio Gonzales. Now please tell me what this is about."

Father John's Gift

"Señor Gonzales, I'm sorry to have to tell you, but your friend Pedro is dead. Did he appear depressed to you when you saw him last?"

"No, he didn't. Why do you ask?" Sergio was digging for any information he could get. He knew Jaime would ask him for details.

"I can't be sure, but it looks like a suicide."

Sergio was shocked. He liked Pedro, and Sergio couldn't believe what he was hearing. "A suicide? I can't believe it." The officer made some more notes.

"How did he do it?" Sergio asked.

The two men looked up at the apartment just in time to see Pedro's covered body being wheeled out on a gurney to the ambulance. Absent a body bag, the ambulance driver had placed a white sheet over Pedro and a large blood spot was visible on the body twenty five feet from the curb where the two men stood.

"It's the strangest thing. It looks like he shot himself in the abdomen and then bled to death. Most suicides shoot themselves in the head. The coroner will know more later if you need it, but I'm afraid our coroner is pretty backed up. He might have the report ready in a few weeks."

"No, thank you officer. That's all I need to know." Sergio turned and walked back to his car before the officer could get his phone number. He went straight back to his house and called Jaime to report what he had learned about Pedro.

The aliens had been faxing the Vatican for years and they let the officials know they had killed Pedro Garcia. The Vatican made note of it, but no one in the Vatican was the least bit interested in the death of a Mafia hit man. The aliens also informed them that they had taken Father John, which was recorded in the church logs at the highest level. But the Vatican saw no need to tell anyone inside or outside the church about the abduction. The church officials knew they would be notified if and when John was returned, even if he was returned years later. The aliens had always made them aware of such important events in the past, and the church never had a say in what they did, or how they did it. One could not argue with a technically superior species. Like them or not, the aliens were diligent, efficient, and unlike their Catholic contacts, they were always honest about what they did.

Bishop Hernandez did not know about the aliens, and he was never told of Father John's abduction. The Bishop entered his residence at six PM after spending a long day in his office. He checked his fax machine and found a short note from the Vatican which read:

> **(For your eyes only. Please dispose of properly after you read this note.)**
> Stato della Città del Vaticano
> Gino reports his work is completed and do not worry, he cleaned up his mess. Double payment was made to Gino's Rome account yesterday as planned.

The Bishop became sick to his stomach and ran to his bathroom as soon as he read the fax. He leaned over the toilet and vomited twice. He cleaned himself up in the sink and retrieved a package of matches from a drawer in his bedroom desk. He returned to the bathroom, burned the fax over the toilet, and flushed away the ashes.

The next day Bishop Hernandez entered his formal office on the West side of the Rectory to address his personal secretary.

"Maria."

Maria turned away from her desk to greet the Bishop. "Good morning Bishop."

"Maria, I'm afraid I have some bad news."

She looked up at him with some concern. The Bishop had never spoken to her that way, with such a strange tone. "Oh? What's wrong Bishop?"

"I just learned Father John died yesterday in Batopilas."

Maria was stunned. "Oh my God! I can't believe it! What happened, Bishop?"

"I really don't know all the details Maria, but apparently he had a heart attack in a restaurant there. I didn't know Father John had a heart condition, did you?"

"No Bishop, I didn't know either." Tears welled up in her eyes.

"Maria, I'm sorry to have to ask you to do this, but can you call the newspapers for me? I want to schedule a Funeral Mass for Father John next Wednesday evening, at say, six o'clock? I want it to start late in the day so we can get as many in the parish to attend."

He handed her a hand-written note he had scribbled the night before. "Here is a statement regarding Father John's death which I would like for you to release to the Batopilas and Tarahumara newspapers. Please clean it up. Correct my spelling like you always do."

"Certainly Bishop."

"Then, please call the Rodriguez Funeral Home in Batopilas and make arrangements for Father John's casket to be sent here Wednesday morning. I want to make sure it gets here long before the start of the Funeral Mass. Can you do that for me this morning?"

"Yes. I have their number." Funerals were a regular event at St Josephina and Maria knew all the funeral homes in the area. Maria looked directly at the Bishop as she wiped her eyes. "And I'm so sorry about Father John." She finished drying her eyes and looked up sadly at the Bishop. "He was here for so long and was such a good man. I just can't believe it. Can you?"

"No, I can't either Maria. I'm shocked too. I know it will be hard for all of us." The Bishop touched her shoulder in sympathy. "Thank you for your help Maria. I know it is an unpleasant task." The Bishop turned around and returned to his office.

The Bishop's statement said Father John died of a heart attack in the Hacienda Restaurant last Friday afternoon in the town of Batopilas and a funeral Mass would be held at six PM on Wednesday evening at the St Josephina Catholic Church. There was no mention of Carlos Martinez, or even why Father John had been there. Everyone assumed Father John had business in Batopilas and he had stopped for lunch at the restaurant.

Back in his office Bishop Hernandez sat down behind his desk and dialed Jaime."

"Jaime?"

"Yes."

"Bishop Hernandez here."

"What is it Bishop?"

"I have scheduled Father John's Funeral Mass here at St Josephina for next Wednesday."

"Bishop... that might be hard to do."

The Bishop was surprised. "Why is that?"

"Because we don't have Father John's body."

"He's not at the Batopilas Funeral Home?"

"No."

The Bishop was at first confused, but he was now beginning to understand the fax comment from Rome about Gino cleaning up the mess. "Do you know where John's body is?"

"No, I don't know. But don't worry about it Bishop. I'm sure he is dead." Jaime was his usual blunt, insensitive self. "There was lots of blood."

It was more information than the Bishop wanted to know, and he didn't care to know any more. He thought about the situation. "Well, I will just have to have a funeral Mass for a closed casket. Can you tell the funeral director to properly weight the casket? I don't want the pall bearers to know the casket is empty."

Jaime cracked a smile at the Bishop's idea. "OK Bishop. I can do that." Jaime loved the Bishop's attention to detail. He thought if the Bishop wasn't already employed by the church, he would have made a good addition to Jaime's Mafia team. It was nice to deal with someone who could think for himself and wasn't afraid to contribute good ideas.

Jose Requena, the Batopilas funeral director, never questioned Jaime's orders. He always did as Jaime instructed, and his lead mortician was sworn to secrecy. The funeral director obeyed Jaime not because he was fearful of the Mob and knew Jaime was a ruthless killer, but because the Mafia was good for his business. Everyone has to die sometime, he reasoned, why shouldn't he profit from it? He was a funeral director after all, and attending to the dead was his business. The Mafia had come to town six years ago, and his business went up an average of seven percent in each of the following years.

Bishop Hernandez made sure the church promptly paid for Father John's funeral expenses, and as usual, the funeral director gave Jaime a small kick-back for bringing him the business, which in this case, was particularly nice since there was no body to be prepared for a burial. Embalming fluid was expensive and had to be ordered, but fifty pound bags of sand were cheap and available at every hardware store in town.

Father John's Gift

The next Wednesday Bishop Hernandez said Father John's Funeral Mass to a packed church filled with tearful parishioners. At the homily break in the service, the Bishop stood at the church podium, looked sympathetically at the packed church. He pulled out some notes from his breast pocket, unfolded the papers, and began the Father John story:

"I'd like to say a few words about our Father John. About ten years ago, God sent St Josephina a special gift from St Andrews Parish in Chicago, Illinois. His full name was Father John Albert Danek. I got to know Father John well and I learned he did not request the transfer to our little town. I doubt any of you know that Father John had a pretty good life in Chicago, and I was told he really did not want to leave the United States. But our Holy Father had other plans for Father John, and John readily accepted the transfer to Mexico without question or reservation.

Before he served at St Andrews in Chicago, Father John did missionary work in South America. Thankfully for us, it was there that John first learned to speak Spanish, and I believe this was one of the reasons why John was sent here. Once he arrived, John improved his Spanish, and he worked hard to get to know all of us. As you might imagine, it was not easy for him to make the transition from a big town like Chicago, to a small town like Tarahumara, but John never complained. He accepted his new calling, and he preserved. Father John was instrumental in helping St Josephina to become the successful and loving community church it is today. As I'm sure you all know, Father John was a good priest. He cared for the spiritual and emotional needs of all of us... including me." The Bishop looked down at his podium before continuing. "The fact that we are all here today is testimony to how much we all loved Father John, and of all the good work he did for us." The Bishop's soliloquy was good, and he now heard muffled sobbing by some of his female parishioners in the packed church.

"Finally, I want you to know Father John recently inherited a large sum of money from a friend who died about a month ago in the United States. Even though Father John was under no obligation to do so, he used this inheritance to start plans to build the first hospital in Tarahumara.

Although these plans are not yet final, we have been given authorization from the church to continue Father John's work on the hospital. We will proceed with the hospital construction as soon as possible, and I am told it could be up and running as early as March of next year. It will be named, "Father John's Hospital" in honor of Father John, and it will be built in the large vacant lot next to the church.

I can think of no better use for that land, and we all have Father John to thank for his extraordinary vision, for his loving kindness to the people of Tarahumara, and for his wonderful generosity. The hospital will be a lasting legacy and tribute to Father John, and when it is done, I hope we all will remember him every time we step foot in the hospital he so generously gave to us."

When the service was over, the entire congregation filed out the church and walked to the cemetery on the side of the church opposite where the Father John's Hospital would soon be built. All were present when additional prayers were said and Father John's weighted casket was lowered into the ground. No one present doubted Father John had gone to heaven, including Bishop Hernandez. Like Father Mark before him, Father John was loved by the people he served.

****

Chapter 38: **The Conclusion**

It was now June 10, 1980. Eleven years had passed since Father John's faked death and funeral.

The City of Chicago had sold Chicago General to the Catholic Archdiocese, and the church decided to make a public splash to commemorate the event. Each of the five Chicago TV stations had been invited, and each had sent a small camera crew and a reporter to record the ceremony for broadcast on their nightly news. All had been told Mayor Allen would participate in the ribbon cutting ceremony. Mayor Allen was Catholic after all, and Catholics represented thirty five percent of the registered voters in Chicago. Anything Mayor Allen did publically was big news in Chicago.

A small stage had been built fifty feet from the entrance to the hospital and thirty rows of folding chairs had been assembled to seat the audience in an area of the parking lot blocked off with plastic yellow tape for the occasion. The stage microphone was positioned so the hospital entrance provided a nice backdrop behind the speaker and a telephone link was established with the clergy from the church of St Josephina who would rename Father John's Hospital in Tarahumara, Mexico.

A crowd of four hundred people: Chicago dignitaries; Catholic cardinals; bishops and clergy, hospital administrators, staff, nurses and doctors were all in attendance. Bishop Hernandez, now in his mid-seventies, was flown in from Mexico City for the Chicago ceremony. Catholics throughout the Chicago metro area were all notified of the

Father John's Gift

dedication ceremony at Mass on the previous Sunday. Local Catholics, who worked near the hospital, took the afternoon off or came on their lunch hour to witness the event.

Christine O'Roark arrived just before the start of the ceremony with her precocious ten year old daughter, Anna Danek, and not wanting to generate any attention, they headed towards the back row of chairs. Christine had never lied to Anna about Father John. Christine had told Anna at age seven about Father John, and that he was her natural father. Anna knew only that her father was somehow special, and that the Mexican newspapers had reported he had suffered a heart attack before she was born.

While Christine suspected foul play, she did not know the Mexican Mafia and the church were responsible for John's death. Neither was implicated in the Mexican newspaper accounts of John's death, and even if they had been, it would have made no difference to Christine. After all, what could Christine to do about it, and what difference would it have made? As far as she knew, her Father John was dead.

It was a beautiful day in Chicago. The sun was shining, the sky was blue, and a gentle seventy two degree breeze blew off of Lake Michigan. Everyone grew quiet as Chicago Mayor Thomas Allen stepped up to the microphone to address the crowd. As a seasoned politician and speaker, the Mayor tested the microphone by gently taping on it and satisfied it was working, he then looked directly at the TV camera man standing in the back row who understood his glance, and with a pointed finger the Major signaled him to begin recording.

"Ladies and Gentlemen, and members of the Catholic Archdiocese of Chicago… and the Catholic Archdiocese of Chihuahua, Mexico, Honored guests."

"It is fitting that we stand here today on what would have been Father John Danek's sixty first birthday. For today, we have three reasons to celebrate. First, we want to celebrate the recent canonization of Father John Danek by Pope Lucias X in recognition of the miracles performed by Father John here, in this hospital, some twenty years ago. Secondly, we celebrate the renaming and rededication of the St. John Sister Hospital in Tarahumara, Mexico which many of you may not know was actually started by Father John just before he died. And finally, we want to celebrate the sale of Chicago General by the city of Chicago to the Catholic Chicago Archdiocese by turning the hospital keys over to Cardinal Ritter."

The Mayor turned to face the still seated Cardinal Ritter. "Cardinal Ritter, can you please come to the podium to accept the keys to your new hospital?" The Cardinal stepped up to greet the Mayor and accept the keys. Handing the keys to Cardinal Ritter, Mayor Allen turned back to the microphone for all to hear and said, "Cardinal Ritter, here are the keys to your new hospital."

Cardinal Ritter shook the Mayor's hand, accepted the keys and stepped up to the microphone. Looking back at the Mayor he said, "Thank you Mayor Allen!" The audience cheered and applauded. Cardinal Ritter turned back to address the audience and waited for the applause to die down. He opened a few pages of notes he had prepared, and he began.

"It is my great pleasure to accept the hospital keys from Mayor Allen today. We honor the church, the staff, the nurses, the doctors and the memory of a humble priest who some of you may remember only as, "Father John". First, I want to personally commend the hard work all of you are doing here, and hope all of you will continue to work hard for us, despite the change in ownership and the name change of this great hospital. We want and very much need you to continue the work you are doing for the people of Chicago and for the many sick people who come from all over the world to seek your medical care. I also want you to know the church does not intend to make any significant changes in the day to day operation of the hospital and there will be no layoffs as a result of the sale. But since the canonization of St John by his Holiness, Pope Lucias this past year, it seemed only fitting for the Catholic Church to acquire the hospital where Father John performed many, if not most of his documented medical miracles, so many years ago. And, although it is not yet completed, the church has commissioned a Chicago artist, Luis Fairchild to create a life size bronze replica of Father John which will stand at the main entrance to the hospital, for all to see when they enter here.

Cardinal Ritter continued. "Therefore, Pope Lucias has instructed me to bless this hospital in the name of St. John Danek. I will bless

Father John's Gift

the hospital now with a prayer, and then Bishop Hernandez from St. Josephina's Church in Tarahumara, Mexico will bless it with a sprinkle of holy water. Finally, I will give the signal, and the new signs above both hospital entrances, one here in Chicago, and one in Tarahumara, Mexico will be uncovered at the same time. Please hold your applause until the signs are uncovered."

Cardinal Ritter was a showman. He was ever mindful of his television audience, and he knew the effect of showing the new hospital sign on camera with applause in the background would be the better than any television commercial the hospital could ever buy.

Cardinal Ritter and Bishop Hernandez walked to the edge of the platform where a large vessel of holy water had been placed. The Cardinal faced the hospital, and as he made the sign of the cross he said,

"May the blessings of Almighty God and St. John Danek protect and defend St. John's Hospital and all who work in it. We pray that all patients who enter this hospital be cured of their sickness, or healed of their injuries. Equally we pray that Almighty God and St. John Danek protect and defend the sister hospital which was started by Father John in Tarahumara, Mexico twenty years ago which was then called, "Father John's Hospital" but is now renamed as, "St John's Hospital". In the name of the Father, and of the Son, and of the Holy Spirit." Cardinal Ritter then turned to Bishop Hernandez and said, "Bishop Hernandez, please bless the hospital with this holy water."

Bishop Hernandez turned and dipped the hand held sprinkler into the bowl of holy water, raised it over his head and shook it three times in the direction of the hospital. The water drops fell on the hot black parking lot asphalt and quickly evaporated in the Chicago breeze.

Cardinal Ritter returned to the microphone. "Ladies and Gentleman of Chicago, I now present to you St. John's Hospital." He turned and waved to the local priest and said, "Please uncover the new hospital signs now." Priests at both locations tugged simultaneously at the supporting ropes and two large tarps, each covering their respective new signs fell to the ground revealing the new name, "St. John's Hospital" above both hospital entrances.

Everyone applauded. Coffee was served to the doctors, nurses and administrators with hors d'oeuvres catered for the event. Cardinal Ritter and Bishop Hernandez drank champagne and ate rice crackers, caviar, and brie with Mayor Allen.

When the main ceremony was over, Christine did not stay for the festivities, but as she and Anna started to leave, Christine was shocked to see Mrs. Johnson, Lamar's mother, approach her and Anna at the back of the crowd. Mrs. Johnson looked at Christine, and then down at Anna, and then back at Christine.

"Christine? Do you remember me?"

"You're Mrs. Johnson, aren't you?"

"I'm afraid I wasn't very nice to you when you saw me last. Is this your daughter, Anna?"

"Yes." Christine was surprised. How could she know Anna's name?

"It took me about a week but I finally got over my anger and read Lamar's letter. It said I would find you both here on this day. The second page is addressed to you, but you can read all of it." Mrs. Johnson handed the now twenty year old letter back to Christine. Lamar's mother then turned and disappeared into the crowd without saying goodbye.

Christine pulled Lamar's letter from the opened envelope which read as follows:

Dear Mother,

I want you to know that I am sorry for all the trouble and grief I caused you, and that none of it was your fault. I know you did everything you could to raise me right. But nothing could stop me from doing all the things I did. I had to do them. The voices I heard were from the aliens, and they made me do them, and I believe it was for the better.

Please give this letter back to Christine at the dedication ceremony of St. John's Hospital in downtown Chicago on June 10, 1980. The rest of this letter is for her.

I love you Mom.
Lamar

Father John's Gift

Dear Christine,

You and I never met, but the aliens told me all about you and Anna. Your Anna is special, and you must use your money to send her to medical school. The future of the world depends on it since the aliens told me she is destined to make a major medical breakthrough in cancer research after she graduates.

Although you have not heard from Father John in more than ten years, he is not dead. He was rescued from the Mafia by the aliens in Mexico, and you will see him again sometime soon.

When you see him, tell Father John I wasn't sorry for killing that man. I wasn't sorry I did it, but I was sorry I had to do it. And, of course, I am... that is, I was scared of dying. But by killing the drug store owner, I know I changed human history by stopping an evil man from killing hundreds of people and starting a terrible chain reaction of death and unhappiness that would have lasted for many generations. ✓

John will remember I asked him if he believed in free will on my last day. Tell John there is no free will. The freedom we feel for choices we make is just an illusion of life. We all do what we are predestined to do. Each of us has our unique parts to play, and we all must play our parts.

The aliens have time travel, and they know everything that will happen given the current state of the world at any point in time, and I believe they make whatever changes are necessary to keep the world on track for the greater good of man.

Father John should use the healing gift the aliens gave to him. It is a rare gift which they give to very few people. Father John can and should use it to help good people, like he did in Chicago.

Christine, keep this letter to show John as proof of all I have written. Father John will remember I gave him this letter to give to my mother so long ago. The aliens told me he will remember it.

I hope you are well.
Lamar Johnson

They have seen our future.

R. Allan Worrell

The End

[This page intentionally left blank.]

Author's Note: The Quest for ET

The story of Father John's Gift raises interesting questions about the existence of aliens or Extra Terrestrials (ET) in the known universe. When I think about the search for ET, three separate but related questions immediately come to mind:

1) Do advanced civilizations exist on other planets throughout the universe?

2) Will or can we make radio contact with advanced aliens, if they exist?

3) Have we ever been visited by extra-terrestrial beings from outer space?

Obviously, questions two and three are moot if there are no advanced civilizations. If there are none, then we are truly alone, and we have only each other for company. I believe, if that is the case, then it is disconcerting given the size and scope of the universe with its hundreds of billions of galaxies and countless numbers of stars. However, if we find there are other advanced civilizations elsewhere in the universe, then how we view ourselves and our place in the universe will forever be changed. This is the premise behind the Father John story.

How can we begin to answer any of these important questions? In his book, *Cosmos*, the late astronomer and astrophysicist, Dr. Carl Sagan used the Dr. Frank Drake equation[5] to calculate the number of planets in our Milky Way Galaxy which might contain intelligent life. "Intelligence" in the Drake equation means intelligent enough to be able to broadcast a radio signal into outer space to greet and communicate with other intelligent species anywhere in the universe.

To do the Drake calculation, you only have to be able to multiply seven numbers together, and it helps if you can handle numerical exponents, so you can multiply very large and very small numbers. You can do the calculation using a scientific calculator, and the equation is easy to understand. But making the assumptions before doing the calculation is the hard part, because the assumptions one makes can either make, or break, the calculation. Allow me to explain.

There is an old computer axiom acronym called "GIGO" which applies here. That is, "Garbage In, Garbage Out". It means, if the assumptions we make about the data are wrong, then it may appear that ET is everywhere in the universe, or conversely, the calculation may show we are truly alone, and there are no other civilizations anywhere. Both of these results would be earthshaking and hard for many people to accept. Therefore, making the right assumptions is critical to the calculation, and is therefore critical to the results of the equation.

Fortunately, Dr. Sagan made the hard choices for us by carefully selecting the parameters in the Drake equation. Sagan calculated the number of planets between one (only us) and 10,000,000. He reasoned that if there are millions of planets with intelligent life in the Milky Way Galaxy, there should be lots of radio signals for us to hear. Dr. Sagan calculated the average distance to these potential planets to be 200 light years away, where one light year is the distance light can travel in one year (One light year is about 10 trillion kilometers or nearly 6 trillion miles).

Radio waves are electromagnetic signals which travel at the speed of light through the vacuum of space. Therefore, given Dr. Sagan's assumptions, a radio wave would take 400 years to make the round trip to an average distance planet in the Milky Way, just to say, "Hello". Imagine how long it would take for us to carry on a conversation of any length! We can only guess at how long a lifespan ET might have, that is, if he, she, or it exists at all.

What about receiving signals from other planets in other galaxies? The distances in outer space are so vast they are hard to comprehend. The nearest galaxy to our Milky Way home is the, "Canis Major Dwarf" (CMD) and is reported to be 25,000 light years away. A round trip "hello" message to a planet in CMD galaxy would therefore take the radio wave 50,000 years to get there and back (assuming someone was listening and they answered us right away). And that's the closest galaxy!

Father John's Gift

How far away is the most distant galaxy? Wikipedia reports the most distant galaxy is, "NGC 4945", and is reported to be 11.7 million light years from Earth. (The round trip "hello" would therefore take 23.4 million years.) It helps to remember that Earth civilizations with writing (Cuneiform) have only been around for about 5,000 to 6,000 years. (These early civilizations were in Mesopotamia and Sumeria in the Bronze Age beginning at about 4000 BCE). Given these numbers, it is clear we will never communicate with ET from other galaxies with radio waves. The galaxies are just too far apart, and mankind as a species is very young. As far as we have come, we are still in our technological infancy. It was only yesterday that we split the atom, built a computer, or discovered antibiotics.

But what about traveling faster than light? Einstein taught us the speed of light (186,000 miles per second or 300,000 kilometers per second) is the universal speed limit. That is, nothing can travel faster than the speed of light: not a radio wave; not a space ship; not a subatomic particle, not anything. Physicists have proved again and again with particle accelerators such as the CERN Cyclotron in Geneva, Switzerland that Einstein was right about light being the universal speed limit.

Einstein's Special Relativity equations show that time slows down when matter is accelerated to near the speed of light. Strange as it seems, the deceleration of time at speeds approaching the speed of light is Nature's way of throwing on the brakes. That is, the closer you get to the speed of light, the more time slows down. You can get close, but the laws of Physics will not let you get to the speed of light, no matter how hard you try, or how much energy you expend. It is a losing battle. Einstein's equations show that your inertial mass goes to infinity as you approach the speed of light. Nothing can go that fast except light itself. Mother Nature won't let you.

The search for messages from ET began in earnest in the 1960's in the former Soviet Union, and in the 1970's in the USA with the SETI project. Both have thus far yielded nothing. While that fact in itself is discouraging, it doesn't mean we should stop looking. To make a simple analogy, suppose you were digging for gold, or looking for oil. If your first efforts failed to find any, should you stop looking and conclude the gold or oil does not exist? Of course not. It only means you haven't looked in the right place, or you didn't dig deep enough.

There is one other remote possibility, and that is you don't know how to detect what you are looking for, i.e., gold, oil, or intelligent signals from outer space. However, if ET does exist, and they have transmitted signals to us, we can be confident they could figure out an easy way for their signal to be detected. Even if they were to send a repeating arithmetic sequence like 1, 2, 3, etc., it would be unmistakable signal against any background noise in outer space. The hard part would be deciphering their language, although they could start with their alphabet and follow it with the laws of Physics or Mathematics which are believed to be universal in nature. They might create a version of the Rosetta Stone which would allow us to decode their messages and communicate with them. Or if they already know and understand English (or any other Earth languages) from our radio transmissions, then it seems reasonable they would use one or more of our languages to communicate with us.

It is now 2017. SETI efforts continue to this day, albeit with private funds. If the SETI scientists have found intelligent signals from outer space, they have not told us about it. Conspiracy theorists might think signals from ET have been discovered but have not been revealed to the general public. Some may say there is a giant USA government cover-up to hide the aliens from the rest of us. (Remember Area 51?) However, I am not cynical enough to believe any organization could keep such a discovery secret (if they did find something). In my experience, scientists and engineers always get so excited by their discoveries, they immediately want to tell the whole world what they have found to get credit for their work.

Scientists love to be first to make a discovery. Why? Because we all remember who was first to do anything, but being second never counts for much. Everyone remembers Alexander Graham Bell as the inventor of the telephone. But outside of Western Electric, how many people know the name of Elisha Gray? Elisha reportedly filed a patent office claim for a telephone device just a few hours after Bell, and almost no one remembers him. No, it is unlikely there could ever be a cover up by scientists who have already discovered or are currently communicating with ET.

Time Magazine published a double issue (September 8, 2014 and September 15, 2014) which they titled, "The Answers Issue – Everything You Never Knew You Needed to Know". In this issue, Time devoted most of a page to the question, "How soon will we discover alien life?" What was their answer? The author stated we will have examined 10 million planets by the year 2040 thereby "making it highly probable we will find someone or something" by that time.

Their only assumption was that scientists will double the rate at which they can examine planets in the Milky Way, " about every two years for each two-year period between the year 2014 to 2040. Though not explicitly stated in the article, I believe the assumption was based on Moore's Law which states our computers double in speed about every 18 months. Moore's Law has held true since electronic computers were first invented in the 1960's, and it shows no signs of abating to this day.

However, using their numbers, I calculated the odds of finding something interesting or fruitful to be one in ten at best, and one in one thousand at worst. In my estimation, we will need to examine a total of one billion planets to virtually guarantee we will find something. I don't know how long that will take, and of course, we could get lucky and find a civilization long before that.

But if we assume there are 10 planets per star, and since we know there are some 400 billion stars in the Milky Way Galaxy[6], it is sobering to realize there would be four trillion planets to examine in the Milky Way. This means even if we examine one billion planets and still don't find life, we will still have three trillion nine hundred and ninety nine billion more planets to examine in our cosmic back yard before we have looked at them all. (And that's just in our own Milky Way!) It is seems unrealistic to think, with all those planets, that there is no intelligent life on any of them. I don't believe we are alone.

While I will always keep an open mind about UFO's and ET visiting us here on planet Earth, I believe it is highly improbable that we have ever been visited. Why? I conclude this due to the lack of evidence. Consider, if you traveled millions or billions of miles to greet a new civilization, wouldn't you make your presence known by landing in a highly populated area? And if you were sophisticated enough to make the trip, would you crash land in a remote location? I don't think so.

My view of an alien earth visit is akin to that portrayed in the 1951 science fiction movie, *The Day the Earth Stood Still*. In that film, a flying saucer landed on a baseball field in the middle of Washington DC. The part of the film I find incredible is that the alien looked exactly like us!

Some day we may make radio contact, or we may find evidence of intelligent life elsewhere in our galaxy. Watch out when that happens, because when it does (mark my words), all hell will break loose here on planet Earth!

References

[1] Dr. Carl Sagan, *Cosmos,* Carl Sagan Productions, Inc., Random House, Inc., New York, 1980, p193.

[2] Albert Einstein, BrainyQuote.com, Xplore Inc, 2017. https://www.brainyquote.com/quotes/quotes/a/alberteins100298.html, accessed April 18, 2017.

[3] John Adams. BrainyQuote.com, Xplore Inc, 2017. https://www.brainyquote.com/quotes/quotes/j/johnadams134175.html, accessed April 18, 2017.

[4] *Unknown author,*"Anointing of the Sick", http://en.wikipedia.org/wiki/Anointing_of_the_Sick_%28Catholic_Church%29 , accessed December 13, 2014. The form established for the Roman Rite through the papal document *Sacram unctionem infirmorum* of 1972.

[5] Dr. Francis Drake, The Drake Equation, Retrieved from Website: The SETI Institute: http://www.seti.org/drakeequation, accessed December 13, 2014.

[6] Dr. Carl Sagan, *Cosmos,* Carl Sagan Productions, Inc., Random House, Inc., New York, 1980, p10.

Made in the USA
Columbia, SC
20 April 2017